Curious Stories
of Diverse Places

Curious Stories
of Diverse Places:

The Cod's Earring, The Click of The Reindeer,
and Other Adventures and Even Some Poems

Richard Reichbart

IPBOOKS.net
International Psychoanalytic Books

International Psychoanalytic Books (IPBooks),
Queens, NY
Online at: www.IPBooks.net

Interior book design by Maureen Cutajar, gopublished.com

ISBN: 978-1-949093-41-4.

For Nansie, my love,
who makes me laugh and endure.

Acknowledgments

Thanks to the following people who have given me encouragement along the way by reading some of the short stories or poems here: Nansie Ross, the late Thrae Harris, the late Henry Seiden, Luba Kessler, Carmel Osborne, Elena Reshetnikova, Leide Porcu, and Joan Fiorello.

I am also grateful to the members of the Arts and Society Committee of the Institute for Psychoanalytic Training and Research (IPTAR), particularly Rena Greenblatt, for providing a forum in which to share some of my poems and stories.

Thanks to my son, David Reichbart, for letting me use his painting for the bright cover for this book; to Kathy Kovacic for the cover graphics; to Robert Seidman, a gifted author in his own right, for his encouragement; to Arlene Richards, who has always been a source of support; to Willie Sneed for his courage and graciousness; and to Catherine Satterlee, talented editor, who has been a delight throughout the process of finalizing this book.

Poems: "I carry my death" was originally published in Riversedge, (2007) Vol 20. No.2. p.85; "Love with a hint of Shakespeare" was originally published in Riversedge (2007) Vol. 20, No. 2, p. 85; "The hero with a thousand faces" was originally published in The Lyric (Spring, 1989) Vol. 69, No.2, p.44.

Table of Contents

Table of Contents

Stories

The Cod's Earring

The sea was not rough that day, finally, so they could go out. The visitors stood around the beach, all but one, a girl of about ten who was seated in a wheelchair. The sky was a grey white, the sea a grey blue, and the beach filled with small hard grey stones. Although Labrador was across the water, it was too far for the naked eye to make out, so that the sea seemed endless.

It was easy to tell by their clothes who the visitors were: they were the family dressed in what looked like new down jackets, bright blue and red, and red-laced hiking boots with not too many scuffs on them, and apparently with Vibram soles, the tell-tale yellow swatch on the bottom revealing itself as the young boy of the family, standing on one leg like a bird, tried to pull a pebble out of the tread.

They were waiting at the edge of the sea for the fisherman in his cod boat to come closer; milling about near them were the fisherman's wife, his boat mate, and two women who were apparently friends. Ordinarily, the cod boat would be gone from sight at day break; but these were no longer ordinary times. Cod had all but disappeared from beneath the dark waters and, devastatingly the Provincial Government had banned commercial cod fishing, until the cod replenished, if they ever did. The fisherman – Gavin by name – was trying to make money by tourism, which was permitted, during the summer, and so he was taking out this American family, who had seen his pink handwritten leaflet taped up at the only grocery story in Rocky Harbour, promising: *Newfie Cod Jigging: Learn How to Jig for Cod in the Sea.*

3

The small boat, puttering away, came up to the decaying pier. The boat mate tied it down; and assisted the mother and father onto the boat but the boy did not want any help and jumped in by himself. The girl, whose name was Jenny, was left alone on the dock in her wheelchair with the fisherman's wife. "O.K.," said Gavin, leaving the steering wheel, "We're all set for you." He and the boat mate, Robert, took hold of the wheelchair to raise it. Her father yelled to them from the boat, frantically: "Don't pick it up by the footrest. It will come off in your hand." Jenny in her chair was lifted off the dock, over the wooden side of the boat and placed in the back, next to a large coil of salt-whitened and frayed rope. "Can you see?" asked her father. She craned her neck to look over the side. She could see an unending expanse of water, although not the water just beneath the boat. "Yes," she said.

The two women, who had been waiting on the pier with them, were the last to climb into the boat. Then Robert untied the boat rope. A gangly man, he jumped in, with a thud but with the strange grace of a large animal. Gavin pushed the throttle, the engine now made a constant roar, and slowly the boat moved from the pebbled beach. Jenny could see over her shoulder the dwindling of the pier and the fisherman's wife, who had turned away from them. As the boat moved, the wooden houses that lined the shore, dull white and small, leaning in different directions, and at uneven intervals, became apparent. Jenny watched as they gradually got smaller and smaller, until they looked like toy houses, and then they disappeared. The boat and its passengers were alone in the long sea. For a long while, everyone was quiet.

Eventually, they came to a spot that looked to Jenny no different than the rest of the ocean, but now Gavin cut the motor. Silence. Jenny could hear the pleading cries of three or four seagulls that had followed them from shore. The boat seemed very small to her in the ocean. Intermittently, a long swell splashed softly against the sides and rocked them. "You never quite know where the cod are," said Gavin, breaking the silence, "but Robert has the best sense of them all; he can sometimes tell by the look of the water." As Gavin talked, explaining to them how he was a fisherman like his father before him, and how never before had cod fishing been banned, Robert was gazing downward at the dark water. He had gotten out a long line, filled with hooks, hooks that looked surprisingly large to Jenny. He held it over the side of the boat.

"You don't need bait," he said, to no one in particular. "The cod just swim up to it. Now he let the line of hooks into the dark water. He stood there, holding the line, looking downward and moving the line up and down. He paused. "Not sure that they are here," he said. After a while, he pulled up the line but the big hooks were bare. "Guess not." Looking at him, Gavin nodded and started the motor again. It made a throaty sound that broke against the grey clouds. They moved on to another spot in the vast ocean, and now, looking for Robert's signal, Gavin stopped the boat again, with a dying muffle that sounded like a sigh. Again they tried. No luck. They moved on.

One of the women started up a conversation. She was a thin woman with a tight fitting low-cut t-shirt and black jeans, black bouffant hair, and arched blackened eyebrows, as well as large gold hoop earrings. Her name was Gazelle. She had climbed aboard with her mother, a bland faced woman wearing a heavy kerchief, whose rheumy eyes teared with the sea wind. Gazelle was from Rocky Harbour originally and knew Robert and now she lived down the coast. She had a loud voice and laughed loudly, saying that she had not been out on a cod boat since she was a child. Robert asked her about how her business was going, and she told him and Jenny's father, who was sitting next to her, that she was doing very well. She pulled out of her front jean pocket a small bright red leather case, and extracted, with her equally red nailed fingers, a business card. She handed it to the father. It said: *Gazelle's Traveling Beauty Parlor and Hair Salon.* Jenny's father leaned forward and closer to the woman to look at the card. Jenny noticed that her own mother, at the other side of the boat, looked away toward the dull seemingly unending ocean.

5

"You see," said Gazelle, now actually leaning against her father, "I had worked in a beauty parlor in St. John's but I missed home, and I got this idea. Why not have a traveling beauty parlor? The towns are far apart here, and it seemed to make more sense to go to people, rather than for people to come to me. So I bought this van, and outfitted it. Now I make house calls, me and my girl friend. I do the hair and she does nails. See." She held out one hand with the bright red long nails for him to admire, as if she expected him to take her hand in his. "People come right into the van," she said, "It works out well." Her father said something about it being interesting.

"Alright," said Gavin, again cutting the engine. "We'll try here." They were at a spot without markings in the water that seemed indistinguishable from the others, but this time after Robert put in the line and jigged it up and down, he grunted. "I think this is it." He gave a heave, pulling hand over hand quickly upward, and four of the hooks had cod on them. To Jenny's dismay, each fish hung from its hook like a piece of clothing, a large grey shape with dark eyes and a vulnerable white underbelly, as water dripped from its body. There was no flapping, although sometimes they moved slowly, suspended there against the sky. They did not even thrash around and only then become resigned to their fate, because there was never any fight in them at all. Fat and dumb – it was as if they accepted the outside air and death, whatever befell them, as easily as they accepted swimming in the sea. Seeing her staring at them, Robert said, as if in response to her silent question: "They're cod. They don't fight." When he took them off the hooks, which had entered their bodies through their sides and their bellies not just their mouths, they just lay on the bottom of the boat, sometimes moving but slowly. They made Jenny uncomfortable.

Her brother, Daniel, however, was delighted. He was three years younger. "Let me see, let me see," he said, all but dancing on the wooden floor of the boat. "Can I touch one," he said to his mother. He had let go of her hand, his initial shyness once he had jumped on the boat apparently gone. "Yes," she said. He knelt

6

down and reached over and touched one of the fat cod that was lying in a corner on the bottom of the boat. "It's rough not smooth," he announced to his mother. She smiled at him. Jenny saw that the smile came across her mother's face like sunshine but as quickly disappeared.

On and on, Robert let his line into the water, and the fish came up from the deep. "It used to be," Robert said, "a line like this would have twenty fish on it." Nonetheless, each time he pulled the line up, half a dozen fish, as fat and slow as the first, hung from the big hooks. Between jigging, Robert moved quickly around the back of the boat, throwing the cod into two large metal tubs, where some of them still moved slowly. When the cod coming up from the deep on each try were fewer, Gavin started the boat again and they moved to a new spot, which was as good as the previous one initially had been. Now Robert turned to her, and said, "Do you want to try your hand." Jenny shook her head, but her brother said, "Can I?" Standing next to Robert, he held onto the line, and when he pulled up, with Robert's help, he was greeted by three cod. He smiled: "Look," he said, "I did it." Jenny's mother and father praised him and Gavin jokingly said, "I think he has the touch."

After a while, the wind blew stronger, and the sky became darker. It was time to turn back. The cod boat chugged toward land, the houses rose up again – as if by magic – on the thin line of the shore; finally, Jenny could make out the broken pier. Mary, the fisherman's heavyset wife greeted them, and helped Robert carry the two tubs of fish to a rough plank of wood mounted on saw-horses on the stony beach that served as a makeshift table. The passengers left the boat. Finally, Gavin and Robert raised Jenny in her chair once again to the pier. With some effort, because the wheelchair would not move on the pebbled beach, they brought her toward the table. "Come, "said Mary, "bring her near me. There." Jenny was encamped now next to Mary. She watched her father and her brother throw a battered, rubber football that had washed up on shore. Her mother – seated on a large rock – was trying to read something in their guidebook, but the wind was blowing the pages. The others were gathering driftwood along the beach.

"Ahhh," Mary said. She single-handedly grabbed one of the tubs from the pebbled ground and heaved it onto the plank table, which shivered briefly with the sudden weight. She reached over to the other side of the table and picked up a large knife with a blackened blade. She was getting ready to clean the cod. She looked over at Jenny.

"What's your name, dearie?" she asked.

"Jenny."

"I'm Mary. I'm glad you're keeping me company. I'll show you how to clean a cod."

"O.K." said Jenny.

Mary started to reach into the tub with one hand, but then paused.

"Tell me, dearie," she said, looking at Jenny again "if you don't mind my asking, how come you are in a wheelchair?"

"I have spina bifida," said Jenny and waited, for that fraction of a moment to which she had become only too attuned, to see whether she would have to explain.

"What a shame," said Mary. "My sister-in-law's sister has a son, Jamie, born with that; we get so much of it around here, you know. I just don't know why. The world is not a fair place, no matter what they say. And the poor thing, he's had to have all these operations. What about you dearie?"

"I've had six so far."

"Acchh, it just isn't fair. But you're a beautiful girl, you know, and look at you: such a soulful face." She had dropped the knife and moved from the table to Jenny. She brushed Jenny's hair back, blown by the wind with her palm, appraising her. Jenny felt somewhat embarrassed with this attention, and yet strangely warmed. She smiled up at her.

Mary returned to the table and set to in earnest. Her arms bulged beneath her frayed green sweater, as she grabbed at each cod as if it were a block of wood despite its flapping softly and slowly. She took her knife in her right hand, held the large cod in her left, and with a swift motion, cut into its white underside, dropped the knife, now reached in and removed the guts, and then placed the cod on the rough plank table. Picking the knife up again, she severed the head, tail, fins and sides. With a sweeping movement of her arm, more than half the fish was suddenly gone: swept aside, off the table, blood and little grey dollops of intestines still lying there. All that was left of the fish was the edible center portion. Jenny watched with horror. Over and over, Mary performed this operation, sometimes heaving a recalcitrant head into the surf. A stack of white flesh, like misshapen plates, began to form on one side of the table.

After a while, Mary paused in her working, put down the knife, and stretched her short arms upward. "My back is hurting me again," she said.

"Why didn't I think of it? ," she said suddenly. " I have a surprise for you." She turned her attention to the table once again, ALet me show you."

With the next cod, after disposing of the excess, she left the head on the table, and with her thick fingers reached right into the head, ripping and tearing. "The cods have ears," she said. "Ahh," she said. "I cannot find this one; it must be small," and she suddenly heaved the head into the distant surf.

She grabbed another slowly moving fish, eviscerated it, cut it, and severed the head. This time when she reached into the head, fumbling with her thick fingers, she removed something from each side. "There," she said, "those are pretty good."

"Hold out your hand."

Jenny held her small hand out, and Mary supported it with one rough bloody hand. From her other hand, she carefully dropped into the girl's upturned palm two delicate and pure white shapes that landed lightly. To Jenny, they looked like two tiny serrated leaves, miniature white Xmas trees, with flecks of blood on them, so different from the fat and sluggish cod itself.

9

'See,' said Mary. "You can make earrings out of those. That's what they do with them. Just glue a backing on each one. They'll look real pretty on you. Take them." Then, she said, "Wait, there's a little blood on them."

She took the otoliths back and walked solidly toward the sea, her long green sweater swinging around her large backside. When she got to the surf, she bent over and swished her hand in the water, then returned.

"Here," she said, "They're fine now."

Jenny looked at the delicate ivory shapes in the palm of her hand, bright with water drops.

By now, night was coming. Robert and Gavin put the gathered driftwood into a rusted old barrel, poured on gasoline, threw in a lit match, and with a whoosh, they had a fire, sparks flying into the darkening sky. On the pebbled beach itself, they had started a smaller fire, with a metal grill on it, for cooking. The weathered plank on which Mary had sliced and eviscerated the cod had been washed clean with seawater. It now had plastic plates on it, plastic forks and knives, and bottles of beer and cans of soda in a large battered red cooler, and bags of potato chips. Mary puttered around the fire, cooking, and singing something to herself in a surprisingly high voice, moving big pans of cod.

Night fell. The black sky was spotted with stars, and the moon shone through the dark clouds. They drank beer, and ate the cod that Mary had fried. The adults were drinking more heavily now, her father flirting with the hairdresser, and they all seemed a little drunk. The flame from the burning driftwood in the oil barrel lit the scene and one or two figures that stood near it, more than the others, who were in dark shadow – the figures changing places as they talked and laughed, like in a dance; and along the level sand their huge moving shadows were thrown.

For Jenny, stolid and perforce unmoving in her chair, there was a moment when she saw all of this before her clearly. She knew better than most children her age from the unmitigated and irre-ducible deformity of her young body that the world was a scary

10

place, that there were limits to what she could control. When her father approached her, in the dark, and looked deeply into her face (he looked strange, she thought, in the flickering light; perhaps it was because he was a little drunk) and held one of her hands in both of his, he asked: "Are you o.k. ?" "Yes, dad," she said, pretending an annoyance. "Your hand is cold," he said, rubbing it between both of his. "I'm fine, dad," she said. He nodded and returned to the party. But she wasn't o.k.

She had seen the uncertainty of it all – the quickness with which life could be taken and the matter-of-factness of its taking. She shivered as she remembered the flesh and viscera of the cod thrown into the black sea by Mary. And yes, she had seen without quite knowing it the flitting shadow of a possible future, in her father's too great attention to the hairdresser. Where she wondered was the solidness she held so dear – what would be rescued from this day? As much as she loved this vacation, the adventure, momentarily she found herself feeling alone in the darkness despite the presence of others. She wished to return from here to her home in the suburbs of New Jersey, where the streets were aligned and quiet in the night; and outside her window, the only noise was the rustling of the leaves of an oak tree.

It was very dark now. The stars shown against the black sky, and the sea was black, except for the little white line of foam of each wave as it came ashore and announced itself gently in the remaining light from the fire of the oil barrel and then silently receded. Jenny reached into her coat pocket with one cold hand and found the two otoliths nestled there. She clutched them tightly, with all her heart.

Dank

Somehow he had landed here. He didn't know how, and it fit no plan of his. He lay in the dank house – that was his first impression when he opened the shuttered doors with the skeleton key from the rental agency, impulsively flinging them wide and imagining them to be the great doors of a long neglected castle – the smell of dankness. It lay inside as if the house were swaddled in wet wool, a dank cool smell that rose from the stone floor. In fact, when he inspected the house, he found there was no basement. Instead, a small waterway empty of running water but wet, its bottom black with mud, ran right underneath. Here, he knew, the dank smell began.

The house was an amazing affair. It had once been a mill; he did not know what had been ground by the massive millstone that now served as a makeshift table in the back garden. The first giant room of the interior, which was both living room and kitchen, had a wood-beamed ceiling that rose two stories high and more. The walls were of stone, punctuated at intervals with windows both small and large. The tall front of the house itself was one giant wall with a set of shuttered windows near the bottom but with only two or three unexpected small openings on top, looking out as if it were an impassive face upon the rows of corn that stretched before it and beyond that a rolling hill where there was a sudden and surprising yellow carpet of sunflowers.

The setting was beautiful, but inside the darkness and dankness impressed him. It did not seem to bother Susan. She had shouted with joy when he opened the door and they stepped into the darkness, clapping her hands together. "Isn't it wonderful!" she said, and she flung her arms briefly on him, her body against his, and kissed him hard on the lips, and then as suddenly she was gone, almost dancing through the house, commenting on the stone walls and the massive stone fireplace and the long wooden table in the kitchen, saying, "Look at this," and, "Isn't this magnificent." "Let's open the shutters, Charlie. Hurry," she said. They had moved through the house, opening each window and then each pair of shutters, making satisfying dull clunking sounds in the darkness as each metal bolt was thrown back, and then pushing the shutters open so that the sunlight outside, the green grass, and trees around the house were revealed. In some cases, to his surprise, the window was level with the grass, and this immediately troubled him as he envisioned a person or a furry animal walking through the window into the house as through an open door. As had the dankness, it made him uneasy with possibilities. And in addition, there were no screens.

And now he lay in the stone house, not quite believing he was here in France, only a quarter of a mile down a thin road from a seemingly ancient village, as the early morning light came through the upstairs window. They were sleeping on an open loft raised above the kitchen which surveyed the vast living room (if they shared the house with anyone, for there was another bedroom downstairs, dark and dank, in which he had not wanted to sleep, how would they have had sex without other people hearing them? he wondered). But now he lay quietly, gazing at the texture of the stone walls, and at Susan, asleep, lying nude in a disarray of white sheets.

She stretched. "Hmmm," she said, her arms going upward, and her breasts rising so they became flattened against her. Her eyes opened, and she smiled at him. "This is the day," she said. She stretched further, then flopped her arms down upon the bed. "Are you ready for the caves?"

Her movements, in their spontaneity, intrigued him and made him envious, and in fact, he felt a fluttery feeling in his chest - that sense of anxiety that had attended, intermittently, this entire visit since it began - but he answered as evenly as he could, "Yes, I've been waiting for you, just watching the morning light."

"Hmmm," she said again, "I'm so glad we came. I cannot believe we're really here." And in a quick and graceful motion, she rose up from the bed, first from the waist, and then standing completely nude "like a goddess," he found himself thinking. And then, surprising himself, "God, how much I love her." Her body was touched with freckles, almost like someone had scattered brown petals upon her, and he was bemused by them (when he had first seen her nude he had been startled by their profusion) as she stepped to the bathroom.

Breakfast was like a soft dream where everything was so perfect that he felt as if it were unreal. They sat opposite each other at the long board table. Together, they had prepared an abundance of new foods they had bought at the local town market the day before: a crusty French baguette; assorted soft goat's and cow's milk cheeses (whose names he did not know) in different shapes (cylindrical, rectangular, pyramidal), some of them white, some touched with speckled black, some still in their paper wrappings, so that they sat upon a blue ceramic plate like just-opened gifts; olives of different sizes and colors in a small earthen bowl; and a large plate of scrambled eggs with bright red tomato slices around it. He wanted the moment to stay still, for time not to pass or pass so slowly that it would seem to go on forever; and he felt a terrible ache inside his chest. She was looking at him. Her brown hair, he noticed, was barely contained by a barrette in back so that it straggled outward, and he could not decide if he liked it or was annoyed. She was talking animatedly about their visit to the Prehistory Museum in the neighboring town of Les Eyzies from the previous day, her words spilling out, and he could feel her trying to pull him along with her as she had when they had visited, going from room to room to look at stone and antler and bone preserved from tens of thousands of years before. Suddenly, as he looked at her, the image of Marilyn, his wife, flashed before him and their suburban kitchen in New Jersey all bright and cool and

14

antiseptic, and he felt so disoriented that it was as if he had the wind knocked out of him. The unreal beauty that attached to the present was gone. He tried to reconjure it but could not.

"It's so amazing," she was saying, thumbing through the book of photographs they had purchased at the museum, "to see these things, and what's best for me, you know, is seeing how they seem to have worshiped women." He looked at her abstractedly. "Charlie?"

He caught himself. "Yes. They had a different kind of religion, I guess."

"It's not just that, Charlie. Look at this. It's that Venus we saw yesterday." She had the book open to a photograph of the rough-cut bas-relief of a heavyset woman standing naked, implacable, the features of her face indiscernible, which they had observed together the other day in the cave next to the museum. The photograph made the figure appear life-size, when, in fact, it had been only a foot tall. "Can you imagine?" Susan continued, "Maybe it's not just Woman, you know, with a capital W, but a specific woman: maybe the woman this sculptor loved who modeled for it. It just gives me the shivers: 18,000 years ago, she was standing where we stood yesterday."

He could not restrain himself. "Standing in that cave nude, she probably had the shivers too . . ." which prompted her to look at him with mock disapproval. More soberly, the image flashed across his mind of the nude drawings of his mother, before she had gained so much weight, that had been on the staircase of his childhood home. He found himself offering lamely, "Actually, I can't quite imagine it."

"Why not?" she countered. "Come on, Charlie, all this phallic worship of our culture; all these Western male gods with their horned heads and their brutal sacrifices, and here it is a fertile, naked woman (and maybe one man's woman) we see on the walls, and those little naked Venus statuettes, which maybe men carried around like pictures of their lovers or like crosses to protect them . . . or like pacifiers." He felt himself bristle at this last. She smiled exaggeratedly at him.

He laughed. "Serves me right," he said, sotto voce.

"And these, look at these," she went on without waiting, pointing to a series of triangular shapes, again beaten into different rock walls or drawn, that represented women's vulvas. "Look at them, Charlie." Despite himself, he now found himself actually blushing. Maybe directness was not really his forte, he thought. And yet, he both loved and distrusted her for wanting to engage his intellectualism. It was exactly what had intrigued him from the very beginning about her, as if she had looked through the manifestations of his image — his expensive silk tie, his inscribed Rolex watch, his off-putting need to sound like an authority — and had barely noticed them; as if, instead, she chose to address the ghost of what he had almost forgotten about himself, a shadow that walked with him through daily life that he had learned to ignore.

It was, after all, how he had met her, how she had engaged him right away, assuming without question that he understood how she thought and was part of her world. And it began by impulse too, just as the decision to rent this house for two weeks. He had finished a hard session of negotiations with an old client in the City, and rather than go back to New Jersey, he found himself wandering. It had just rained, the footsteps of pedestrians were muffled by a looming gray sky overhead, and the dark streets were bright with reflections from streetlights and storefronts. Everything seemed suddenly fresh to him and new. He passed by the plate glass window of a coffeehouse, and although he thought the people inside somewhat young, he felt an urge to be part of the City as he had been when he, too, was younger, before he moved to the suburbs. He quickly found himself inside, seated at one of those impossibly small tables, drinking an espresso, and completely entranced by the sound of people talking and the jazz that was being played through the loudspeaker. It beguiled him, making him feel as if he wanted to be nursing a scotch in a smoky club. He found himself feeling very mellow. When the waiter came by again, he asked him whether he knew who was playing. As the waiter started to say no, the woman seated at the little table next to him, said, "It's Ben Webster on the sax, I think." He turned, looking at her for the first time. She had just been a barely-noticed presence before, dressed in black: black shiny skirt, black ribbed sweater.

"Isn't it marvelous," she said. "It's all in the timing; when you're in the mood, it's like he is caressing and then pinching you. It has such a bodily feel to it, like a mother who is singing to her child." This last analogy seemed a little strange to him after the pinching analogy, but she continued to draw him in. Her hair was somewhat straggly, and he noted that the cuff of her shirt from beneath the sweater was frayed, but it was her eyes he looked at, direct in their gaze and seemingly sunken, and the darkness of the skin around them.

"Well, it certainly gets to me," he said.

"You know," she answered, "I think during the day, we cannot hear this kind of music properly; your body is out of time. During the day, your body is in pace with your watch, so to speak, and now when the evening is coming, there's a chance you can feel it. Life's like that a bit. We miss so much, don't you think, because our bodies are running at the wrong pace." And it was certainly true that at most times he would have listened at a distance, or pulled himself back from engaging with such a seemingly impulsive woman, and caught his evening train, and forgotten the moment. But this evening, for some reason, he did not; everything slowed down for him. Something in what she said went to his core; he thought with a sigh how he needed things to slow down. At that moment, he dimly felt that he willed their affair to start, although she had been more than willing.

He knew she represented something he had left. When he was younger, he had been ambitious for things artistic and intellectual. His mother (he remembered her sometimes with a smoky cigarette smell attached to her like an unseen veil and wet kisses smelling of sickly sweet liquor placed on his childish cheek) had dabbled with one artistic flirtation after another: once it was taking wax sculpture lessons with a Madame Baryknikov, a Russian emigre who lived in a dark studio apartment overly filled with Oriental carpets which he dimly remembered visiting when he was eight, and as a result little wax heads and wax figures of satyrs and naked women by his mother began to sprout like mushrooms in the glass-enclosed cabinet in their living room; another time it was painting landscapes on panes of glass (he remembered being constantly afraid as a child that he would knock into one of these works that stood in the middle of the same living room so that it could be viewed from both sides), but basically, his mother combined her flirtations in art with flirtations with artistic men. It was this that troubled him. Apparently she posed nude for them because nude pictures of her periodically appeared on the wall near the staircase. He had never met these mysterious artists nor seen her pose for them, but she tended to walk around in various stages of undress at home, which made it difficult for him to feel comfortable inviting friends over as he got older. And he had heard the arguments between his father and mother late at night. "Andre," she would say, "you're overly sensitive."

And his father would grumble something like " 'In the interest of art' my foot," or "I'm going for a walk," and the front door would slam. He never knew whether his father really went for a walk or where he went at all, but he did worry that he would not return. He also sensed that he felt somehow ashamed for him. His father was a taciturn man who worked in his law office late or at home late into the night, and Charlie found himself increasingly taciturn with him as he got older. He liked his company, liked the smell of his pipe, liked to sit with him in his study as he worked at an antique desk, but they said very little to each other. It was his mother he sought to please, as if he wanted to be one of those mysterious men in her life. And when he went to Yale (the walls of this old mill surrounding him now reminded him of the stone buildings at Yale but here the stones were more disorderly), he found himself drawn to the Yale Drama School – acting, playwriting, and involved with one girl after another, sexually more seductive and promiscuous than he ever could have imagined he could be. When he flunked out, his father was deeply disappointed. He could see it in his eyes. Scrabbling back took years; he had tried to live in the Village for a year, taking odd jobs and joining an erstwhile theater group, but he was really living off his father's money. He became increasingly frightened for himself, and so he gave it up, made his way back in a different college, went to business school, married Marilyn, and founded his own business in New Jersey. His father died before he was really a success. When he thought of this, he always got a sunken feeling in his stomach. At intervals, Charlie found himself flirting with secretaries, carrying on affairs that went nowhere, with women who were impressed by his wealth and who offered, in effect, to relieve him of his uncertainties. For these affairs (they were not even affairs, he told himself, just once or twice clutches in a hotel room or in a car, from which he then disentangled himself), he felt terrible guilt. He would look in the mirror as his face changed over the years and wonder why he no longer saw the life in it that he used to see. He looked respectable, pleasant, but it took an effort he knew to keep from letting his mouth be drawn downward. He wondered whether he was looking more and more like his father. One thing was certain: he had not chosen a woman like his mother to marry. He had almost consciously avoided the kind of women who had fascinated him in college and in the theater. Steadfast, involved in routine, good-hearted but unexciting, Marilyn could be relied upon. Long ago, she had given up teaching elementary school, and now she confined herself to volunteer work. She was a good mother, he thought to himself. At least he had provided his two sons with that.

And now he found himself here, with a woman who aroused in him the excitement he had vowed never to give in to again. What was he doing? he wondered. Things had quickly (too quickly), gone from one thing to another, and this time it did not end after one or two clutches. He found himself thinking about her all the time. When he entered her for the first time, he felt such softness that the stiffness of his shaft seemed new, even a little frightening, to him. It was almost as if he were being reborn or transported back to when he was younger. When he had to go to the City on business, he extended his evenings so he could be with her or went to her apartment. Her apartment was a mess: he knew there were always clothes strewn about and sometimes dishes left in the sink. But there were also books everywhere, not only in book shelves that went floor to ceiling but open on the bed, on the kitchen table, on the floor. There were sensual photographs of nudes on the walls, he recognized Georgia O'Keefe in one of them; and sensual photographs by Robert Mapplethorpe of flowers, which looked stunningly phallic. Scraps of paper here and there were pinned on the wall near her desk, sometimes just with certain words that she must have liked, sometimes with lines of poetry. She worked, in fact, in a small theater as a publicity agent and what seemed a general factotum, and, at times, they let her have a small part. She had published some of her poetry and said she was working on a play that the theater might produce. It seemed strange that she was at all interested in him.

She kidded him about living in the suburbs, which he tried to take good-naturedly, but when she said, "I bet you play golf," and he acknowledge it, he saw how her facial expression went blank and surprised, momentarily. He felt annoyed at her on the one hand (why should he have to apologize for this?) and on the other, he wanted desperately to remove her distress.

He joked, "But not very well," and then he found himself confessing to her that playing golf was probably the one thing he had been able to do with his father where his father seemed less withdrawn, almost, at times, ebullient. Now when he was on the golf course, he sometimes imagined for a moment that his partner standing near him was actually his father, resurrected with golf club in hand. When he told her this, Susan's face changed: she smiled and put a hand to his head, tousling what there was of his hair and kissing him gently on the cheek. He felt such a wonderful warmth inside when she did this. It was so strange how he just confessed things to her, things that he barely acknowledged to himself, and how these things then became a part of their being together. They just came blurting out of him with no apparent hindrance and very unlike his other experiences in life or his experience with Marilyn. In the same way, he began to talk about how he had been involved in the theater when he was young, and memories of things he had hidden away from being at Yale and the year he spent in New York returned. They talked and talked, compulsively, animatedly, about plays and movies — it was as if he could not get enough, as if he was trying to assuage a hunger he had not realized he had — and he started to come home later and later. He always wondered whether Marilyn suspected anything, but she seemed oblivious.

Then there was this unexpected business trip to France, which he had intended to take with Marilyn. But Marilyn's oldest sister in Georgia, who was alone since the death of her husband, became seriously ill and Marilyn (who did not particularly like to travel to begin with) said she wanted to take care of her for the week. She urged him not to cut short his trip to France; she knew he would have a good time. Surprising himself, he invited Susan to join him, and, equally surprising, she immediately accepted. He booked into two separate rooms in a hotel in Bordeaux, but when Susan fantasized about a house in the Dordogne region, he got onto the internet and found a site that specialized in just such rentals, but everything was taken for their dates except one hideously expensive manor house. He called the agency directly, hoping he might at the last minute negotiate a lower fee, and a woman with a very proper British accent stated immediately that she was sorry but the rate could not be altered at all. He felt the wind go out of him, but then, after a seeming pause in the conversation as if the Fates had reconsidered, she said, "Wait one moment, please." When she returned, she said that they had a cancellation that very morning; it was an unusual house, and it might be what he desired. He booked immediately. The internet photo of the house was dark and unprepossessing, but he told himself it did not matter; it wasn't until they stood looking at the great stone face of the house in the summer light that he realized how fortunate he had been.

*   *   *

They cleaned up the breakfast things, shuttered the windows, and stepped outside into a warm morning sun. The red rental car, bright against tall green grass, stood by the side of the house. He fantasied that this was their own country home, which they had purchased, and their own car. As he got in, his trouser leg brushed against a spider's web ripe with dew among the weeds and became splotched and wet. Susan reached up to the skylight in a sensuous motion that again exposed her underarms. "Ahh," she breathed as she opened the skylight revealing a blue sky that seemed without end. They smiled at each other for a moment, and then he turned the ignition key. A soft cloud of dust rose from the dirt road as they drove along, and the warm wind played through the car.

"It says the electric train goes into the cave for over a mile," Susan said, her head bent over the brochure of the Grotte de Rouffignac. Their cave visit would not be on foot, which he regretted, but it, apparently, promised many cave drawings. An electric train running deep into a cavern was intriguing; he had a brief incongruous vision of his electric toy Lionel train from childhood and a styrofoam tunnel. They drove on and Susan continued to read aloud. As they went under some large overhanging trees, the car fell into shadow, and he suddenly remembered that he had a disturbing dream last night. He had been lost in a cave and, not knowing which way to go, felt chilled and afraid. He remembered that he had awoken from the dream disoriented sometime during the night, and for a moment had thought from the dank smell that he was still dreaming and still trapped beneath ground in his dream; he would have to struggle another time to truly wake up. He felt the panic (which he sometimes got when he traveled) of not even being sure where in reality his body was sleeping. He had thought that if he could not remember or envision where he was, maybe he would never awaken at all. Then he realized – which was itself so strange – that he was already awake; to his relief the dark interior of the house slowly took shape before his eyes. Apparently, the blanket had slipped off the bed, leaving him exposed and cold. He had then fallen asleep again. They passed the overhanging trees into bright sunlight again, and, as quickly as it had come back to him, the dream left his mind.

They wound their way through French towns, then through a forest and around hills until they arrived at the entrance to the cave. There were cars parked all along the side of the road. They got out and walked. When they rounded an overgrown rock outcropping, he saw a large entrance in the rock face like the dark mouth of an encrusted whale beached far from sea. Inside, in semi-darkness, people were milling about, waiting. There was an incongruous wooden ticket booth along one side, looking fragile and uncertain, and he saw from the sign above it that the train left every half hour. They approached the booth. The ticket seller, a pleasant-faced woman with a sudden streak of grey in her long black hair, smiled at them. "*Bonjour*," she said. Susan paid, but the woman, looking at a large clock on the stone wall next to the booth, indicated that they would have to wait for three quarters of an hour because the next train was entirely filled. They looked at each other with disappointment; he started to say that waiting would not be so bad, but then the woman said, "*Mais, non. Attend un moment.*" She looked over her papers again, and then said there were just two seats left. Charlie was reminded of how luck seemed to accompany them on this trip. Happily, they paid and waited for the train.

A sudden harsh screech, then another, and a third, and a continuous clacking, and at last a train of sorts emerged from the dark tunnel. "It is more like a string of long hand carts," Charlie thought, each one with a series of long metal benches mounted on it. The metal was damaged in places, and he could see that the dark green paint was chipped and there were rust spots. "Thousands of people must have sat here," he thought, "on this almost derelict conveyance, which, in itself, was thousands of years more advanced and alien to the people who had walked here in animal skins and painted with burnt wood from trees long gone." They approached the train and he lowered himself uncertainly onto a metal seat next to Susan.

The train took them into the cave, sometimes traveling close to the jagged rock walls, sometimes far away. As soon as it started up, Charlie had a helpless feeling. His expectation of enjoyment began to dissipate. Instead, he found himself feeling controlled and captured, and even wanting to stop the train to get out and walk. The little train clicked and clacked along, and the dank chill of the cave began to envelop and seep into him. A conductor at the back of the train slowed the lurching movement and stopped the train periodically, usually close to a wall where, at first, Charlie could see nothing but rock – impervious, dark, sometimes shiny black with water, almost too close for comfort – and then the conductor used his flashlight to light up the wall. Markings appeared, unexpected shapes, the outlines of animals small and large. There would be a sigh from the people in the train, like a soft rendition of the collective sigh that comes when a firework display blossoms in the night sky, except here they were deeply underground. At first Charlie did not know what to make of the markings. It was hard to follow the lines and shapes they made, as they were crisscrossed by natural marks in the rock face, marks from other drawings which overlapped, and even scratches in places, long series of scratches high up on the walls, which the conductor attributed to ancient bears standing on their hind feet drawing their sharp hard front claws against the softer rock. This last image troubled Charlie, too, as if the bears had wanted to claw their way out of the darkness.

They went deeper, lurching along the track, until finally they came to a large central cave where the conductor asked them to leave the train. Charlie was glad of the opportunity to walk, but he found the rock floor uneven. The conductor gathered them all into one place and turned off his flashlight; they stood there, dark shapes in the darkness, hearing each other breathing and shoes scuffing on the rock floor. Someone coughed and the sound echoed. Then suddenly, the guide turned on his flashlight again, lighting up the low ceiling that spread above them. There was a profusion of scratches in the black rock, and Charlie could make out animals large and small: tens of them, mammoth, bison, horse, and ibex. He heard a gasp and realized that it had escaped from him. Susan leaned with her back into him, and he put his arm around her, and they both stared upward, up, up at the animals in the close stone sky. Eighteen thousand years ago ("Too many years for it to really register, 18,000 or 5,000, what difference did it make?" he thought)rough people clothed in animal skins struggled here in this deep dark cave to incise these delicate marks into the ceiling, breathed the same fetid air as they did now, and cast (as he imagined it) onto the cold walls giant shadows of themselves thrown by the smoky fires they used to light the darkness. "They made their mark," Susan punned. He laughed but without enthusiasm, and wondered sadly to himself whether he in his time would ever make his. Despite his profound awe, once again he could not shake a feeling of foreboding, which seeped into him with the dampness.

It came to a head in such a simple way. When they returned to the train, Susan wanted to sit closer to the conductor, and, reluctantly, Charlie followed her onto a different metal bench. There was a young and dark long-haired man who averted his eyes already sitting there alone, which required them to squeeze by him. Susan said, "*Pardon, s'il vous plait,*" trying a smile on him which he seemed to ignore. After uncomfortably sliding by, Charlie lowered himself into his seat and found himself wedged tightly, his thighs pressed against the young man's on one side, and Susan's on the other. He felt even more trapped. He glanced over at the man's angular face, his thin languid body, sensing the hard thigh against his, and he became conscious of the too large roll of fat around his own middle. "I'm just a balding middle aged man sitting between two youngsters trying to pretend he's young again," he found himself thinking. "What a picture I make!" He felt the need to adjust his collar.

Susan, for her part, seemed oblivious. As the train gathered speed, she leaned her head against his shoulder once again so she could look upward, entranced by the innumerable scratches on the wall and the dark stone shapes. The train's lurching, accompanied by the harsh rasp of metal against metal, only made Charlie more uncomfortable, for the motion alternately increased and decreased the pressure of the young man's leg against his. The hard metal top edge of the bench cut repeatedly into his back. "God, I wish this ride were over," he thought, trying to gauge by the shape of the cave's walls how close they were to the beginning, but nothing looked familiar; he could make out no landmarks in the dark.

"I wonder if we will come back here ever," Susan asked, sitting up and turning to face him. He did not know how to respond. She glanced toward the young man who momentarily looked at her. "*C'est magnifique*," she said to him, *n'est-ce pas?*" He seemed to smile slightly, which evidently pleased Susan as if by the pure force of her personality she had roused him, but beyond a mumbled assent, he said nothing.

The train screeched around a turn, throwing Charlie into Susan. "I doubt it," he said. She did not follow, having become distracted.

"What?" she said.

"I doubt we will ever return."

"We're here!" she said, ignoring him. "See we're at the entrance."

At this point, she got up as did the young man, who quickly exited and was gone in the crowd of people leaving the train. Susan, however, did not wait for Charlie. She started to slide past him, which only annoyed him further ("She could at least let me leave first," he thought), and in doing so she stepped on his toe.

Glancing backward, she said, "I'm sorry, Charlie," and in the same moment, not watching where she was going, she stumbled out of the train, falling down to the stone ground in a kind of pratfall accompanied by the sound of tearing fabric.

"Damn," Charlie said out loud. People stopped, turned to look, which for some reason embarrassed him, and a white-haired old man nearest her, probably unable in actuality to be of any assistance, said something to Susan which Charlie did not catch. She shook her head, thanked him in French and staggered up. The old man smiled and moved on as Charlie came up to her.

"How clumsy of me," she said. He could see that her skirt had a rip in the flowered pattern, exposing a naked white thigh, and there was a slightly bloody bruise on one knee.

"Are you alright?" he asked.

"I'm fine," she said.

"What about your knee?"

She looked down, then stuck her leg out a bit to see better. "It's just a scrape," she said, flexing it. She started to search through her black leather bag, which Charlie now saw had a deep scratch on it that he was almost positive had not been there before, evidently looking for a handkerchief. Finding it, she put down the bag and dabbed at her knee. "There," she said, admiring the effect of her ministration, then bunched up the handkerchief and threw it into the bag.

"I'm afraid your skirt is ripped too," he said.

"Where?" she said. "Oh, I see. That's too bad. Maybe I can sew it, but I think it would show." She held out the fabric from her body and examined it.

"You know," he found himself saying, "if you hadn't been so impatient to get out, you wouldn't have fallen." She looked up at him very directly with her dark eyes. "You really should be less impulsive," he added.

"Charlie. . ." There was a pleading tone in her voice.

"But," he continued anyway, "it was so . . ." He was going to say unnecessary, which he knew would sound old fashioned, but she interrupted him. She was annoyed now.

"Charlie, come on, don't ruin things. I'm just so happy you brought me here. Who cares about this silly skirt?"

He felt himself relent. But then the darkness inside him came surging back. "It's just the fact that everything of yours always seems to be half-torn. Your bag too, you see," he pointed to the scratch. She looked down at it, saying nothing; he thought he could sense her taking a deep breath, and he had a sinking feeling, but he blundered on anyway. "Sometimes I don't understand how you manage." He was going too far and he knew it. What had gotten into him? It was as if being angry was better than the uneasy feeling he had been having all morning. And then, but he couldn't say it; he knew it, but he just couldn't say it: there was that long-haired young man she seemed in such a hurry to follow.

"I've gotten along fine up until now in case you hadn't noticed," she said sharply.

"In a manner of speaking." He hated himself now.

She looked at him, her eyes wide. "I can't do this," she said almost to herself, and walked away.

He looked after her, at the damp spot in the center of the back of her white peasant blouse and her swaying hips. Outside the mouth of the cave, he followed her down a grassy hill to the car. He felt like a child, walking single file. They did not speak.

It was worse in the car driving back. Their argument seemed to have a life of its own, like a wild animal that they had invited inside that began wrecking havoc and which they could not now get rid of. He was grateful when evening came and, barely speaking, they climbed into bed. They lay there without touching, and after a while (he did not know how she could do it), Susan slept. He felt utterly alone, staring at the stone ceiling above him, listening to the sound of the wind rustling the trees outside, wondering what was going to happen to him. When he finally managed to sleep, he had a dream which began with a sense of relief. He was back on his club golf course in New Jersey, in dwindling evening light, the grass very green and uniformly cut; it was pleasantly warm, almost balmy. He was standing in a sand trap looking at his golf ball beneath his feet, holding in his hand an old battered sand wedge, not at all like his own club, that reminded him of his father's favorite from decades ago. He felt a peculiar sense of confidence. But then, a wet smell like rotting leaves rose to greet him, and he realized as his shoes sunk into the sand, that the sand was only a thin layer over thick, black mud. He became concerned that he would sink into it farther. In a hurry, he rushed his shot and missed the ball, splattering mud all over himself. He tried again with the same result, and it was as if he were digging a hole. The third time, his club struck something soft but solid with a thud; the sensation that went up the thin shaft to his hands made him queasy and he suddenly became convinced that there was a dead body buried just beneath him. He awoke with a start, his heart racing, struggling to realize where he was, and slowly recognizing the dank smell from the stone house, which seemed to envelop him, and beside him the dark form of Susan sleeping.

The morning began no better. When he awoke, Susan was nowhere to be seen. He called downstairs for her, but there was no reply. Showered, dressed, he descended the stairs; the windows were thrown open, a breeze blew through the house, and there was a fresh emptiness to everything. There were broken egg shells in the sink, crumbs of cheese and bread on the worn wood table. He noted to himself again her messiness. He cleaned up, made himself coffee, devoured the bread and cheese with particular pleasure, while leafing idly through the book on Paleolithic art. He hoped for her return, but nothing. He went to the heavy front door, opened it, and stepped outside into bright sunlight. There was no sign of her. He gazed down the thin dusty road until it disappeared in a turn at the end of the cornfield. "She must have gone for a long walk," he thought, stretching. Not knowing quite what to do, but feeling lazy, he wandered toward the rows of corn. Curious, he went in a way (the stalks clattered as he walked against them), stopped, then pulled at one of the ears with delight; the corn silk, soft, fragrant, and stringy, made a shredding sound and revealed almost white kernels. Engrossed, he realized that there was a clattering of corn stalks near him; he was momentarily convinced that an animal, a big dog or something similar, was there. He started to yell to scare it away when the clattering suddenly increased, only to reveal Susan walking toward him. He had started in fright. "Jeez," he said now. "Jeez, you scared me.

She grinned at him. "I just went for a walk in the field," she said.

"God, don"t do that again," he laughed, holding one hand to his heart. They looked at each other, smiling, and he embraced her, feeling a surge of overwhelming love, relieved that the feeling had returned to him, as she held him gently. "I'm so sorry, Susan. I've been ridiculous," he said. Her hair felt warm from the sun; he smelled the dirt and the corn and sensed that he was in the midst of a landscape that itself was like a wild animal. He knew with deep gratitude that their argument was over.

The two days they had left were as wonderful as at the beginning. Their last night, they decided to go to Le Bugue to have just desert and coffee, and they found a perfect terrace restaurant that overlooked the Vézère River. Everything seemed to symbolize France for them, from the way each couple was seated side by side at a small table rather than facing each other as in the States, to the delicate but pungent cheeses, to the wine, to the chocolate mousse that was made to look like a jewel and tasted bountiful. "Let's take a walk," Charlie said as they got up.

"Yes, please," she said. They found their way to the cobblestone street. The river now stretched black beside them, with the street lights silvering the water here and there and a full moon in the night sky. The water lapped against the sides of the river, and when he stopped walking and turned to embrace her, the softness of her lips was like a welcome into life itself. "Come to me," she seemed to be saying with her lips and her slight body against him. "Come to me." For a moment, he felt the tightness in his own body give way, a tightness he had not even recognized, as if he were slowly opening hands that he had unknowingly tightened into fists. They continued to walk. He felt young, like an adolescent, swinging her arm; they giggled and he pulled her closer to him so that she now was walking against him. They were passing by some buildings with narrow doorways, and suddenly, she pulled away from him.

"Look at this," she said. In a small open vestibule, there were posters of pastels by an artist whose gallery apparently was in the building, pastels that were explosions of color, mostly still lifes of flowers and fruit, in a style that swirled. Under the single doorway bulb, they were vibrant splashes of color in the dark. Across the posters, the name of the artist appeared in script, "Jacqueline," just her first name, "An affectation," Charlie thought to himself, and the sign indicated that the gallery was open all day. Apparently, it was upstairs, as a large green door stood open at the end of the vestibule and a narrow stairway could be seen.

"Aren't these beautiful," said Susan, peering more closely. "Charlie, let's go look."

"But it's almost nine, it's probably closed."

"Come on, Charlie, don't be silly. Let's try. Where's your sense of adventure?" Where, indeed? he wondered; it seemed that Susan constantly challenged him to loosen up. He followed her up the narrow staircase, where they were met by another seemingly anonymous door. Susan knocked. After a moment, when he did not know whether there would be an answer, the door opened. An attractive middle aged woman, her hair in a kerchief, opened the door.

"*Bon soir,*" she said. In halting French, Susan explained that they had come to see the pictures. The woman switched to English. "Come in, please." They entered what was clearly an artist's studio: there were paintings on the walls, on the floor, an easel with a pastel of flowers in progress, a large box of pastels on a table next to it. To his right, as he entered, he saw there was another room: a large open kitchen with a red-and-white patterned oilcloth on a table and dishes and wine bottles. The smell of food cooking came from the stove, permeating the apartment. In front of him, there was a kind of enclosed porch, all glass, beyond which he could make out in the evening light and a floodlight from the apartment itself, a large open garden on an extended balcony. Everything was a clutter, and yet the pictures seemed to sing their colors and shapes from the walls. The woman extended her hand, "I am Jacqueline Bonnet. Come on in. Can I be of help?"

They introduced themselves. "We saw the posters downstairs," he said, "but I see you are having dinner."

"But no, no. It is sure. This is the way we live. You see, we eat, but the gallery is always open. This we like." At this moment, a deep baritone voice came from further inside the apartment, saying in French something which Charlie did not understand, and then a tall handsome black man entered. "Raymond," said Jacqueline, "they are from *les Etats-Unis*. Charles and Susan."

Raymond came forward and shook Charlie's hand. "Welcome to our home," he said. "Where do you come from in the United States?" Charlie explained while Susan drifted away, gazing at the pictures on the walls.

"Oh, Charlie," she said, "these are just wonderful. Come look." She motioned him to her side.

"I am glad you like," said Jacqueline behind him as Charlie approached. The paintings on this wall were different from those downstairs, not just a profusion of flowers in vases, but some pastels, painted in seeming haste, of black jazz players, striking swatches of black, blue and brown colors.

Susan held his hand. "Aren't they nice."

"Yes," he said, sensing that they must remind her of their first meeting. He touched her shoulder and she leaned into him. Out of the corner of his eye, he saw that there were other pictures, too, on a small adjacent wall; he looked over Susan's head at them. Facing him was a pastel of a nude woman; he saw there were three or four others, but this was by far the most interesting. She stood full-faced with darkened eyes next to a table with a vase of yellow and red flowers. The light on her was so direct that there were few shadows in her skin, just a swatch of rose and ivory-colored flesh. There was something in the picture that reminded him both of the Venus they had seen and of Susan herself: the dark eyes perhaps, the full and uncompromising forward look of the figure, as if daring him to comment on her ripe nakedness. There was a red highlight in her eyes that seemed to pick up the red of the flowers and gave her a feline appearance. Charlie was entranced. "Oh, how much is this?" he asked without thinking. Susan, who had not seen what he was looking at, turned her head.

"Charlie," she inhaled, gripping his hand much tighter.

It was quickly settled. Of course Susan protested, but Charlie was insistent on buying it himself as a gift for her, and the price was more than reasonable. He arranged to have it shipped to Susan's apartment in New York, and he felt really good, expansive, having in some way taken a stance against the inimical forces of his life. He and Susan repeatedly marveled at the coincidence, that the picture reminded them of "their" Venus, as if they had a special relationship to the bas-relief of a woman who had posed thousands of years ago, and that the paintings on the walls of jazz players seemed so suited to them and their first meeting. They both felt this final event of their vacation was symbolic of everything that had happened to them, of their love for each other, of France and its mystical effect.

Raymond insisted that they drink to the purchase, and then, to the delight of both of them, Jacqueline said they should stay for dinner. "No, no," they said, over and over, "we couldn't. We already ate." But of course they did. They were plied with wine, with cheese and bread, with a delicious veal stew. As the evening wore on, Raymond, who was a blues singer by profession born of an American father who had returned to the United States leaving his son (then an infant) behind, got out his guitar and sang in English lyrics that Charlie could barely understand, but it was marvelous nonetheless. When they left, a little wobbly, and Jacqueline kissed him on the cheek and he held this tall black man close as if they had been friends forever, Charlie felt content. The tensions of the last few days, their argument at the cave of Rouffignac, his sometimes unexplainable discomfort, were forgotten. "How could I let myself get so upset?" he told himself. "See, love does change one's life, look what is happening to me, what has happened to me." They drove back to the stone mill under a black sky filled with points of light. It was very dark when they got there. "Home," he said to Susan as he approached the front door, feeling how much that word meant to him with Susan beside him. Their shoes scraped the gravel in front of the house. He worked at the door for a moment and then the hollow clunk of the metal bolt broke the deep silence as he opened it for what was really the last time, he realized; the only other sound came from the crickets and the leaves rustling in the tall trees. They entered the great space. The dank smell assailed him once again, but this time he found it familiar, enveloping, belonging to them.

They flew out the next day. Charlie looked down upon the fields of France as the plane gained altitude. It was such a flat country, he mused, and so seemingly soft and endless. One could fall into it as if it were a rumpled quilted bed, and, indeed, it had been that for him. Somewhere down there was the mill house and the field of sunflowers. He glanced over at Susan, who smiled at him, and he felt happy. The flight was uneventful. All the while, he anticipated with an uneasy feeling their saying goodbye at the airport. He always became flustered when he landed, worried about the baggage and meeting his driver, and everything became rushed just as he feared. One of Susan's bags had come undone somehow, and it was spilling clothes when it fell onto the carousel. He was unaccountably embarrassed, but Susan was unconcerned and did not find anything missing. Over Susan's protests, he had gotten a limousine for her to go back to the City, but at first the driver was nowhere to be found. The air conditioning in the airport seemed non-existent; it was hot and muggy, and he could feel the sweat pouring off of him. Finally, the driver who had gone to the wrong terminal was located, and it was time to say goodbye. "It was wonderful," said Susan. "I love you. Call me." She threw herself into him, kissed him hard on the cheek, and was gone before he knew it.

His own driver, John, reliable as always and always in the background when he arrived with others, had waited patiently through all this and at a distance. Probably he sensed that Susan was more than his usual business companion, but he could be trusted to say nothing, either to Charlie or anyone else. He had an incredibly beaked nose and a thin, lined face, and wore what seemed to be the same black suit, a little dingy and a little frayed each time, but as Charlie turned to him, he realized how glad he was to see him. "Good trip, Mr. Kaplan?" John asked, taking his bags from him. As John's dry hands brushed against his and the luggage was lifted from him, Charlie felt delightfully lighter.

"Yes," he said, "things went well and France is beautiful . . . but I'm glad to be back." He was aware of how mundane his response, but then the mundaneness made him feel comfortable, a ritual performed between them each time he returned. They took the escalator down to the parking lot and then walked silently together to the limousine. It was dark, late in the evening, but the mugginess outside was incredible. John held the back door open for him, and he hunched himself into the cool interior. He shifted in the leather seat and waited patiently. "How's the weather been?' he said once John had settled in front of him. "Like this, hot," John said, his incredibly beaked nose bobbing. "It has been over 90 the last few days."

"I forget each time how muggy it gets."

"Yes," said John, " It's awful."

"And how's your son doing?"

"Fine, Mr. Kaplan, fine. He's really recovered, he's out of rehab and he's going back to college in the fall." John's son had been in a motorcycle accident. It was hard to imagine this thin and dutiful man with a son so impetuous as to ride a motorcycle, hard really to imagine any of his life, which Charlie thought must be as dingy as his suit.

"I'm glad," said Charlie. "I'm glad."

"Kids," John said.

"Yes," said Charlie, accepting that shared understanding of adult men who now have to shoulder the unremitting burdens of life, and he leaned back against the dark leather as the car began to gather speed, signaling the completion of the ritual. John, like a giant bird in front of him, fell silently to his task.

He leaned back against the dark leather, enjoying the glow here and there of lights in the car: the dashboard with its colored lights, the lit outline of an ashtray, the glow of a light near his polished black leather shoes. He felt safe, enjoying the dark silent form of John in front of him, seemingly so solid.

Outside the window, the scene now had turned unearthly: they were passing the vast oil refinery near Newark, and there were strange metallic shapes rising skyward, towers and cauldrons, plumes of white smoke, rows of white lights. He felt privileged in his limousine as if this strange show were for him. How far away the house in France now seemed: the sun-flowered hill, the corn-field, and the ancient town were like a dream, as if they had never happened, as if he had been momentarily transported to another century and now had returned to the present. Deeply he breathed in the smell of the leather seat, to his surprise feeling completely relaxed for what seemed the first time in weeks.

But he became aware that he was troubled by a pungent odor from the refinery. He pushed the button next to him to make sure the window was tightly closed, and as he did so, he suddenly knew without any of his usual equivocation that he could never live with Susan. It was over. That was the way it had to be, the only way it could be. He should have known all along; he had almost fallen, and now he would pull himself back from the very edge; he would save himself. He envisioned how the painting would arrive at her apart-ment, all wrapped in brown paper and French stamps on it; and she would tear off the brown paper in her impulsive way and place it on her wall, but that he would never see it hanging there. He dreaded telling her. At least, he thought, and he knew foolishly, he had given her that memory of France (they had given each other some memo-ries), but he did not know why he had not seen things clearly from the beginning. It was like he had stepped briefly into a different world which he had learned to avoid as an adult: an adolescent landscape of uncertain shapes. There was no way that it could ever work out. He remembered with clearness how she had been impa-tient with him, how her hair straggled so often from her head, how her life was really so disordered. Most of all, he remembered being so out of control with her – it had been truly frightening. Everything had been a little out of kilter: the dank smell of the house was really

36

pretty horrible, like decaying matter, like a sign of death; and that whole experience of the caves, while interesting, had been so marred by their argument. No wonder he had been feeling so uncomfortable while he was there, for he must have begun to realize the extent to which Susan lived a life of uncertainty, of impulse, where things could collapse at any moment. Whatever had come over him, he did not know, but now it was passed; he knew it; he felt that he was thinking clearly again; he felt strong again. He would return to his old life with renewed vigor so that it was not "old," so it was filled with the essence of his experience in France, perhaps that was the lesson he had learned: return to his work, to his wife, predictable as she might be and as certain. He realized how much he relied on her, after all, to keep his home going, to take care of things. For some reason, he had an image of Marilyn now, opening the clothes dryer and taking the clothes out, which he knew was silly and mundane, as mundane as his conversation with John, and together their putting the still warm sheets into the linen closet after she folded them. Who was Susan to ridicule the life he had fashioned so carefully for so long, or his golf, or the suburbs? Doubtless, underneath, she envied the stability he represented.

There was a stinging sensation in his eyes, probably the chemical smell from outside had entered the car, and so he pushed the button again, almost frantically, wondering to himself whether the gas — whatever it was from this surreal landscape — was toxic. There seemed to be a momentary pause, everything unchanged and un- changing; the dull sound of the tires on the road going on and on like the sound of a distant ocean. And slowly it dawned on him: he would cry. His hands curled into fists like those of a small child, and then the tears, from some deep source within him that had lain hidden for what seemed his whole life, welled-up hot and relentless in his eyes. They came without end. He had difficulty breathing and his chest felt tight because he did not want to make a noise. He thought, with surprise and a clarity so brutal that he felt he had been hit, "I am so unhappy. I have been unhappy for so long." Soundlessly, wordlessly, so John would not hear, he cried all the way home.

Ya-ta-Hey,[1] John Yazzie

or The Richest Indian in Fort Defiance

John Yazzie, the almost blind owner of the laundromat in the small town of Fort Defiance, Arizona, was sitting on the porch of his house. The house was right next door to the laundromat. John could make out that a red pickup was parked on the packed dirt in front of the laundromat, and he saw when a black pickup drove up and stopped. He could just make out that an old woman (she was dressed traditionally in a red skirt and black top, her hair tied in a bun) was in the back of the black pickup, and that she descended from there with a large bundle of clothes wrapped in her arms, while the driver – he could make out his cowboy hat – got out of the cab.

"*Yah-ta-hey*, John Yazzie," the driver yelled to him. John responded the same way, but he was unsure who it was. It looked like Big Joe Burton from over Chinle way, by his size and the way he walked so slowly, who would have been visiting his mother who lived on the outskirts of the Fort, but he could not be sure They went inside the laundromat and John leaned back in his rickety chair, reached over and picked up the coffee cup on the wooden box that served as a table next to him, and took another sip. It was black and hot, which was the way he liked it. The dry semi-desert air, still a little chilly this morning and filled with the smell of dirt and sagebrush, felt good, and John was content.

---

[1] Ya-ta-hey: "Hello" in Navajo.

He thought about last evening. It had been a strange one. The Delany sisters, Mary and Delores, from just down the road, had been at the laundromat late, and he had invited them over. Delores was already a little drunk, which was usual, and it had probably been a mistake to invite her in and offer her some of the Wild Turkey he saved for just these times. John did not really drink and he often took a lot of ribbing for it, which he was more or less used to.

"John Yazzie, how come you don't drink?" said Delores as she grabbed the bottle from him as soon as she entered the house and took a swig, dribbling some on her chin. She paused for breath. "You're not *Dine*²," she said, looking at him, and then she took another swing. Then she went up close to him, looking him in the face, "You're not *Dine*," she repeated. "You're Mormon. They must have secretly adopted you when you were not looking, John Yazzie." And she laughed.

"Let Mary have some of that," said John, trying to get the bottle away from her, but she pushed off him. She took a third swig.

"I know, you, John Yazzie. Them Mormons, they gave you back, that's it, they gave you back, but not before they made you hate Wild Turkey. They gave you back 'cause you weren't a good enough Indian for them." She laughed again, so much so that her whole body seemed to shake. "You weren't good enough." And then, looking pointedly down at his jeans, which was somewhat wasted on John Yazzie because he could not make out exactly where her eyes were staring but he could hear the now sweet provocation in her voice, "Are you good enough, tell me, John Yazzie. Are you good enough?"

Delores was a big woman. John Yazzie could remember when she had been a little thing, but she had gotten progressively fatter and now she looked matronly. The sudden seductive sweetness in her voice seemed strange given her huge size. In contrast, her

---

² Dine: Navajo name for the tribe, translates as "The People."

younger sister Mary was a beauty, thin and buxom with her black hair straight and skin that seemed unblemished to John's eyes.

John had once, when he was much younger, been married but it had not worked out. His wife claimed that all he cared about was making money and that he was no fun, and she had gone off with a rodeo man from Lukachukai way. That was long ago. Now he owned the laundromat and this house and another house down the street, which he rented out, and, on the other side of town, the only gas station in Fort Defiance, with a convenience store attached. He knew he was not liked much, but he told himself he did not care. For a half-blind Indian, he figured that he had done pretty well for himself. Unlike other Navajos, he thought, he did not really need anyone. His parents had died and he had one brother, who had gone off to Riverside, California, and he never visited his aunt, his mother's sister, and her family who lived in a hogan on the long dirt road the other side of the Fort.

But he was lonely. And Mary seemed so inviting with her long hair and quiet manner, unlike her sister's, and her beauty (which he could vaguely make out when she was standing very close to him). He had known her for years and he had always been interested in her, even when they were both married. She had gone off with her husband, who was part Zuni, to live in Albuquerque years ago, but they quarreled all the time and she had returned to the reservation alone maybe three years back. It felt as if she and John had been circling around each other ever since, but he did not know whether she thought of it that way. She had had a number of boyfriends and had a job over at the Navajo Tribal gift shop in Window Rock, which he knew she had recently quit, where he was sure her beauty did no harm with the tourists. Maybe he was too old for her, he wondered. Besides, he was set in his ways for sure.

Delores kept waving the Wild Turkey bottle around, not giving it back to John or over to Mary. "How come you never got married again, John Yazzie," she said, staggering a bit and holding her bottle hand up and out for balance. "You forgot how to use it?" she giggled. "That's it, you forgot how to use it." She managed to plop herself down in the one big chair in the living room, almost missing it, and holding the bottle out to her sister Mary at the same time. "Here," she said, magnanimously. "Here, you have some of this, sister." The bottle almost dropped, but Mary grabbed it. She, too, took a long swig, but it seemed to John that as she drank, she was looking over the end of bottle to him and smiling at Delores's goings on, as if she and John understood each other.

"Delores, you've got to go now," he said.

"Why?"

"You're drunk, Delores," he said. "Go sleep it off."

"I ain't drunk, and anyhow, I'm good you know. You wouldn't know what to do with me, I'm so good." She grinned.

She staggered up from the chair.

"Come on, John Yazzie. Where's your bedroom. I'll show you."

"Delores, " he said, "you need to go now," but she was lurching toward the back of the house, looking in the rooms.

"Is this it? No, is this it?" She giggled to herself, looking in each room.

John tried to guide her back to the living room, grabbing on to her shoulder, but she twisted drunkenly away, laughing. She had found his bedroom. "It's dark in here," she said. "Where's the light?" and she made large swipes with one hand on the side of the door without encountering the light switch. "Ohhhuh," she said, the motion of her arm unbalancing her, and she stumbled backward until her lower legs hit the side of the bed, which she then fell onto.

She broke into a fit of laughter, her whole large body shaking, as she looked up at the ceiling. Her feet were splayed outward. "Ohhwee, I sure found your bed," she laughed, and then, "and this is the right position too, John Yazzie," which only brought on another paroxysm of laughter.

It took a long time, but with much persuasion and cajoling, John and Mary finally managed to get Dolores through the front door, urging her to go home and sleep it off. John closed the door tightly behind her, but once through, Dolores just stood unmoving on the porch, her bulky back to them. Then she turned around and stared at them through the glass door panes, as if in a daze. "Go on home, Delores," John said for what seemed the twentieth time, raising his voice so he could be heard through the door. Finally, she moved away. After a while, he could vaguely see her in the light from the lone street lamp as she crossed the parking lot in the direction of the Delany hogan. He breathed a sigh of relief. "She sure didn't want to go," he said to Mary. And then he added, "I'm glad at least that you're still here."

"Me, too," she said, leaning against the hallway wall. She had such a graceful way about her, which he could make out in the broad outline of her standing there. "I think I need some water," she said, and they moved into the kitchen. He took a glass from a cabinet, ran tap water into it, and handed it to her.

They sat down at the small formica kitchen table.

"I wonder why we never seem to get together, John," she said.

"I don't know."

"It's been this way for so long."

"I guess I just been busy."

"I even remember when we were young and you came out of a sweat lodge with nothing on"

He laughed.

There was a sudden sound of breaking glass from the living room. "Oh, no," said Mary. She put down her glass of water on the table and they hurried toward the noise, both of them knowing what they would find. For Delores was back on the porch again, and now she was reaching through a shattered pane in the front door to turn the doorknob from inside. Her hand was bleeding. The door opened and she staggered in.

"You locked me out," she said accusingly. "You shouldn't have done that, sister." She was weaving into the room.

"Oh, Delores," said Mary. "Let me see your hand. It's bleeding."

"Why?" said Delores, and she looked at her hand quizzically and saw the blood. She moved her hand up closer to her eyes, trying to focus on it. "It's a scratch."

"Let me see it, " said Mary, and she guided Delores to the living room couch, where she plunked her down.

"It's nothing, sister," Delores kept saying. "Why'd you lock your big sister out?"

Blood from the cut was very slowly making its way down Dolores's arm.

"John, do you have something for this," Mary said. "She's bleeding."

John went to the bathroom and brought back a towel. Mary staunched the flow.

"Delores, we should go back to the house. We need to take care of this."

"We can stay here. Why not?"

"No, Delores, it's late. Let's go back. We'll go back together."

John felt disappointment, but there was really no help for it. It was not even clear that Delores would leave.

"Come on, Delores," said Mary. "Let me help you up."

"We're not staying?" said Delores.

"No, let me help you up."

Mary tried to push her up. John Yazzie went on the other side of Delores, and together they got her standing from the couch.

"You come back with us, John," said Delores, but she was rather subdued now.

"No Delores, this is fine. You need to sleep it off. Let your sister take care of you. Sleep it off."

"Ok, John Yazzie," she said, "but we have a date," and she giggled as she stumbled out the door.

Mary held her on one side and nodded to John.

"Thank you, John" she said.

He tried to watch their merged form walking away, but they disappeared into the night. It was dark now. He stood at the door briefly, smelling the dark night, and then closed the door. Then he went into the kitchen. He made himself some coffee and sat at the table there, silent, his arms propped on the cool surface, leaning forward. His shoulders felt heavy. He was tired. He would have to go to bed soon. He stayed like that for a long time, thinking to get up but half-asleep.

Then there was a sharp knock on the door. He pushed himself up from the table and went to the door, opened it. Mary stood there, smiling at him. "Would you like to let me in?" she said. "I snuck out."

He was surprised and pleased and stepped aside. They sat at the formica table again and talked of the past. He could feel how happy he was to have her there. "Do you remember," she began, and then a litany of early events came from both of them: his trying to lasso a goat as a boy without success until he mistakenly lassoed her; the time they both tried to push Larry Yazzie's pickup out of the mud when the spinning tires suddenly caught the dirt road and they fell completely flat together in the mud; the time that his uncle Zuni Yellowhair prepared a roasted goat for them to celebrate his graduation from high school and everyone came from miles around. She touched his rough hand lying on the formica table with hers at that point and it was so soft, he thought; and when he leaned forward to kiss her, the softness of her cheek felt so wonderful. She held his hand tightly and then said, "John Yazzie, let's go to bed."

It was more than he expected, the whole thing. And despite Dolores's teasing him previously, "it" worked just fine, he thought, rather proudly. When they were done, Mary lay there against him. He could hear her breathing, but in the darkness he really could not see her. He was reminded of what it had felt like years ago when his wife lay beside him, but he tried to push the thought away. They began to talk again.

"John," she said, at one point, "I heard about your trying to rent that house of yours to that *bellagaana*[3] lawyer from Window Rock.

"Oh," said John, "what a coyote. I really don't want to talk about it."

"I heard he fell through your ceiling."

---

[3] Bellagaana: Navajo name for "white person."

"He didn't 'fall.'"

"What happened, then?"

" He put his foot through is all."

"Put his foot through?"

He thought to himself he did not really want to talk about this.

"Yeh, he put his foot through it when I had him go up to fix a wire. And just as I told him not to step on it."

"You mean your rental house has one of them drop ceilings."

"Yeh, that's it. What a stupid *bellagaana*. I got so angry, I just told him to go away. I wasn't going to rent it to him anyway."

"You lost your temper, John Yazzie. Serves you right. I heard you were going to charge him twice the price."

"How'd you know I lost my temper."

"John, we could hear you yelling at him at the top of your voice, down at the hogan. We didn't know what had happened. You even scared the goats over at Claire Begay's. They looked up and shook their heads to get the sound out of their ears."

"OK, Mary. All them goats care about is eating."

This, John did not like, but then he took a breath and decided to bluster it out. "Well it would have served him right. He was one of them slick lawyers from back East that don't know a thing, come out here for what? We don't need more lawyers out here."

She was quiet for a while.

He relented. "You know," he said, "it was funny anyhow. You should have seen it. I couldn't see it very well, but you know, it sure did *sound* funny when he went through the ceiling."

They both laughed.

It was so nice having her here to talk to, he thought to himself; he really did not want her to go home. They talked some more, but finally she said, "I better go, John. They're going to wonder what happened to me, although they probably could guess. I will see you in the morning. This was nice."

"Yes," he said, "it was."

Early next morning, he was back on his porch, sitting in his chair, his coffee cup in hand. It was a brisk day and the dust swirled a bit here and there, and once in a while, pieces of tumbleweed skittered along the dirt road. From the Delany hogan, he knew smoke must be rising. He could smell it in the air. People were already up there, apparently. Eventually, a figure left the hogan. He could tell from the way it moved that it must be Mary. She was making her way to him. Finally she stood on the dirt driveway, looking up at him on the porch.

"John, I'm going up Shiprock way to help my sister, you know Denise, who just had her baby. I don't know how long I will be gone. They say there might be something for me there."

"Eeyah," he said, standing up. They were both silent.

"John" she said and stopped. She did not say anything more.

"Was that a question, Mary?"

"You know, John Yazzie, it didn't sound like it, but it was."

"If you've got to go, you've got to go, I guess."

"What about the question?" she said.

He was silent.

"Is there anything to come back for here?" she asked.

He thought about it, and then he started to wonder whether maybe one of the nurses at the Public Health Service whose trailer had been washed out in the flash flood two weeks ago might need a place to stay, and he could rent her the house.

"John?"

"Mary, I reckon if you come back this way we would see each other again."

Mary looked up at him.

"My sister said there may be a job at the convenience store I could have up there. I think I might be staying."

"Eeyah," he said.

They were silent a little longer. It became painful.

Finally Mary said, "You take care, John Yazzie."

"You too, Mary," he said.

He sat back down in his chair and watched her going away. There was a nice sway to her walk. For a moment, he thought of calling out to her, but then the impulse passed. Through the evening, he just sat on the porch in the cold air. After a while, night fell. Now, looking up he could not quite make out the stars, but the moon was full. From the Begay family hogan, across the way, there came the odor of burning pinon and the sound of voices. He breathed in the pungent aroma. It felt like a beautiful night, but he could not entirely see it, and he laughed to himself. Here he was a *Dine* whose whole existence intermeshed with the beauty of the Reservation, and from birth he could not really see that beauty. "With beauty before me may I walk, with beauty behind me may I walk, with beauty above me may I walk," he said to himself. He had heard the song at the Beauty Way ceremony so many times, intoned by the medicine man, but it would never apply to him. It did not matter. He did not need it.

The Click of the Reindeer

The black and white photograph was old and tinged with brown. It showed a group of Russians, some seated and some standing, in what seemed to be a forest clearing. At the center of them was a rustic table on which stood a very large samovar, and there were some white ceramic cups, looking almost too delicate, next to it. Some of the standing men casually held long rifles with the butt ends on the ground, and all the women were dressed in long patterned dresses, some of them with their heads tied in kerchiefs. They all, at least in the photograph, looked healthy and happy, as if they were on a camping trip. In fact, they had been exiled to an uninhabited Siberian island near Vladivostok as punishment for their revolutionary activities. This was where they lived, in rough cabins, and the rifles were not for sport so much as to kill food that they needed to survive.

Seated on the right side was a slim young man with glasses and somewhat large ears and an almost amused and quizzical expression on his face. Standing next to him was a buxom and short young woman who stared at the camera as if she were challenging the nameless person taking the picture to a duel. These were my grandparents. I had pulled the picture out of my backpack where I had carefully placed it between the pages of my Norway/Sweden guidebook, and I stared at it now in the early morning mist.

It was a little chilly and my hands were cold holding the picture. The only other person up was Irwin who was seated cross-legged not too far from me, sketching in watercolors. It was quiet; the mist covered the small lake before us, the tall grass was a little wet with dew, and the sky showed up here and there a light blue.

Our blue tents spotted the meadow in a random pattern. Every once in a while there was a noise from a sleeping reindeer shaking its tether.

The reindeer were lying in the tall grass, only their antlered heads and their shoulders visible. It was cold enough that their breath could be seen in puffs. It seemed magical for the moment to be here above the Arctic Circle surrounded by reindeer and tents, so far from home – from a home of city noises, skyscrapers, hustle and bustle, black soot and garbage bags left on the street. All that was far away.

I looked at the old photograph again, with a feeling of some satisfaction. How I had loved my grandfather. Impractical always, always with a book in his hand, arrested for passing out revolutionary pamphlets in Kiev, he and my grandmother had endured their banishment for two years, only to escape the island when the winter was particularly cold, and the water had frozen over, and eventually (I really did not know how) make their way to America, past the Statue of Liberty, to Ellis Island, and then the Lower East Side of Manhattan. He had never seemed a man of action to me and yet, look what he had done. In the summers, while my grandmother supported the family with the restaurant that she had created in the Catskills, my grandfather walked among the pine trees there, his hands clasped behind his back, looking around at the beauty of the forest or at the brown pine needles beneath his feet, entirely in his own world. Sometimes he would take me with him, and then he would talk to me in his Old European voice, sometimes teasing me because I was so skinny then, calling me a "skinny marink," and at other times telling me how much the Catskill forest reminded him of his exile in Siberia. He told me how they had to hunt for their own food, how they always tried to have the samovar filled with hot tea in the morning and at night, and how they planted and tended a vegetable garden. He told me how the mummers would come to the island and entertain them in a clearing, how they read Tolstoy and Turgenev to each other on cold winter nights, and how they sang and recited poetry from memory in the darkness. He described how the reindeer that populated the island were almost friendly because they had no previous awareness of people, and how they came near the camp, moving in small herds with a kind of quiet dignity. Most of all, he told me how important it was to dream about the future, and how his dreams had come true when he came to this country, how freedom was so wonderful, and how I, his granddaughter, was part of his dreams even back then.

When I was ten I wrote a story about him for Mrs. Winograd's fifth grade class. I labored over it very carefully, recounting everything he told me in my careful cursive handwriting, in ball point pen on the lined paper of my writing book, which I then removed so the teacher could see it. But before doing so, I showed it proudly to my mother, who was baking in the kitchen. She had flour on her hands, which she rubbed on the dish towel that she had over her shoulder, and there was a smidgen of dough in her black hair. I can still see her, looking down over the pages on the counter. I waited expectantly. And then she said, looking at me, that it was very nice, but you know, she added, there were no reindeer. "Yes," I said, "that's what granddad told me."

"Oh," she said, "he probably was just trying to make the story interesting; you know how granddaddy is."

I felt confused. I was almost sure that was what he had told me, but I did what my mother asked, and I carefully re-wrote the story leaving the reindeer out. I handed the paper in and got some grade on it, I do not remember what, but a few weeks later, when granddad was visiting, I told him I had written about his experiences for school. I gave him the paper. I can still see him sitting on my bed in my bedroom, hunched over the paper held in his large and gnarled hands, reading it. When he looked up, his grey-blue eyes focused on me through his glasses. "A beautiful job," he said. "Beautiful. But, my skinny marink, where are the reindeer? You forgot to put them into your story." And in that moment, I could feel a sudden emptiness in my stomach, for I realized I had listened to my mother and betrayed my grandfather, betrayed us together in some way. I did not dare tell him that she had told me to take them out. I was too ashamed. I just said that I guess I had forgotten them.

And now, now here the reindeer were: six of them, lying mostly obscured by the tall grass in front of me. They were smaller than I had imagined. Soon they would be loaded with our cooking gear and the blue tents, including the one large one, and we would begin our trek across the mountains into Norway. I could hear voices now from the tents, and the air was getting a little warmer. Irwin got up from his spot in the grass and came toward me, holding his sketch pad in one hand, and a tin of watercolor paints with a small brush in the other. Irwin was the one reminder of home here. He too was from Manhattan and although we had signed up for the tour separately, we had naturally gravitated to one another.

The rest of the hikers were from Minnesota, garrulous and noisy, not at all my kind. There was one exception, whom I found woefully intriguing. He was Norwegian, tall and dark looking, very thin, and seemingly in his late thirties. His name was Jacov. He wore a grey and black woven Norwegian wool skull cap and with his high cheekbones, unshaven cheeks, and black eyes, I had trouble not staring at him. Woefully intriguing because this was just the type of man for whom I invariably fell; my romanticism seemed to take root on the tall, dark, and sullen looking man before all others. It was not at all what I wanted on this trip, for I was trying to leave behind the memory of just such a man.

After a quick breakfast of hot tea and oatmeal, we took down our tents, and rolled them up, so each one fit into a tent bag, and then we gathered together at one spot, where the tall grass had been worn down. Lennart, the Sami leader – a stolid looking man with a slow smile and a matter-of-fact manner whose hiking clothes were no different than those of the rest of us and gave no hint of his Sami background – reminded us that we would hike for four days and camp three on a route that led between Sweden (where we now were) through the high mountains to a town in Norway near

Narvick on the sea. He warned us to be careful of the slick black rock when we got higher up because it was slippery and to try not to stray off the path. As we hiked, there would be two people per reindeer. It was important not to hold your reindeer too tightly with the thick rope that attached to a halter, in order to give each reindeer his space so that he could negotiate when he walked down hill or across a stream, but to be prepared to pull on the rope to prevent him from becoming too engrossed in eating grass or tree leaves as we moved. Reindeer often could be difficult, but these were generally well-tamed. When we got up higher in the mountains, we might see many wild reindeer and perhaps at night we would see the Northern lights. We would not go that far each day, perhaps eight miles.

We waited a little restlessly for Lennart to assign the reindeer to us. I had been hoping to be with Irwin, but, on the other hand, I had noticed that Irwin seemed to have taken to the youngest of the Minnesotans, a perky girl with a blonde pony tail, whom he was talking to even now. Maybe Lennart had seen that too because Lennart now looked at me and at Jacov and said, "Julie and Jacov, you take Sivu." He then gave the rope that hung from the neck of one of the larger reindeer to Jacov. The reindeer was placidly munching grass and paid no attention to Jacov. Then Jacov came closer to me and I felt both a twinge of excitement and a shyness.

"Here," said Jacov, handing the rope to me. "You can start. Take Sivu."

"Are you sure?" I asked.

"Yes," he said.

"Thank you," I said.

I took the rough rope from him. All of us started out then, in a long line, with Jacov and me and then Sivu bringing up the rear. The morning mist had burned off, the air was crisp, and the sky was unremittingly blue. Our boots crunched on the forest floor as we walked.

The Minnesotans, further ahead, talked animatedly to one another, and I had the desire to go slowly so that we would be further back and hear them less. Jacov and I spoke hardly at all as we walked. Once in a while, I would stop to look at the mountains ahead, which, through the few trees that existed here, still seemed far away, and Jacov would stop as well. I might remark how beautiful they were and he would agree. He did not offer much when he spoke, and he was very polite. Because the path was so thin and sometimes barely discernible, we walked single file, and, as he was in front of me, it gave me a chance to observe him: his fine chiseled features, the simple, even lithe way he walked, his lips that seemed pressed together as if he wanted to speak but would not let himself. I had the feeling that his careful silence concealed loneliness.

Eventually, I suggested we change places, and gave him the thick rope that attached to Sivu's halter. When I did so, our hands brushed. This transfer of Sivu's rope between us continued. And so it was that we walked on, murmuring at times about things in the landscape: a distant hawk, a small stream that gurgled near us. And behind us: Sivu, with a soft kind of lumbering, walked, his reindeer face looking gentle yet severe and his whole attitude mutely accepting. As he moved each hind leg, there was a click, and then another, and another – not unlike the slow sound of a clock – caused by a tendon in the lower leg rubbing against bone. It was a natural sound, common to all grown reindeer. Perhaps the click had survival value, permitting reindeer to find each other as they walked in the snow blinding blizzard conditions above the arctic circle. But there was no snow blizzard now, and still the clicking continued as we walked along: measured and strangely calming, like an accompaniment to the relationship between Jacov and me.

After dinner, sitting on the ground outside our tents, which we had pitched away from the Minnesotans, I told him why I had taken this trip and showed him the photograph of my grandparents in Siberia. He took the photograph and looked at it for some time. I could not tell what he was thinking. When he handed it back to me he said, "Exile must have been hard."

"Yes," I said. "But you can see at least they had each other."

We were quiet for a while. Finally, he asked, "What was he like – your grandfather?"

I described my grandfather with some joy, and then I asked, "And your grandfathers?"

"No," he said, "I did not have. I was raised by my mother only. So I missed that experience. When I hear you talk as you do, it is perhaps a little hard for me. But my mother, she loved the mountains here. We used to take many hikes together, not here, but further on. Just the two of us."

"It is wonderful that this beauty was part of your childhood."

He did not say anything.

There was a burst of laughter from the Minnesotans, who were talking together animatedly. Darkness had descended by now. Crickets sounded. It felt that Jacov and I were in a different place than the others. I wanted to ask why he had not known his grandfathers, but I sensed he did not want to elaborate.

He continued to be silent, as if the little he said was more than he wanted. I talked on as I do sometimes when I am nervous. I talked about New York City, how it was sometimes hard to find yourself there and how I had come to these mountains because I wanted to get away; I did not tell him that I was alone because I had a lover for two years of whom he reminded me – Greg: moody, sometimes ethereal in his speech (but speak he did sometimes, going on for what seemed hours), in fact, a would-be writer who was alternately open and closed, a man whose sudden and often immense insularities had ultimately driven me away and whom I mourned. And I did not tell him that his dark eyes reminded me of Greg's.

What I did say was that I felt I needed silence and vast space and a sky where I could see the stars instead of a sky you could barely see between buildings. I felt alive here, wondrously alive. To my surprise, despite his quietness, his aloneness, which I sensed and which worried me, I found him easy to talk to. He bent his head to listen. And he asked me questions carefully.

Then he took out a pack of cigarettes from his jacket pocket. "Is it ok?" he asked. Normally, I would have said no, but I thought, "He is European," and beside I wanted him to be comfortable.

"Yes, of course," I said. He offered me one, but I shook my head. He lit his cigarette. The smoke mingled with the cool mountain air, and the end of the cigarette glowed orange in the dark. I laughed and said that the light of the cigarette reminded me that I wanted so much to see the aurora borealis tonight. Together we looked up at the night sky.

"It is not quite the right time of year," he said, "but you never know." He paused. "Yes, you are right, the sky is large here."

"Life is strange," I found myself saying. "I come from such a different place."

He laughed. "Such differences may make things harder, you know."

I said they could, but they also make things more interesting. It seemed that he did not quite agree. We joked with each other, realizing that the differences of which we spoke really involved us. In kidding him, I brushed his hand playfully with mine. And of course, one thing led to another. I knew that I wanted to touch his body, which looked hard and muscular and compact. His kiss, when it finally came, was remarkably soft, though, and he seemed even a bit shy, and that smell of cigarette smoke, which ordinarily I did not like, was exotic in the coolness. I knew I was being entirely too impulsive, but it was such a remarkable setting, so romantic, and I felt that it should be shared. Really, I just could not resist.

We did not get to see the Northern lights that night, although we stayed up late and snuggled into one another as it got colder. The night sky never lightened with color but just seemed to get a deeper grey. The laughter of the Minnesotans had died away and all was quiet, when, together, we went into my tent. It was cold and it was not easy making love, with our hiking clothes and the sleeping bags, but he was the way he seemed: hard, determined, as if he wanted to do a good job, and even a little rough. I loved it and fell asleep quickly.

During the night, I had a strange dream. I was a child, maybe ten years old, and I was with my grandfather; it was night and we were running. Something, some animal, was chasing us. I could not see it in the dark, but I heard it crashing through the bushes behind us. My grandfather held me by my hand, and, although I was running as hard as I could, I just was not able to keep up with him. My stride was a small child's. And then to my distress, my hand slipped out of his. And yet, to my surprise, he did not stop. He did not even look back. He just kept running, getting further and further ahead. "Come back. Please, please come back," I screamed, but to no avail. He had disappeared entirely into the darkness, and I now heard that the crashing of the animal was much closer to me. I was terrified. And then the sound gave way to another, a clicking sound, except it was anything but comforting. It just got louder and louder, as if the animal – or whatever it was – was about to pounce on me. I awoke with a start, my heart pounding in time to the clicks.

I lay there as if to catch my breath, waiting for my heartbeat to slow. Then, thank goodness, I felt Jacov beside me in the darkness, asleep, snoring slightly. I touched his arm, muscular and warm, for reassurance. He stirred but did not wake. Eventually, I calmed, and, for what seemed forever, I listened to his breathing and the crickets outside and a light breeze that pushed against our tent. Finally, I must have fallen asleep because I did not wake until the morning sunlight had brightened the tent fabric and I heard voices and the distant sound of birds.

There was an easy familiarity between us now. It was nice, for a moment, to lie there with him before we got up. We joked about how we had fumbled the night before and how we had tried not to make too much noise so that others did not hear us. We packed up, and at morning coffee, which was hot and wonderful in the cold, we sat next to each other on a large rock. Irwin and the Minnesotans made passing comments to us, but I am sure they knew.

The hiking proved to be different now: there were fewer trees and grass and we were into the rocky mountains. Walking was more difficult, and we had to climb steep rock inclines at times.

More than once I slipped but managed to catch myself. Sivu, although burdened with our equipment, of course had no problem at all, although I kept wondering why his hoofs did not slide. Often, it was hard to even make out a path along the rock faces, but Lennart just led us along, a line of bright-colored parkas and backpacks against the rock faces. The sky shone an amazing blue, and, even though it was summertime, there were patches of snow on the distant mountains. Then we came to a large jumbled field of rocks where there were wild reindeer scattered here and there, grazing, moving along at their own pace and whim, and paying us no mind.

After lunch, we continued onward. We were now into the mountains themselves, and there were snow patches in the rocks. It was late afternoon when we came upon a gray wooden sign, weathered and unassuming, that indicated we were passing from Sweden to Norway. Further on, in a declivity along the side of the trail, rocks had been formed around the remnants of a tall wooden box, maybe three feet in height with the open side facing the trail. Some of the rocks had tumbled to the side. The whole thing was covered with ivy and moss and clumps of grass at the bottom, so, obviously, it had stood here for a while and been taller at one time. Lennart stopped beside it and the rest of us spread out in various attitudes of waiting, while the reindeer, with their heads down, munched clumps of grass along the trail. "This," said Lennart, "is a Nazi sentry box. You will find them all along these mountain trails as we get nearer the Norwegian coast."

We stood there, looking at the remains of the box, and then Lennart started to move on. The group followed him. I did not move. I was reminded of how harsh this part of the world could be – the Nazis with their hatred of everyone, of anything foreign to them, and then the Russians who had condemned my grandfather to exile in a cold land not so far from here and not so different. Jacov stood next to me. "Let's go," he finally said.

I did not want to move yet. "I cannot imagine this," I said to him.

"Imagine what?" he asked.

"Imagine a young German soldier standing here, stationed here, in the cold, in the middle of nowhere, waiting for people to come along this trail. For what? To tell them they could not flee to Sweden, they could not escape from the German army, to turn them back or to kill them if they persisted in walking forward."

"It was wartime," he said. "You should not try to imagine. You are from a place too far from here. Your country's boundary is the sea; there are no sentry boxes; you are protected from occupations, even from wars themselves. Here, things are very different. We are Europeans. You cannot understand." He drew on his cigarette and then looked at me directly, his head up, and blew the smoke into the cold air, as if dismissing me with it. He was suddenly so different and maddening.

"So I cannot have an opinion?"

"You can of course," he admitted after a moment, and then after another moment, "but it is without meaning." He took one more drag on the cigarette then threw it onto the rocky trail and stamped at it twice with his booted foot. He turned from me and started to walk toward the others who by now had moved out of earshot down the trail. I did not know whether I was more taken aback by the white cigarette butt – which he discarded so unexpectedly, so nonchalantly into this pristine setting – or by his indifferent, cutting words.

"Wait. Wait." I said, and then, without thinking, "What is wrong with you?"

"Nothing is wrong." He stopped and waited. "We should join the others."

"No. Tell me. What is wrong? You cannot say these things without seeing that something is wrong."

He did not respond. He just stood there, looking at me, waiting to see if I was finished.

I came up to him. "Jacov," I said, "you seemed so thoughtful yesterday, and even happy, and now something has happened and I do not know what."

"Nothing has happened. This is foolishness." He was quiet again. Then, "Let's go."

Perhaps I should have stopped there and accepted what he said, but I remembered those moments that we had connected the previous night, remembered the feeling of him: how we had woken up in the morning next to one another. I wanted to protect those moments from this seemingly transformed person. And at the same time I realized how little I knew him. It was too early. Probably I had invested too much, too soon, as I all-too-frequently did. I approached closer to him and put my hand on his arm.

"Look," he said, pulling away, "you are entirely too emotional about things you do not understand. It is an American trait, I think."

"But I *want* to understand," I persisted. "All I wondered was what was it like for a young German soldier, far from his home in these mountains, possibly alone, who probably did not even speak their language but had to police the poor people – the Norwegians, maybe the Swedes, the Sami – who came by him on this path. Standing sentry duty, for a miserable regime, in the middle of nowhere."

"He had his orders. Like any soldier, he obeys. That's his job."

"I cannot believe you think that way."

"What good does it do to imagine?"

"But, Jacov, we *do* have to imagine. It is the thing that makes us human, makes us able to connect with one another, the way I thought we were starting to connect."

"No more," he said in a loud voice.

And because I did not know what was happening, because I did not know, I instinctively put my arms around him to hold him.

He gave a sudden cry as if in pain. And with that, he shoved me away with both hands and with such sudden force that I fell over. I felt a twinge in my left ankle as my foot caught on a space between the rocks on the path – I too gave a cry – and then I was flat on my back on the ground. Fortunately, my backpack cushioned my fall. Jacov had started down the trail. He heard my cry, turned, looked at me, and then turned back and continued down the path toward the others.

I struggled clumsily to get up, stood, and realized that the pain in my ankle was not too bad. I thought it would probably go away.

I knew that the others must have heard when Jacov raised his voice, although they may not have seen. I could not bear to talk to any of them, however, so I pretended that nothing had happened. I was miserable. We all ate dinner around a large campfire, but I avoided Jacov, did not even look at him. Irwin came over to me, no doubt to try to cheer me up, and it was nice to hear his New York City voice, but I barely made conversation. The fire threw our shadows and the shadows of the tents and those reindeer that were not sleeping against the bare rock in large patterns that were beautiful and strange, but for me they seemed almost sinister. The wind blew. It got colder. I excused myself from the Minnesotans, who were laughing and talking, and went into my tent. Jacov's tent was far away, across the campfire near a small tree. I fell asleep wondering what had happened and feeling terribly, terribly alone.

When I woke in the morning and crawled out of my tent, I saw most of the Minnesotans were up, chattering away as always, but then I noticed that Jacov's tent was no longer there. Instead, it was rolled up into a perfect blue cylinder, standing on end, leaning against the tree. At first I thought he must have gotten up early for a walk. I did not see him around the campsite though. The Minnesotans were talking in their usual excited way, but I noticed they glanced over at me. Lennart walked over and said, "Jacov left early this morning, before anyone got up."

"Left?" I said. "How will he get back from here? How would he ever know the way?"

"He will know. Don't worry," Lennart said.

"But I don't understand, Lennart," I said, and I knew my voice was pleading.

"We will talk, you and I," he said. "Later. This evening. I can explain. Meanwhile, we need to have breakfast and get started. Hopefully, the weather will hold."

The whole day, I tried not to think about Jacov. He had said he hiked in the mountains with his mother, so perhaps that explained how he could find his way along the trail to Narvik. But it seemed such a strange and dangerous thing to do, and why?

I plodded along. Eventually, the sheer beauty of where we were, and the fact that I had as a companion Sivu, whom I now had to handle entirely by myself, calmed me down. I began to feel that Sivu was a silent companion, and, having to look out for him with his unchanging serious but calm face, took my mind away from Jacov. Late afternoon came, and we camped one last time, building a fire again. I even found myself joking with the Minnesotans. But my ankle hurt now more than it had before, and I was limping slightly.

"Come," said Lennart, startling me. I had not seen him walking toward me. "Let's talk."

We moved away from the others and sat on a rock.

"Are you ok?" Lennart asked.

"Yes and no," I said. "I twisted my ankle and it hurts a bit." And then I could not stop myself, blurting out what had happened. And I ended by saying, "Lennart, why did he get so upset. Why? It was almost as if he were a Nazi himself."

"You did not know," said Lennart. "You couldn't have. And there was no way for me to tell you. He is a war child."

"A war child?" I asked.

"I recognized the name when he signed up for the tour – I had heard of him. He returned to live in Narvik where his mother was originally from, but it has been very hard for him I am sure. His mother was a Norwegian who took as a lover a German soldier stationed in Narvik. These children were ostracized growing up in Norway."

I felt a chill. I remembered a photograph, another photograph that I had once seen, made in France at the time of the liberation, in which a mother, her head shaved, held her small infant as she walked through a village street, and all around her the French townspeople were yelling at her and ridiculing her, no doubt shouting traitor.

Oh Jacov, I thought.

We sat silently for a long while. The fire was going down and it had gotten chilly. Lennart gazed into it, his hands playing with a yellow piece of rope used for tying down the gear on the reindeer. Stars dotted the black sky in a profusion I had never seen before. I rubbed my ankle, which hurt and seemed to be stiffening.

"I can try to help your ankle, if you want," he said.

"Yes, that would be wonderful."

He left, found his backpack, reached into it, and then returned holding a white tube.

"This is a cream we use in Sweden. I can try to massage your ankle."

"That would be fine, Lennart."

I removed my boot, and Lennart rubbed my ankle with the cream. It felt remarkably good, warm, and he massaged it with sureness and strength in his fingers.

"Did you learn massage?" I wondered to him.

"No," he said, "but I have been told that I am good at it." He continued rubbing.

"You know," he said, "there is more to it than I am saying."

"What do you mean," I asked.

"My grandfather was a shaman of the Sami, but he had to hide it because the Swedes forbid it; they forbid us to practice our ceremonies, they sent us to Christian boarding schools, children were forbidden to speak our language, they even sterilized some of our women. They tried to destroy our heritage and our culture. And they destroyed the drums that the shamans used. My grandfather had been known as a great healer, but he could no longer practice."

"I did not know," I said. "I'm sorry. Did he have to give it up entirely."

Lennart looked down. He did not answer. He just kept moving his fingers along my ankle. Somehow, I sensed that his grandfather may have defied the rules. But at the same time, I had the feeling that whatever the truth was, Lennart remained scared even now in his own country.

Lennart then said, "Some have said that maybe I have some of his power when I massage. I am not sure it is true."

He continued to work on my ankle. I suddenly felt a warm flash, like a spark, which was as quickly gone. He said, "Did you feel that?"

"Yes," I said.

"Maybe that was something," he said.

It came to me how careful Lennart was and, in a way, how humble, for it seemed to me that something, indeed, had happened. I looked at him. His head was down as he looked at my ankle, which he kept on massaging with his strong fingers in a workman-like manner. "There are such different men in this world," I thought to myself, "and so many so unreachable. Why did I not seek out the Lennarts of this world?" I wondered. It was almost as if, in his simple healing of my ankle, I felt another healing. I relaxed and, for some reason, felt like crying, but I did not.

We sat there together and I felt content. The Minnesotans had gone into their tents and we were alone. Lennart then said, "It's strange, you know. On the one hand, this Western culture tried to destroy us, on the other at times, it has honored us too. Very strange, don't you think?"

"What do you mean?"

"You know New York City. You are from there, yes?"

"Yes," I said.

"In Central Park there, at the center of Manhattan, that great place of trees, rocks, and meadows surrounded by buildings, you know it?"

"Yes, of course," I said, having no idea where he was going with this.

"In that park, there is a large statue of a dog, I have seen it when I visited years ago."

I was surprised he had been to the States, much less to Central Park, but I did not say it for fear that he would be insulted. Instead I said, "Yes, I have even seen it. I think it honors a dog that

63

brought medicine to save those in Alaska who were dying of a disease."

"Well that dog was named Balto. It was brought to America by the Sami to help bring medicine to the Inuit in Alaska by dog sled. The Inuit were dying of diptheria. Balto was the lead dog, and the Inuit were saved as a result. And Balto himself was named after a Sami, Samuel Balto, born way north of here, in Karasjov. Samuel Balto skied across Greenland with the explorer Nansen in the late 1880s. And then he went to Alaska with other Sami reindeer herders, where they actually taught the Inuit about reindeer herding. So in the center of that great city of yours with its skyscrapers, there is a statue that pays homage to our way of life, although it may be no one realizes it."

"Yes," I said, "it is strange."

He was looking upward. "Look," he said.

The grey sky had become alive, with a curtain of color over near the mountains shimmering green and purple and yellow – the Northern lights. I sat transfixed, letting out a long gasp.

"It is amazing," I said.

We watched together for a long time, the undulating, translucent curtain. At one point, I rubbed my ankle. Lennart saw me. I nodded and smiled at him in the dark, our eyes meeting.

"At times like this," Lennart said, "I remember my grandfather." The wind blew in a sudden gust, as if in response to his thought. For a moment, I saw my own grandfather in my mind's eye as I remembered him with his gentle smile, his hands behind his back, his head craning up to look at the Northern lights with me, as he must have looked decades ago when a young man. Then the wind quieted, somewhere a reindeer shook its head, dully ringing the bell attached to its neck, and the image was gone.

And so we two sat there even longer and watched the Northern lights. They spoke of something beyond us, beyond time, something which seemed ineffable and wondrous, and bound us together. And yet, and yet at the same time, I could not help but think that here, another and dark part of us also came, as if it would not be denied. Here, in this faraway place, we still could not escape ourselves, Jacov could not escape. To a place like this, my grandparents were banished by Russia, here in this place – the ancestral home of the Sami – the Swedes invaded and assaulted a tribal culture which did them no harm. In this place, the Nazis came with their guns and unspeakable barbarism. Among the rocks, in the mountains, amid the herds of reindeer and the wide blue sky, we came . . . .

Boxball

Boxball was a city game. You needed a concrete sidewalk that had big boxes incised in it, and behind the boxes a brick, concrete, or smooth stone wall. It made a difference whether the sidewalk concrete was smooth or studded with an aggregate of pebbles. Smooth was better because the bounce was truer, and, besides, you were less likely to scrape the tip of your fingers or the side of your hand on the smooth concrete when you went for a low ball. The ball itself was a Spalding, pronounced without the "g" and elongating the last syllable, so it came out "Spaldeen." It was a soft pink color with a whitish tinge to it, smaller than a baseball, made of hollow rubber. You could buy one for a quarter at any "candy" store – really an all purpose little store with a dark green wooden newspaper rack out front, and stationery, candy, pink bubble gum Bazookas and Topps with baseball playing cards inside, and often a counter with tall stools on whose round and cracked black vinyl seats you could spin while you waited for your egg cream or root beer float or thick chocolate malt. The Spalding fit nicely in your front pocket, so you could be in class sitting in your chair (which had a piece of shellacked wood attached to it to make a desk) and feel the pressure of it against your thigh and know that come recess or after school, you could be playing boxball with your best friends. It was a comfort, like a talisman.

The feeling of control once you began to play was a comfort too: holding the Spalding in your left hand (if you were a righty) when you served, knowing if you barely tossed it and sliced it perfectly as you moved forward a bit, it would skim the gray pavement, hit the wall near the bottom, and come back with barely a bounce in your opponent's box. Boxball was a game of nuance and speed. (The other urban Spalding games, stoopball and stick ball, were less subtle.) It was played with three or four players.

In 1955, at Joan of Arc Junior High School (despite the name, a public high school, sometimes referred to as JHS 118) in Manhattan, Daniel, Michael, and Arnold were best friends, but really Daniel and Michael were the best friends, Arnold was the newcomer. Daniel and Michael had gone through public elementary school together. It was a strange friendship because they did not have much in common: Michael, pale-faced with large strong-lensed glasses, a little pudgy, always wearing either a brown or green plaid shirt, was an unprepossessing boy. He did not particularly shine in school or sports, but he had a sweet and ready smile. Daniel was actually smaller than Michael; nonetheless, he was a good athlete, quick, well-coordinated, a bundle of energy, and he excelled academically as well. His parents were both professionals (both lawyers), and they traveled in intellectual, artistic, and theatrical circles with largely secular Jews such as themselves. In contrast, Michael lived in the projects, tall buildings of brown brick farther down town that all looked alike, with metal doorways painted a dark red that had flecked off in spots and dimly-lit hallways that smelled of urine and ammonia, on the edge of a poor neighborhood called Hell's Kitchen. His Italian parents were less educated: his father was an electrician; his mother stayed at home.

Of these differences between them Daniel was very aware. He felt pride in his parents, whom he knew made an elegant couple. His father (tall, barrel-chested, strong and athletic) was almost always impeccably and formally dressed, his mother petite and beautiful. In contrast, Michael's parents seemed almost slovenly. Michael's father would frequently be at home when Daniel visited (Daniel's father was never at home during the day and usually worked late into the evening). His father wore a plaid shirt like Michael's, rumpled pants, and workmen's black boots, and sometimes, to Daniel's surprise, he would appear in an undershirt that did not entirely conceal a large gut that hung out and curly black chest hair that seemed amazingly profuse. Michael's mother, also somewhat overweight, invariably was dressed in a black blouse and pants but wearing a stained apron, and usually plied Michael and Daniel with food from the small kitchen, not really much bigger than a closet.

Although Daniel felt happy in the parents he had, even superior, he was vaguely aware that he actually envied Michael. Michael's cramped apartment was always lively and noisy: Michael and his younger sister were always arguing, his baby brother would be in his high chair laughing or crying or toddling around the living room, his mother and father (when the father was home) would be talking continuously. The few times Daniel stayed for dinner by himself (Michael's mother always tried to persuade Daniel's mother to have him stay) he ate the most wonderful food, lasagne made with green spinach noodles, spaghetti with sausage and meatballs, things that his mother who was a terrible cook never prepared. It was all a tremendous contrast to life at his larger apartment uptown where, in the evenings, his mother listened to classical music on the record player and read, lying on a couch in their elegant living room, and Daniel, an only child, stayed in his room doing his homework.

Most of all, Daniel felt in awe of the giant fish tank, in Michael's apartment which occupied almost the whole of a wall of the small living room. The water in the tank was usually brownish, the green water plants thick and decaying, and there was usually a pungent fishy smell coming from the tank. A school of neons flashed through the dark water; there were catfish and large snails adhering to the sides of the tank; and guppies, mollies and gold fish floated between the plant fronds. Michael showed him how to clean the tank by siphoning the crud on the bottom through a thin tube. Michael knew all about the fish and how to care for them, which he had learned from his father, and which Michael in turn explained patiently to Daniel. When the father was home, he would tell Michael to feed the fish, and seated on the corduroy sofa opposite the tank, his hammy hands around his big gut, he would watch with satisfaction as the fish excitedly swirled about. "Those fish are something," he said each time, and Daniel silently agreed.

If Daniel could have explained his friendship with Michael, he would have said that he found in Michael's steadiness and faithfulness, even the fact that Michael did not offer real competition in school or at play, a sense of security. For his part, Michael was content to enjoy Daniel's attention, for he greatly admired his friend, and wished, too, that he could share in Daniel's achievements, which he did by contiguity. In boxball, which they played between just the two of them, Michael could never quite beat Daniel, although sometimes the games were close, but, nonetheless, the two friends were inseparable and played almost everyday at lunch time or after school against the brick school building. Unbeknownst to either of them, their apparent contentment with each other was to come to an end.

Exactly how it began, what came first, seemed unclear in retrospect. Arnold came, of course, in the first year of Junior High School, actually, in what was called the "Rapid Advanced Class" that Michael and Daniel were in (which was for academically "gifted" students who took seventh, eighth and ninth grades in two years rather than three). Arnold was a thin, gangly, very pale boy with a shock of blonde hair and a toothy grin, which was sometimes preceded by a smirk. Despite his almost sickly appearance, he was, in fact, very strong athletically and he did well academically too. In time, he began to join Michael and Daniel at lunch time, and then after school, playing box ball. The games were much more exciting with three; sometimes even a fourth would join them, and much closer too. And as Arnold learned to play, he began to beat Daniel once in a while, and then, gradually, all the games were close, Arnold winning almost as frequently as Daniel. Daniel found himself surprised at this, and perhaps the difficulty he had in accepting this new state of affairs is where things began. But that was not all.

For the fact was that, at the same time as Arnold's appearance, tensions began to show in Michael and Daniel's relationship, and this was for a reason whose significance Daniel could not anticipate and of which Michael could not have known. Daniel was at that point in his life when he felt that he was getting older and was no longer just a boy. It began with a change in his voice. His voice had been high and squeaky, but now he had the ability to speak in what sounded to him like a deep voice. Really, he could not quite figure out how he wanted to sound. He hoped to sound like his father, whose deep voice often seemed to come out of him like the plaintive blare of a foghorn, slow and solemn. It commanded respect. When Daniel tried to sing, he no longer could quite hold to a pattern; he tried to sing "Old Man River" in what seemed to him a deep base, but he could not quite get through it without his tone going up. He tried, too, to talk to his friend Michael with a deeper voice. Even more, he started to treat Michael in the way his father treated him, with solemn authority.

It began with his starting to help Michael with his school work, which he saw as part of taking Michael under his wing. "See," he said to Michael one day when Michael's notebook with scrawling pencil marks and misspellings was open on his desk. He opened his own notebook, "See, I go back over my notes and I underline them, and then I put a heading. Look, here in red crayon on each part so I can remember what is important. You should do that too." Michael looked at him but did not say anything. He slowly closed his own notebook.

That day, when the three of them played boxball, Michael kept on trying to smash the ball and it would end up going long. "Wait until it drops further before you hit it," Daniel observed on retrieving one of the smashes from the far end of the playground.

"Yeh," said Michael, and then proceeded to do the same thing, and this time the ball almost hit Daniel in the face as it caromed off the wall.

Arnold laughed. "Looks like the lesson's over," he said. It made matters worse when Arnold then beat Daniel on a skittering last

70

shot that barely bounced so that Daniel scrapped his fingers trying to get it just before the recess bell rang and they returned to class.

"Nice shot," Daniel said reluctantly.

"Yeh, it was," replied Arnold, "wasn't it?" Daniel noticed that Michael smiled and seemed to walk closer to Arnold as they headed toward the double doors that led inside. Daniel felt annoyed, but he was determined as ever to be a true friend to Michael, a better friend than Arnold whose sometimes cutting humor Daniel felt was simply wrong, something of which his father would never have approved. And so, he just increased his efforts. In the cafeteria at lunch, when the three of them often sat together, Daniel openly disapproved of Michael's tendency to fart (he sensed but did not say that Michael tried to make a virtue out of something he sometimes could not control), but Arnold only laughed each time Michael let loose. And the following day, at lunch, they got into a heated discussion about their home room teacher, Miss Barshonski, whom Daniel very much liked and for whom Daniel was a favorite. She had curly red hair that she tied in a pony tail with a red ribbon, and she smelled of peppermint when she leaned over his desk to look at his work. To Michael that day, she asked what had happened to his notebook, which looked splotchy with red marks, and he said embarrassedly something about spaghetti sauce. Unsolicited at lunch, Daniel told Michael (trying in a measured voice to be helpful as he imagined his father would) that he found it was better never to have a notebook around the table when he ate, but Arnold remarked that Miss Barshonski probably only chewed peppermint gum for dinner and never ate spaghetti, which explained why she was so flat-chested. "That's not a right thing to say," Daniel said, but by then Michael had already begun laughing.

Their boxball games gradually became more contentious too. When there was a questionable shot, such as whether the ball had actually hit the wall before the sidewalk on a very low shot, and they argued, Michael now invariably took Arnold's side. On a day when it seemed clear to Daniel that he was going to win without any problem, he said, "Arnold, this is not your day," an expression his father used, and then Arnold seemed to hold on, making one defensive play on a wide shot where he actually fell, that so surprised Daniel that he missed an easy return, which only provoked Arnold to go into a paroxysm of laughter as he lay on the ground, his trouser knee torn, clapping his hands together over and over. Michael went over and helped him up, and thumped him on the back. Then to Daniel's chagrin (Arnold's play now almost perfect) Daniel missed a series of shots and Arnold went on to win the game after all.

Even worse, it was Michael, not Arnold, who ribbed him after his loss, "I thought you said you were going to win, didn't you? Maybe you didn't concentrate hard enough." (In fact, the day before, Daniel had carefully explained to Michael, in a slow voice imitating the patience of his father, that he had probably been missing his shots because he wasn't concentrating.) And Arnold gave out with one of his laughs.

For Daniel, now boxball was no longer much fun, although he could not fully admit it to himself. He said nothing. Each day they played, it seemed to get worse, and he felt like the two of them, Arnold and Michael, were increasingly ganging up on him. And yet, the more desperately he tried, by giving measured and helpful advice to Michael, to keep their special friendship alive, the further he seemed to drive Michael away. He played now not as much out of enjoyment but out of a kind of dull determination. One day, when the weather was particularly balmy, they were at it again, and Daniel was playing poorly. Arnold was kidding him about how he couldn't hit anything right today, which only made Michael giggle, and then he remarked that he had really tanked it. "Yeh, sure," Daniel replied, "it isn't over 'til its over."

'Naw," said Arnold, "you have tanked it; in fact, you stink today, like a fish tank." Michael laughed at that, and Arnold hit him playfully on the shoulder, and immediately Daniel knew for a certainty that Michael had invited Arnold to his house and he had seen the fish tank there. Michael felt numb and hollow inside. He had known that he had not been invited to Michael's house for a while (he had wondered about why not), and now this, which explained it. Now he just did not know what to say so he played on with renewed intensity, avoiding looking at either of them, afraid to make eye contact, as if all that concerned him was the boxball game itself.

And he did manage to catch up in the game until he was almost at the point of getting even. And still, all the while Arnold kept on teasing him about how he thought he was going to win but he would not. Then Arnold hit a sliced return to Daniel's serve; the different spins he put on the "spaldeen" were often hard to handle, but this one Daniel hit sharply, so it just touched the edge of Arnold's box, the third box, but was obviously in, at which point Arnold shouted, "Out!".

"Oh, come on," said Daniel, "it was a great shot and it was in."

"It was out," said Arnold.

"It was in, it hit right here," said Daniel, moving to Arnold's box, past Michael, and pointing down at the spot.

"It didn't," said Arnold. They had never gotten into an altercation of this kind before. Daniel was flabbergasted.

"Come on," he said, turning now toward Michael, "tell him it was in, Michael."

"No," said Michael, "it was out."

"That's ridiculous," said Daniel but he then said, reluctantly, because it was two against one, and they had a history of resolving things, "we'll do a do-over."

"I don't think so," said Arnold. "It's two against one. It was out." This really was too much.

"Come on," said Daniel, "come on."

"But it's my point clearly," said Arnold, and then Michael piped in, "Yeh. No do-over, I saw it."

Daniel tried to reason with them, thinking of his father; he tried to explain with careful and patient logic that they had always done do-overs in the past, so they should do one now. But it made no difference.

"It was clearly out," continued Arnold, "clearly, clearly, clearly, and when it's so clearly out, no do-over."

"Arnold's right," chimed in Michael.

"Yeh, and beside," added Arnold, "the problem is you don't like to admit that you stink today." And Arnold laughed. "You just don't like to admit that you're just a loser today."

"Yeh," said Michael again.

Something finally broke inside Daniel, quietly and suddenly, like the sweet and painful snapping of a ligament in his chest. He felt it before he could think about it. It released him, and he did not realize that a cry of rage escaped his lips at the same time. He charged fully toward Arnold. He saw Arnold's fist come at his face and felt the blow against his lips and teeth, rocking his head dully, but there was no pain. He realized he was hit, but by that time, he was upon Arnold. The force of his tackling him knocked both of them to the ground, and, in a moment, he was on top of him. With a feeling of power, he felt Arnold writhing beneath him, and he grabbed his head with both his hands. The pebbled pavement was there. All Arnold could do, at that moment, completely help-less, was to stop fighting and laugh. "In a second," Daniel thought, "I will smash his head fully upon the pavement and truly hurt him." He imagined the pulpy sound of the back of Arnold's skull on the hard surface. And knowing that, knowing how much he could truly hurt him, he realized he could not. It was not in him. It was a moment in his life when there was no one to consult, that kind of moment everything slowed down suddenly, when you do the right thing almost despite yourself, without any hope of rec-ompense except from your own conscience, your knowledge that you would always have your own memory to carry with you, no matter what the world might think. And he knew, too; it did not matter anyhow. He had lost before the fight began because he had already lost Michael's love, lost the battle for Michael's affection with Arnold, and smashing Arnold's head into the rough pave-ment would not change that or soothe his terrible pain. At that stilled moment, a teacher grabbed him from behind and pulled him off Arnold. The teacher apparently thought that he had stopped the fight, not realizing that Daniel had stopped a moment before.

A group of boys were milling around, watching. He heard one boy say, "Did you see how he got walloped right in the mouth?" He felt tears in his eyes, and he knew that the teacher, who bent over to see his face, thought he was crying from the pain of the punch. but Daniel silently shook his head when the teacher asked if he needed help; he picked his books up from the ground where he had dropped them and walked off. He trudged home, his eyes still filled with tears, his chest tight. Every once in a while, despite himself, he felt a sob come out of him, relieving the tightness, followed by an uncontrolled trembling. He could taste saltiness from blood in his mouth. His eyes continued intermittently in tears. He was bereft.

His mother tended him gently at home with warm water and a pink washcloth. He told her that he had gotten in a fight, without elaborating. When his father returned late that evening from work and asked Daniel what had happened, he wanted so much to explain, explain the whole thing, but before he could get up the courage, his father interrupted his effort, "I know what you need," he said in his deep voice, "I know exactly what you need. You need to learn to defend yourself, and I am going to teach you." He looked his father in his face; it was a strong face: full lips, sharp features, a shock of a mustache, and it commanded attention. His father stood there in his business suit, his silk tie still carefully knotted with the Windsor knot he had already taught Daniel to make, looking down at his distressed son, and taking charge.

Daniel looked again into his father's face, which he so loved, and knew then he could not tell him what he so wanted to say. He could hear himself say the words in his mind, to plead them, "I lost the love of my friend because I tried so hard to be just like you." But he could not say them. He could not even tell his father that he had really won the fight but then did not want to seriously hurt Arnold. Why he could not tell his father these things, he did not know exactly. Perhaps it was because he needed to protect himself and his father from the knowledge that he had learned that day. And perhaps it was because he knew that his father would not be able to understand. Instead, Daniel silently prayed that maybe his father would have the wisdom to ask and to probe gently, would wonder to him aloud about why the fight had started, and would coax Daniel to tearfully reveal his secret: that he had tried to treat Daniel as his father treated him, that he had so much wanted to be like his father, but that somehow it had not worked at all – that he had loved Michael and aspects of his life (even aspects of Michael's father) that were so very, very different.

But his father continued to talk about the importance of learning to defend oneself and how he would buy boxing gloves for his son so they could practice together. And so that moment between them, a moment rich in possibilities, passed silently away and did not return. His father bought the gloves and began his son's practice the next day.

Praying Mantis

When a thing is impossible, it cannot be so.
Charles Brenner

They were arguing about it again – discussing really, as they always did – at breakfast, the sunlight streaming through the large windows and outside the ornamental grasses of the garden shining, swaying in a slight breeze, while their cat sprawled on its back on the sunlit paving stones, seemingly unfazed either by their recent absence or now their return from vacation. They both felt how good it was to be home again – the familiarity, the comfort of the expected, even the unimaginative American breakfast itself after the cheese, sausage, and tarts of Burgundy, and the French coffee. It had been typical of their vacations, where they tried to challenge themselves and to learn about different cultures – this time biking along the Danube from Vienna to Budapest and then staying in a *gite* in a small village in Burgundy. But now home, the inevitable argument began again. He could not see how she would not see things his way, how she did not acknowledge the unseen strands that sometimes guided their lives, and she, amused if not despairing, about how his usually logical self (she would, to herself at least, give him that) fell victim again, no, repeatedly, to fuzzy, fantastical thinking. This time, of all things, it focused on insects, well one type of insect really. He began again making his argument, putting down his thick mug of American coffee that he took with two sugars and milk.

"You see, " he said, "it all conspired from the same thing."

"Conspired?" she interrupted. "From the beginning, you have already reached a conclusion. Conspired . . . ."

"Let me explain first."

He looked over at her. She gave him that skeptical look, her head inclined a bit, one eyebrow raised. "O.K., go ahead," she said, somewhat reluctantly.

"'Conspired' may be the wrong word," he conceded. "But look at it this way. I am working on my book on 'free association' and one of the quotes that I use is this statement by Robert Frost that I discovered that no one else, as far as I can find out, has alluded to in the psychoanalytic literature, that a poet freely associates like a 'grasshopper' jumping from one thing to another. And in addition, I have been focusing on that exchange between Freud and Romain Rolland in which Freud – somewhat lost soul that he was despite everything – says he has never had an 'oceanic experience,' that he does not know that type of religious-like experience, nor, for that matter, could he enjoy music in that way, and by implication that he does not know of 'love' in that way."

"Very strange."

"Yes, I agree. And it makes one wonder about the underpinnings of Freudian theory when such an important part of human experience is unknown in the founder of the theory himself. At least on that we agree."

She spread a bit of jam on the American bread she was having with her tea, wishing for a piece of baguette instead. He waited until she finished.

"O.K. Now as I see it, this all began when we were biking in Hungary, the Danube to our left, on the way, as I recall, to Esztergom, and we stopped biking at a cross-road with a plowed field on one side to figure out our directions from the always confusing map guide that the touring company provided us."

"Yes, I know all this," she said impatiently, but he just went on.

"And then I feel something on my left leg, and I look down, and it is a brown praying mantis. Now, I have not seen a praying mantis since childhood – I do not know what happened to them in our part of the world because I always used to see them as a child."

"I know, " she said, "me too. So you see a praying mantis. Not, incidentally, a grasshopper."

"Well, yes. We'll get to that. Anyhow, this praying mantis just crawls up my leg, and then, when I put my hand down, on to my hand, just sitting there, its heart shaped head clearly visible and carefully cleaning itself. It does not fly away, just sits there contentedly."

"So?"

"And I am excited. I take it as a kind of omen."

"Exactly. For no reason... whatsoever."

He chooses to ignore this.

"Except we then move on and maybe ten minutes later we have to stop again to figure out directions, so we pull into that gravel parking lot of a closed restaurant. There is a long blank wall on this side of the restaurant. I'm looking down at the map guide, and when I look up, what do I see right near my head on the wall of the restaurant – nothing else there at all – but another praying mantis, even bigger than the last one, although green in color not brown like the first."

"It's coincidence."

"Well, that is the typical hypothesis. But there is more."

"Wait, not so quick. You are making assumptions to imply that this event was unusual, assumptions that you do not know are true."

"Okay. What assumptions?"

"Well," she said, and now she took her time. She could see he was getting impatient. "Well," she said again, taking a slow sip from her cup, with a certain degree of pleasure.

"Yes?"

Finally.

"You are assuming that praying mantises are as rare in that part of Hungary as we have found them to be here. Maybe they are very common – for some reason – so that they can be found at almost any cross-road or any field near there."

"Admitted. It is a possibility. But there is more still."

"O.K. Go on."

"You know what I am going to say. After all, you were there."

"Maybe. But I prefer to hear you spell it out."

"And make a fool of myself . . . ."

She smiled at him, and took another sip from her cup. "Go on," she said.

"Well, after our bicycle trip from Vienna to Budapest, we fly to France and end up in that *gite* in Burgundy where we simply relax for a while and hike."

"And find no praying mantises."

"Yes, find no praying mantises. Until. . . ."

"I know you where you are going with this, but there will still be no praying mantises at the end."

"Bear with me. Until our French friends drive all the way up from Bordeaux to spend time with us and take us to Vezelay."

"Ahh," she said, "Vezelay ... it was wonderful. The 12th century Romanesque church and the grounds . . . ."

"And the Zervos Museum there, established in the house where we discover (and here is another surprise) Romain Rolland had lived – 'Maison Romain Rolland' they call it – and which we knew nothing about before our French friends decided to take us."

"So, you are going to tell me that because you were thinking of Romain Rolland and his conversation with Freud, this is some type of Jungian serendipity or synchronicity."

"You are depriving me of the ending here, as you indeed know."

"OK. Go on, but it will make no difference."

"Now, there we are in this wonderful home that has been converted into a Museum, where the Zervos's lived after Rolland lived there. They knew many artists. There are Picassos on the wall, Miro, Leger; a real gem of a small house with white walls filled with magnificent paintings and the sprawling French countryside outside. A house with such history, too, because Rolland, before the Zervoses, also knew everyone, not just Freud but Ghandi, Herman Hesse, Gorki, Stefan Zweig. So there we are, walking around in this small museum, in this wonderful place of culture, and we turn a corner and *Voila*! We come face to face with a large oil painting of . . ." and here he paused briefly for effect, " a stylized giant green insect that looks just like a praying mantis. The picture

80

is by Max Ernst. So this is my point exactly. Things *conspired* in a parapsychological way to connect all these things."

"Except," she laughed, "you know Max Ernst did not paint a stylized praying mantis. It was supposed to be a grasshopper!"

He fell momentarily silent. He took a sip of his coffee, then he said, "Still, the first sense for both of us when we saw the painting, the first sense we had, was that it was a praying mantis."

"You know," she said, evincing more exasperation than she really felt, "you insist on making of coincidences something more than they are. After all, what are you saying? What is the meaning of these supposed connections?"

"That's partly the point. I don't know exactly why these connections took place. We don't know exactly why they do in general. But the facts are there. They call out for an explanation . . . beyond coincidence. Maybe we are all connected to the world in ways we do not entirely understand; and our minds and wishes interact with the world or create it in some way. Maybe the world, even the animals and insects in it, join with us in some way. Maybe the animism of tribes, which Western culture thinks of as superstition and, with a sense of misplaced superiority, has discarded, maybe that animism has something to say for it; and maybe we communicate with the animate world in psychic ways of which we are not aware."

She smiled and said, "You are such a fuzzy thinker in this regard. What is misplaced is your passion. A coincidence is a coincidence. By definition, a coincidence is something that looks meaningful but is not and is only the work of chance."

"We will never agree."

"No. We won't," she said with apparent finality. It seemed as if the mood of repartee and friendly argument was over and he worried that she'd had it with him. Repeatedly, they had this kind of discussion, with other facts that he felt begged for explanation as these did, and each time the discussion ended the same way.

Now she got up, carefully smoothed her skirt, and started to go into the living room, which only confirmed his apprehension. He wondered that perhaps she was really annoyed with him.

"I have something for you," she said, from the living room. She returned, stood near him, and smiling, said, "But don't misunderstand it."

"What is it?"

"Don't misunderstand," she said again, apparently awaiting his response as a condition of giving to him whatever she had retrieved from the living room (he could now see that she was holding something behind her back with her right hand).

"Ok," he said, "I promise. I promise not to misunderstand."

" Good," she said on his acquiescence. And then, " Here." She brought her hand toward him now and gave him a small black framed picture, its back to him. He turned it over. There was a picture of the Max Ernst grasshopper. He was stunned.

He put the framed picture down on the table, got up, took her face in his hands, and kissed her, silently. He held her, looking at her, wondering at her green eyes. "Thank you," he said, "what a wonderful gift. But how?"

"When you had walked away at the museum, I went back and took a photograph of it and then enlarged it as soon as we got home."

"Well," he laughed, "we now, after our twenty years together, have a praying mantis finally – and in the States." He held the picture out for them both to see.

"Yes," she said. "But it's a grasshopper."

They laughed.

They seated themselves again, finishing their breakfast and contentedly admiring how the morning sunlight played through the garden. The cat had disappeared from the paving stones. Then, suddenly, startling them, they saw it, jumping right in front of the window, its paws gesticulating wildly in the air.

For a moment, it seemed as if it had grabbed out of the air a large green insect. Just a quick flash. They could not be sure, and then the cat, its back to them, head held proudly high as if carrying off its prize in its mouth, disappeared into the tall ornamental grasses and was gone. The grasses swayed slightly in the breeze, the sunlight throwing a pattern on the silent stones.

In Martin's House

In memory of Ben Clark

With his shirt off, the kid looked like he had been kicked, like someone had let loose with a well-placed boot tip right in the center of his chest. He was also white, a dirty white, the color of crumpled newspaper, and he had long stringy sinews that snaked around his body just beneath the almost translucent surface of his skin. He must have been stronger than he looked. The sinews showed in his forearms just now 'cause he was holding for dear life onto Memphis, trying to keep him from attacking Tupper. Maybe Memphis would have thrown the kid off, but at that point Josea, who had grabbed Tupper and was holding him back, bellowed in his voice of authority that seemed impossibly raspy, "God damn you two. God damn. Calm down already." For a moment, they, all of them, were stuck together there – grunting, straining, cursing but not really moving, as if Josea's voice were crackling lightning that illuminated them in place – and then I could see the fight slowly go out of them.

The kid's name was Harry. He was from Minnesota, and sometimes we just called him Minnesota. His naked, white, snaky skin stood out because he was the only white one there. This was in Martin Luther King's house in Atlanta, which Martin had vacated, moving his family elsewhere for some reason for the summer – safety, convenience, I don't know – and letting the kids and the "staff," such as it was, occupy the hot, cavernous colonial house that seemed afflicted itself with a drab brown exterior and interior. It was 1965. Hot and dusty. The summer drive to register black voters in the sleepy towns of the deep South was now more than half over.

83

I liked Minnesota. I could not quite explain why. He wanted to learn and he learned quick. But as I watched him, I knew in my heart some stuff he didn't know. What I knew was that he would go and I would stay. He would go back, like all the other three-month civil rights workers, to some town up North after the summer, and I'd never see him again. He would go in a more fundamental way: he'd end his adventure, and eventually even the memory of it would fade from inside him like a flame that sputters, dies, and leaves only smoke. And he'd take his whiteness into some suburban white Northern town, where he'd live and eventually die, and even his bones would go into some cemetery where there were mostly white man's bones; and my sorry black ass would stay here. I knew all that for sure. But for now, for now we were together.

Memphis and Tupper had actually been fighting over a white woman, despite the fact she no longer lived in the house. By this time, the two of them had more or less calmed down. Josea with his raspy voice told Tupper to go outside and cool off; Tupper backed up a few steps, but then he just stared at Memphis. Memphis stared back at him. For a moment it was very silent. I wondered whether the whole thing would start up again. I wanted to tell Memphis, who so liked to talk big, to give it up. You just did not want to keep pushing Tupper, because he definitely had a mean streak – everyone knew he carried a knife (or at least he always talked about it), and Josea was always telling him to get rid of it. Non-violence didn't exactly come easy to Tupper or to a number of his friends in Martin's organization, the Southern Christian Leadership Conference (SCLC to all of us), but it really couldn't be expected to. After all, Tupper had been in and out of Juvenile Hall since he was twelve; he was always trying to steal things and was always getting into fights and not calming down when the cops came – he dropped out of high school as soon as he could. The civil rights movement had probably saved him from going to jail permanently. It gave him direction, a sense of belonging, which was hard to realize because his eyes were cold in a wide, hard face, and he seemed impervious not only to Josea's raspy voice just now but to anybody's words. It wasn't like the Movement could be choosy though – Southern black kids willing, in a full-time way, to put themselves on the line, to risk antagonizing the white police and the white citizens, to spend time in jail and get a long police record, were not all going to be your nice well-behaved "Yes Ma'am" kind of kids. They had to be kids who were willing to challenge the established order of things in some way, and so there were a number of "juveys" among us. And a kid as big as Tupper did have a particular purpose. He would often be at the head of a protest march, or around Josea, just as an added precaution – to give some rednecks pause before they might try something. Josea and Randy (who oversaw everything) and Martin himself (when he was around) might preach non-violence (and they meant it, which was why they preached it over and over and over), but there was nothing that said you could not surround yourself with someone tough-looking like Tupper.

Cursing under his breath, Memphis gave one last long stare at Tupper and thankfully then turned away, making Minnesota, who was still holding onto him by the shoulders, stumble and let go. Memphis wandered slowly off into the other room, kind of rolling his shoulders like he wanted to get rid of a weight on them, to be with his friends who had been standing in the doorway watching the fight. Seeing this, Tupper grunted to himself, turned the other way, and stomped slowly off in the big construction boots he always wore. Josea and the kid were left standing there. Josea put a meaty arm around Minnesota's thin white shoulders and intoned in his gruff voice, "Good job, Minnesota," which made the kid smile like a boy. And they both came my way.

"Bernard, Bernard," Josea said to me as he got closer, shaking his head. "Ever since Maxine . . . ."

"Yeh, Josea, I know," I said.

"What about Maxine?" Minnesota now said, looking confused. "I thought Memphis and Tupper were fighting over which of them had chickened out on the march on the bridge and hung back."

Josea and I looked at each other.

"Yeh," Josea said to him, "that's what it sounded like, for sure, but there's more to it than that. Ask Bernard about it. I gotta go now and check on some things," and he patted Minnesota on his scrawny back and left.

Minnesota now looked over at me. "Bernard," he said, "wasn't Maxine the pregnant one that was here last time I was here?"

"Yup," I said.

There was a long pause and then – finally, "Oh" he said, understanding.

"She just loved our black souls all over," I said, laughing.

Sometimes that was the most important thing we had in this long, seemingly endless struggle: laughter. Black humor. The fact was that there were some white girls who came down from the North who wanted more than to integrate restaurants or register black voters or make black friends. They felt their job was to single-handedly move the movement from A to Z, forget all the intervening steps: they were going to register not only black voters but their protest – against daddy or mommy back home, against their white school mates in the North somewhere who perhaps had ostracized them, making them embrace being an outcast, against American culture, against slavery. They were going to caresss black flesh lovingly with their soft white hands, open their soft white legs and take a black penis inside them; and there were many Southern black kids in the movement who were more than willing to accommodate them, given that for them bedding a white woman, sex aside, was also a terrible cry of defiance, perhaps the ultimate cry for a black man in this segregated South. But all of this could end badly; Maxine after all was pregnant and by whom was unclear. And in addition, all of this could be dangerous in a different sense. Josea, Randy, me, Martin too, everyone in authority knew that. We had a whole elaborate speech and routine to warn these ignorant white folk who came down from the North to help us with registration. For the fact was, if white Southern people saw public affection between black and white, holding hands even, much less kissing, it like to drove them to distraction and could place us all, not just the dewy-eyed pair, in jeopardy – from being attacked to being thrown in jail on some trumped up charge. But then again, as in everything, what was recommended could not so easily be enforced. Practice was different than preaching. Witness Maxine.

*   *   *

I loved being here, and I loved Bernard, loved his black soul all over (if in a different way), at least I thought I did. Each moment down South was new yet familiar at the same time. Familiar because I felt like I knew blackness, like I had returned home into it, like I had flown in after a long time aloft and now could rest my tired wings. They called me Harry from Minnesota (and Bernard and Josea shortened it to Minnesota), but that wasn't really true: I just went to college there. I was really, if anything, Harry from New York City. What was new for me was the South (the black-eyed peas, the grits, the southern fried chicken, the greens, and the pounding spirituals in church, with the exclamations, the back and forth of the congregants), but what was familiar was blackness itself: the soft brown skin, the wonderful transformation of the palm of the hand as it flowered into pinkness, the kinky hair, the intonations of the words. How many white kids from New York City somewhere knew this blackness from babyhood, as I did? Margaret sitting in her flowered dress in our kitchen; Margaret in her immovable patience making me breakfast, when my mother went to work; Margaret, the black maid who could cook in a way my mother could not. There must have been Margarets all over the Upper West Side and East Side of Manhattan, pushing white babies in carriages. Years later, in fact, I would realize that, in some fundamental way, I had been searching for Margaret, who had left suddenly for some family crisis which never was explained – a family whose features I did not know and would never know: did she have children, a husband, grandchildren? Did she cook for them as she did for me? I had been searching for her eyes in the eyes of the black women I met down South, hoping in some magical unconscious way to find her once again.

I had come to know Bernard by luck, I suppose, and gotten closer to Josea, the director of SCLC's summer voter registration drive, and also to Randy (who was Dr. King's right hand man), when the registration of blacks to vote in relatively safe Peach County, Georgia (where I had originally been assigned) began to peter out. Relatively safe, that is, for civil rights workers. You see, it all depended on the state, even the county in the state in which you were a civil rights worker. The deepest South, that is Mississippi and Louisiana, were much more dangerous than Georgia to begin with, but within each state some counties, depending on the nastiness of the sheriff, were more dangerous than others. Peach County, where the civil rights workers from Minnesota were assigned by SCLC, was wealthier, more middle class. The county seat was Fort Valley, which was known for two things: an all-black college (Fort Valley State College) and Red Hawk Body Company. You do know Red Hawk Body Company even if you think you do not and even if the name is a contradiction: the bodies they make are actually all yellow. They are the yellow school buses. Take a look at all the yellow school buses up North and three times out of four you will see Red Hawk Body Company, the manufacturer, embossed on a silver metal swatch on the back or on the side. All those yellow school buses come streaming out of a plant in this small segregated Southern town in Georgia and end up plying the integrated suburban streets of New Jersey or Minnesota, or the potholed avenues of New York City, or the highways of a hundred other Northern places – places where the black kids sit on hard bus seats next to white kids and where their parents, black and white, attend the same polling places together on Election Day. Red Hawk Body Company controlled the Southern town of Fort Valley; it had done so for years. It was the largest employer in the town, and it all but owned the county government. It hired black workers too, of course, but they had separate eating areas at the plant and conducted separate church services there too and, of course, there were few registered black voters in the entire town.

But the last thing Red Hawk wanted this summer – the summer of 1965 when SCLC announced it was going to bring in civil rights workers from the North to register blacks to vote for the first time throughout the South, an influx spawned by the soon-to-be-passed Voting Rights Act – was an "incident." No "We Shall Overcome" marches down the sleepy main street of Fort Valley, no visit from Martin himself, no shotgunned dead body of a young white worker from the North lying in a swamp on top of a mangled dead black body: none of that. It would not profit to have the North and Northern school districts apprised about what kind of place all those yellow school buses came from and how the blacks were treated there. So when a committee of black professors at the college asked SCLC to come to town to register black voters, the folks who ran Red Hawk knew there was a problem. A problem which they solved in a time-honored political manner, and which, in time-honored fashion, was then kept from us – the white civil rights workers from Minnesota (twenty of us in all, mostly students from the University of Minnesota) who were now encamped in Fort Valley for the summer to register black voters. The problem announced itself once we managed to register 500 black voters after going door-to-door in the black community and bringing blacks day after day to the Fort Valley county court house in the white center of the town to wait in a long line in the hot sun to register, fanning themselves, talking and laughing quietly, sometimes in their Sunday best to honor a unique occasion although it was not Sunday, and finally entering the coolness of the stone building where two large ceiling fans clacked away and two elderly white women at a long table slowly took down the registration information. Yes, we reached 500, and more quickly than we thought, at which point the black professors of the black State College seemed less cooperative in helping us, and the registrations at the court house seemed suddenly to get more difficult. The two clerks – never quick – now seemed to take forever, as if they were in a slow-motion film. Old black men and women baked in the long lines, fanning themselves. We got them water, but often the line simply would not move fast; lunch hour seemed to have expanded to two hours for the clerks; and on top of that for no reason, the clerks would close the office half an hour early, leaving many unprocessed although they had been there for hours. We complained to SCLC in Atlanta, to Josea in particular, but they for some reason seemed strangely unconcerned. We thought that maybe they just had their hands filled with other problems throughout the South that summer. Eventually, to our surprise, they said we might as well close our operation in Peach County; some of us wanted to go back early to Minnesota anyhow – and then the few of us remaining were split up to different places. I ended up at Martin's house back in Atlanta, which was where Bernard was too, whom I already knew from when he helped to train us when we first came to Atlanta, before going to Fort Valley. And it was to Bernard I told – my very first day there – about the sudden drying up of registrations when we reached 500 in Fort Valley. He looked at me and just laughed. "What's so funny?" I said.

He said: "I guess they didn't tell you."

"Tell me what?"

"I guess they figured you had no need to know."

"Know what?" I asked again, trying not to be annoyed by his smile.

"They made a deal."

"Who made a deal?"

"The professors at the college and the management of Red Hawk, that's who."

I still had trouble fathoming what he was saying.

Bernard sighed, as if he now had to explain something to a not-too-bright student. "When the professors threatened Red Hawk with hosting SCLC in Fort Valley and registering blacks there, Red Hawk sat down with them, and said, 'Look, we'll have the county authorities let Negro registrations go through, without any hassle, so you won't have to march or expend a lot of your resources, provided that you only register 500 voters.' That's why things were so easy at first and then suddenly became hard, and that's why SCLC – which knew what was going on and really approved it – was not upset when things started to slow down. They made a deal. See."

I looked at him. This time he did not laugh but looked right at me. "Shit," I said.

"Yes," he said.

And then we both laughed.

It was like this all the time between Bernard and me – in his dry way he was my teacher about Southern life, my guide to this different land. Often, he would not answer my question completely and let me slowly discover the answer myself, like he had just done about Maxine. We were so terribly different, from such different backgrounds but it also seemed, at least for now, we were friends.

The night after the fight, I slept fitfully on a mattress on the floor in an unfurnished room of Martin's house, with Bernard on another mattress against the opposite wall. The next morning, Bernard and I left together for Americus, Georgia, farther south than Fort Valley. Things were heating up there, and Josea had told Bernard to go down and organize everyone, whatever that meant. Bernard, as small as he was and as cynical too, had a booming voice, a direct and humorous way with words, and a smile that instantly moved people, and so he was often entrusted to troubleshoot in difficult situations. Bernard asked me to go with him. Besides, he said, his aunt lived in Americus (she had moved from Waycross, where Bernard's family was from) and I could stay with him at her house. And that was how I came to know Thelma and her daughter Miriam, Bernard's cousin, and to spend the next month there.

*   *   *

Sometimes I wonder what it is about me: I seemed to know more than I had any right to know. My daddy died when I was six. He was a drunk who liked to mouth off, and he mouthed off once too often and someone stuck him at a bar down in Waycross, where we lived at the time: "The Tyler Inn" they called the bar, but it was a rundown sad place that all but fell into the muddy river that ran by it and the shacks we called home. The guy who killed him wasn't local, and they said it was close to self-defense, so they locked up his ass for two months and let him walk after that. I never did know his name. But I grew up rough and small, really small, like my dad and he was a good man even if he drank too much. But if I was deficient in height, what I had going for me, beside my considerable smarts, was the gift of talk just like he did. I got it from him, and sometimes I felt that I was in danger of coming to the same sorry end as he did. But I was lucky. My momma use to tell me I could talk a rabbit out of his foot.

It was that gift that got me through school and through life. I could play the dozens with the best of them, and I was funny. And I had to be quick and smart that way because I sure wasn't big. Pure gumption got me through. I made friends. With my best friend, Jayson, who was twice my size – with legs like trunks of trees – we could keep them rolling in the dirt with laughter. We'd go down by the river, a bunch of us, with two or three six packs of beer, and we'd go at each other, but always it ended with just Jayson and me cracking everybody up with our traded insults. And then I realized that there was power in words beyond just being able to entertain people or hold my own. True power.

*　　*　　*

Driving down to Americus was uneventful, thank goodness, although as always, driving in the South with black and white passengers together in the same car was dangerous. Sometimes when cars passed us, the whites inside, when they saw us, gave us hard looks; once or twice they gave us the finger or honked their horn over and over. Black and white were not supposed to be together sharing a car, and besides, they may have suspected we were civil rights workers. We made sure not to stop except for gas in the black part of a small town just north of Americus. When we got to Americus, I found that it was not that different in appearance from Fort Valley. Only scarier. It did not have Red Hawk Body Company to control everything in town and keep things quiet, and on top of that the sheriff, Sheriff McGown, was known for being nasty. Already, there had been one confrontation at the courthouse where some teenage kids started throwing rocks at the white civil rights workers as they brought blacks to register, and the cops did nothing about it until one white woman civil rights worker ended up with a bloodied head. Then the police just moved the white kids away, joking with them and grinning. When the civil rights workers asked these police for help for the woman, who was bleeding all over, the cops threatened to arrest them for blocking the sidewalk. Or maybe they meant bleeding on the sidewalk. Anyhow, this was why Bernard had been called in. SCLC was planning an even bigger voter registration effort in the next weeks and was sending for more workers from Atlanta to come down.

In Fort Valley, we had lived with black families throughout the black part of town, but here in Americus – which was a larger town – there was Hubert's, our freedom house: it was the first thing I saw when I got there – a one-story long brick building, at the beginning of the black side of town with a warped and peeling black sign outside which said, in white gothic letters, "Hubert's Funeral Home." In one large room that was used for services at other times, we civil rights workers met each morning: fifteen or so of us mostly college kids from Georgia, Alabama, New Jersey, New York City all over the place, black and white, to plan strategy, to decide where to canvass for voters to register, and to print fliers (there was a small mimeograph machine and boxes next to it, holding reams of white and light green paper).

For the freedom house to be in a black funeral home was fitting. In the back room, dead black bodies probably lay on cold slabs or nestled into linen-lined coffins, "free at last" for real. The fact was, in what other establishment could we the living, the civil rights workers, be safe in this slow, strange and harsh land? Black cemeteries were separate from white cemeteries. Separateness for black flesh and white flesh, even when lifeless, was the end part of segregation, as if dead white flesh would be tainted by the nearness of flesh so foreign in shade, or as if God himself had a For Colored Only entrance to heaven. No white man would have anything to do with the black undertaker. The irony of this was that, whereas almost every other black institution, even at times some of the churches, received white money, no white money crossed the palm of the black undertaker; and so it was the black undertaker (truly independent of the white man and least threatened economically if he backed the civil rights movement) who could let his place be used by us without any fear of economic loss. An irony indeed: black death sustained us and helped to keep us alive.

That first day was as hot as could be, and my mouth was dry with the heat and the red clay dust that drifted up from the rutted street near the funeral home. I had no idea exactly where Bernard's aunt's house was, where I would would be staying, but right now at the funeral home we set to work as soon as we arrived. A battered white fan hung from the ceiling, clacked away in the large room, and the mimeograph machine was going as well, clacking in a different rhythm and manned by a white kid with bright red hair, almost orange, from Massachusetts whose freckled forehead was peeling from sunburn. His hands were black with ink and there was a black ink smear – like a gash – along his peeling forehead. He was sweating, his t-shirt soaked.

As he turned the handle, the mimeograph machine spewed out one light green leaflet after another, some floating like outsized leaves to the floor. They said: March for Freedom in Americus – Sunday August 13, 1965, and gave the funeral home address. The black color was getting progressively lighter, though – it needed more ink. "Come on, Ethan," said Bernard, "Take a break. I'll finish it." The red-haired kid headed toward the washroom to clean up. Meanwhile, two other kids were collating and stapling the papers with another sheet of paper about how to register to vote, and I was putting all the papers into large boxes, taking them outside, down the sagging wooden steps, to an old Chevy, where I placed them in a trunk that smelled heavily of kerosene. "O.K.," said Bernard, drops of sweat resting on the follicles near his forehead, "This is, like, too hot entirely," and he pulled off his starched white shirt, revealing a surprisingly muscular torso. We all did the same.

One of the two older white women in the group, she was almost in her thirties, who had on a flowered white dress and had been hanging back for fear of getting it dirty with ink, said: "No fair."

"Yeh," said Bernard, "but us men are doing the work."

This brought groans and cat-calls from the four or five women there, but Bernard paid them no mind. Eventually, he stopped the machine, poured in more ink with both hands, but the heavy plastic bottle was coated outside with the black liquid. When he put down the bottle, his pink palms were now completely black. "Man," he said, looking at his palms, "that stuff is black, I mean black," and he laughed.

Then he looked my way. "Minnesota," he said," come over here." I looked at him, knowing ahead of time, but I came to him anyhow. He held out his hands, palms outward and looked me in the eyes. "There," he said as he placed both wet palms on my naked chest, leaving them there for a moment and then stepped back observing his work, like an artist. "You a black man, now," he laughed, throwing his head back. "You got the stain on you and it ain't ever coming off, Minnesota." I felt in that moment proud, proud of those twin black palm prints on my white chest, and that he joked with me, and my wanting in a way to believe what he said. The others laughed too. But many years later, decades later in fact, I thought more about it – this scene emblazoned like a still photograph in my memory – for I realized there was another way this was not funny: the fact was that I would never know what it was to be black in our crazy world. My white skin would be my passport out of there when I chose to use it – back North, back to the city, where I lived in a white world, back to where it was safe for me. The "stain" as Bernard put it, "the stain" which he applied to my chest that day making my skin black could simply be washed away. We both knew that. And that truth was Bernard's joke – and made the joke as dark as ink.

That evening, Bernard took me to his aunt Thelma's house and introduced me to her and her daughter, his cousin Miriam. Before he did so, he pulled me aside, "Look, Minnesota," he said, "Thelma is not entirely easy about this. She works for a white real estate place in town as a secretary, and if they find out she is involved with us, she will lose her job for sure. They probably don't know about me. I just wanted to let you know. I wish it were different, but it is what it is. She is putting us up, but she is scared."

"O.K.," I said. "I understand."

But looking back, maybe I didn't. Can I excuse my age? I was young and impulsive and, yes, unaware. But maybe, too, I was arrogant.

Thelma had a face so open you wanted to fall into it, a ready smile, and a look that spoke both of practicality and heart. In a sense, she took me in tow. She looked me up and down and said, "Bernard, this white boy is skin and bones. What you been doing to him?"

Bernard evinced that "No ma'am, I ain't done nothing to him. He came that way."

Thelma laughed. "Well" she said, "We'll have to do something about that." And so it was, in effect, she fattened me up with grits and fried chicken and fried fish and okra and greens, never making a fuss about it, just doing it, so that each time we sat down at the oil cloth covered table, the food would be piled high without fail. And of course plenty of ice cold sweet tea.

"And this here, is my cousin Miriam," Bernard said, turning to a pretty teenage girl with a mischievous smile, kind of long-boned in appearance, who had a shy way about her, looking downward as she said hello. I was very taken with her, that's all I can say.

This was the beginning of my stay, embedded in the context of Americus. Both magical and sinister at the same time, this Southern town, with symbols of oppression and difference engrained in its roads and its dwellings. You see, in town you could tell on which side of the railroad tracks you were by the streets themselves, paved on the white side of town, red-rutted Georgia clay baking in the hot sun on the black side. It was only when I crossed the tracks into the black side of town and my shoes started to kick up the red dust, which settled on the scuffed black leather until it seemed to be brown, only then, that I, white boy from the North – felt completely safe. The fear *fell from me. I had made it back to the black part of town: ironically the only safe side of a Southern town for a white civil rights worker. No longer did I note each passing car, particularly if it was from out-of-state, which often suggested the possibility of trouble, of someone looking for us (for the whites surely knew we were in town) or observe its license plate automatically (just in case someone took a shot at us); no longer did my heart beat faster when a car filled with whites slowed down near us. For the fact was that cars with whites had little reason to pass through this side of town at all. At night, the streets here were deeply dark; there were no street lights in the black part of town: they stopped as suddenly as the smooth pavement stopped, and only the moonlight showed me the way, throwing the shadows of trees on the now shadowed and rutted dirt. The stars filled the expanse of black sky, and from the shacks on both sides, the sound of black voices or dishes clacking or laughter came, and yellow light fled through the windows. Scrawny dogs were loose here; they growled, barked, and bayed each time I passed. I feared them, particularly the small white mongrel whose ribs stuck out and who snarled and showed its teeth each time I approached; it always lay in the road just before Thelma's house. I envisioned it one day grabbing my ankle, sinking its teeth deeply in, and never letting go. But despite my fear of the dogs, this street was home to me now. Here I was recognized, nodded to by any blacks who passed me in the night, welcomed, and above all, invited into Thelma and Miriam's house.*

In the morning, Thelma prepared breakfast for us, humming to herself as she did so. It was always a full breakfast, grits, eggs, sausage, biscuits and coffee. Thelma had such a easy way about her that everything seemed so safe, and such a contrast to what happened when we left the black part of town. And in the evening, after a day of canvassing for voters, I slept in a front bedroom on a cot next to Bernard. It felt as if I, an only child, had a brother – almost a big brother, although I was actually taller and probably as old as Bernard. There was an ease in the warm night air and the clicking sound of the portable electric fan near our bed and the breeze from the fan that spread over us. I would lie there, wondering how I got here – amazed at a certain fortune that had brought me here, now, to this place that felt at once so far from home and so close. Bernard went right to sleep usually, and slept with the same certitude he brought to being awake: I gazed over at his body, the sheet thrown aside, his muscular arms and chest – he slept on his back – shining in the moonlight that came through the window. I could barely hear his slow breathing.

They had let me into their lives in a way that seemed so trusting, each of them – Bernard, Thelma, Miriam – letting me know how they lived and how they thought. Sunday was particularly special because they went to church and wanted me to join them, even though I was not Christian. And so I said yes. Thelma and Miriam would get dressed up in their Sunday best, Thelma wearing a maroon hat and a flowered dress, and Miriam in a black dress with little polka dots. Thelma would then look at me askance. "OK, Minnesota," she would say, looking me up and down, "time for you to look proper." And she would insist that I wear a white shirt and that my shirt be ironed, which she would do then and there with a practiced touch so it took but a few minutes.

One Sunday just before church I watched with fascination as Miriam put a thick metal comb onto the burner of the stove and turned up the flame and let it heat up. I was ignorant of what she was doing until I realized she was straightening her hair, but I thought to myself that it was as if she were going to brand herself. This was before Afros had become popular, before "black is beautiful" was a watchword, and when there were almost no black dolls available for black kids. I watched her and then recalled a scene from only five years ago – the summer of 1961. I was seventeen, then, and my father wanted to impress me with the business acumen of a distant relative in Brooklyn (I forget, second cousin or something), who owned a toy factory there. My father offered to have this relative show me the factory. I guess he hoped it would spark some entrepreneurial flame in me. So I traipsed out to Brooklyn with him, dressed in a jacket and tie which he thought appropriate, to meet this relative. The factory was in a crumbling brick building among other crumbling brick buildings; it looked like a deserted war zone. Inside, we entered a nondescript office, and from there we walked through a dark corridor, down some stairs. The clicking sound of mechanical equipment got louder and louder until we came upon one large cement-floored room. In the center of the room there was a giant metal cauldron with a flame under it that let loose an astringent fume that made my eyes sting and then water; the room was furiously and steamingly hot, and the flame beneath the cauldron made a huge roar. The workers there were sweating, seemingly in the thrall of this monstrous machine. Those nearest us paused and nodded deferentially to my father's relative, their boss, as we stood in our ties and jackets, observing. The workers were almost all black, the sweat slowly dripping down their shiny faces and their partially nude chests, and their heads were tightly tied with bandannas or stockings. And what was all this for? My relative, shouting above the noise, explained to my father how the system worked, but I could not hear, maybe did not want to. I think the cauldron contained a liquid plastic. Instead, I stared at a conveyer belt that began somewhere near the cauldron and clacked through the room. On the belt, one after another, small naked pink doll torsos moved slowly along, and then on another belt, small naked pink heads, into the next room. In this room, these disparate parts were put together, so that along the walls were shelves of naked, pink, sexless dolls with fat pink legs and without eyes in their fat faces, hollow black spaces for eyes staring outward and hairless too, little holes in their heads for the hair that was to be inserted. The black workers came and went in this room too. And not one of the dolls was other than pink, an embarrassment of naked pink flesh.

In the following room, hair was being applied to these dolls by mostly heavy-set black women seated at long tables – it was sheer straight blonde hair that shimmered in their large black hands as they worked it into each skull. Ans then, finally, they carefully and gently placed glistening blue eyes in the hollow sockets, so the dolls now were lined up as if they could finally and blankly see the world. It was less noisy in this room. My father and our relative no longer *needed to shout at each other. They talked calmly now, like men of the world, the relative explaining with evident pride his business from the point of view of expense and income, as he took a white silk handkerchief out of his jacket pocket to wipe the sweat from his brow. I stood there alone, saying nothing, stunned, my eyes still watering.*

And now, here was Miriam, removing the searingly hot metal comb from the stove top and bowing her head as she prepared to pull it through her kinky hair. I had to ask.

"Why do you do that?" I said.

"Boy," she said, lifting her head and looking at me, "ain't you never seen a woman straighten her hair?"

"No," I said, "not really."

"I don't want it nappy," she said, matter of fact, "so I straighten it."

"But I like it kinky like that," I said.

"Shuuu," she said, with a graceful wave of her hand, and in that expression, dismissed me, and set to in earnest, bowing her head once again and running the hot comb through her hair.

One morning, at the funeral home, Bernard announced that we were to get three more civil rights workers coming in from SCLC headquarters in Atlanta by bus. He said that some of us should meet them at the bus station, and turned to me and four others. The rest of us, including Bernard, were to stay behind in the freedom house to man the fort or to go out and canvas for more voters. But before we started out, Bernard had us all stand in a circle in the big central room, hands joined, and we sang. Bernard led us. Out of his small hard frame, came his deep voice. His singing, our chorus, the swaying, the black hands joined with white – it all spoke of the impossible goodness of life where pain was gone: "We shall overcome, someday," we intoned. It was not just about this moment, this struggle: it felt as if it was about a division inside me, maybe inside each of us, as if we could sing that division away. And then, when Bernard changed it to "We shall not, we shall not be moved" and began the line solo, a line which for some reason always went into me, "Just like a tree standing by the wa-ater, we shall not be moved," I felt as happy as I thought I had ever felt.

The four of us left Hubert's, crossed the railroad tracks into the white side of town, and started toward Elston Street. Walking toward us, swinging her purse in one hand, was Miriam – her lengthy and relaxed stride so noticeable to me. "Whew," she said, "Hot," tossing her hair as she came up to us, and looking at me asked, "Where you all going?"

"To the bus station," I said. "There are some more civil rights workers coming in." I hesitated, then said, "Want to come?"

"I'll come with you," she said.

"You sure?" I asked, knowing that Thelma would not like this. Nor Bernard for that matter. I should discourage her, I was thinking, but I liked the idea of being with her. Beside, what harm could there be?

"Yup, sure," she responded, gently pushing my shoulder.

And so, she joined us as we made our way down to Elston Street.

We were all laughing and talking. Miriam and I were nudging each other as we walked. I guess it was pretty obvious who we were, because as we approached the station, two white men got out of one of the pickup trucks parked there, probably waiting for someone to come in by bus. They stared at us.

"Say, wait a minute," one of the men who had gotten out of the cab said to us as we passed. "Wait one damn minute. I know who you are. You come to this bus station to go back home, where you belong? 'Cause you sure ain't wanted around here."

He was a heavy, short man, in a white t-shirt stained with dirt, and jeans, and a wide leather belt around his middle. His face was unshaven. He turned to his companion, "Johnny," he said, "I think what we got here is them Northern interlopers, who can't mind their own business."

All of us became quiet then. We walked past them, without saying anything. But the short man now stepped in our path. "Whoa, wait a minute," he said. "You ain't got any luggage or anything, do you? I think you're not going anywhere, but what I think is you're here at the bus station to meet some more of you, come to Americus."

We were near the entrance to the bus station by now, so glancing at each other, we hurried our walk a bit. I thought that if we could get through the door of the bus station, maybe they would leave us alone. And, fortunately, we made it through the front door. A short while later the bus arrived from Atlanta, huffing and chugging and making a sudden sigh when it finally stopped. It let its passengers off: a white man lugging a heavy black tool case, a black mother and little girl dressed in their frilly Sunday best, and a single elderly white woman who looked like a librarian, with her glasses on a string, making her way gingerly down the front steps. Behind them, came two young white women – looking around with wide eyes, and a very thin white boy, wearing an ill-fitting black jacket and tie with chino pants. It was clear that these were the three recruits that SCLC had sent down from Atlanta.

By this time, the bus station appeared to have become surrounded, more or less. In addition to the two men who had badgered us on our way into the station, there were other heavy men in overalls and plaid shirts and jeans, one with his thick black hair slicked straight back, another wearing a dirty green Deere cap, another one with what looked like an axe handle in one of his hands, and still another holding a Louisville slugger bat incongruously painted bright red, although the paint had flecked off in spots, which he had pulled out of the bed of his pickup. Their numbers had grown, as if by magic. How the word spread so quickly, I do not know. And they were laughing and sneering and calling us names. Behind them, I could see a young white boy, perhaps ten, observing the whole thing, balancing with one hand an upright silver-painted bicycle and in the other hand holding an ice cream cone. We could see all this through the glass, which was smeared whitish with the touch of hands from people leaving the station. But we stayed inside.

The ticket man of the bus station had come from behind the counter with a large handful of keys, and, looking down the whole time as if afraid to make eye contact with anyone, locked the door – while the men on the other side heckled him – and then he had scurried back to the counter. The result was that just for the moment we were safe – but we were also trapped. Meanwhile, the ticket man was on the phone behind his counter, and I heard him say, "Sheriff," to whomever he was talking to, so I gathered he was calling for help. "So," I thought, "everything may end up being alright."

Sure enough, fairly quickly we heard a siren and three police cars arrived and stopped at the back of the crowd. The police got out and seemed to survey the scene, talking casually to some of the men who had surrounded the station. But they appeared in no hurry to do anything. And then two black cars arrived, parking next to the police cars, and out stepped a bunch of men dressed in suits and ties. They talked among themselves, but they too did nothing.

At this point, I thought I better call for help. I saw there was a black phone in the wooden phone booth against one wall. I picked up the receiver and, after a very long moment, fearing that the men outside might have somehow cut the phone line, I heard a dial tone. I dialed the funeral home, my heart noticeably beating in my chest all the time. The phone rang and rang. Finally, a deep and slow voice answered, saying with careful pronunciation, "This is Reverend Linset speaking. How can I help?" I was so nervous I almost giggled, as if I had at last reached God himself, who would slowly ponder any desperate question I might ask him and then make some wonderful pronouncement in his deep voice, to end our distress.

"Reverend, Reverend," I said, "Please, is Bernard there?"

"Bernard Purdue?" he asked.

We rarely used Bernard's last name. It came as a surprise. "Yes, sir, please." I said, trying to appear calm.

"I will see," he said, and the phone was silent.

Then a voice came on. "This is Bernard."

"Bernard," I said, not bothering to identify myself and knowing he would recognize my voice, "we're in big trouble, here," and I explained.

"Whoa," he said after I finished, "calm down. You say there are Feds there? Are you sure?"

"That's what they look like. They're not doing anything but standing around near their two black unmarked cars. If they're not

Feds they're doing a pretty good imitation with their black suits and sunglasses. One of them is talking to someone in the Sheriff's car now. There must be five or six of them in all. They act like they're watching a ball game, laughing and joking with each other, but as I say, keeping a distance too."

"O.K." said Bernard. "That's good."

"What's good?" I asked.

He ignored me. "Let me see what I can do," he said.

"What could you possibly do?"

"Have faith, Minnesota," he said. "What's your phone number at the booth?"

I told him.

"Just sit tight," he said.

"Like we have a choice," I said.

"I'll call you back soon," he said.

"Wait, wait," I said at the last minute, "before you hang up."

"Yes, what is it?"

"I bumped into Miriam outside Hubert's, and she's with us."

"Lord, Minnesota. You shouldn't have."

"I know. I'm sorry."

"I'll get back to you," he said in a clipped voice and the phone went dead with a dial tone that sounded more ominous than before. We waited. And I worried. Not just about what would happen to us. In the pit of my stomach, I felt an ache. What had I done in letting Miriam join us? Had I jeopardized Thelma's job? Would her employer find out if we were all arrested, which was a possibility, or even if we were not, would someone, one of the county policeman for example, recognize Miriam (it was a small town, after all) and word get back to Thelma's employer? I felt miserable.

* * *

This damn dumb white boy. That's all I could feel at first, the feeling just going through me, worrying about what Thelma would think when she found out Miriam was with Minnesota in this iffy situation, worrying about Miriam, toward whom I felt responsible. But really, really I had no time to think about it. I had to deal with the situation. All I could envision were those white feds in their careful black clothes – I could see them in my mind's eye. And yet, thank God they were there, because if it were the County police only, it would be hopeless. Those police would as soon let those rednecks beat our people up, and then arrest Minnesota and Miriam and everyone for causing a disturbance. It probably helped that it was at the bus station. For – like with the Greyhound buses – the station might be considered part of interstate commerce, where federal law applied, and so maybe that was why the rednecks had not attacked yet. Perhaps just the presence of the feds worried them, although I couldn't see that it would keep them from entering the bus station forever. The crowd was probably just trying to work their courage up to attack, goading each other on. Anyhow, as long as the standstill stood for a while longer, I had a chance to help. I placed a call to Josea.

His gravelly voice came on, and I was grateful to hear it. I explained the situation. "You gotta do something, Josea."

"Hold on, Bernard, hold on. We'll get a line to John Doar at Justice. You know how it is. Just hold on." We all knew that the FBI could only be controlled if we got the word to the United States Attorney General's office. This unwritten agreement between the Attorney General's office and us often saved us, although it never hit the papers. It wasn't in our interest to publicize it because then the rednecks would be in an uproar about it; and maybe the arrangement would not hold. The fact was the Attorney General of the United States did not want any more civil rights workers' deaths. This wasn't Mississippi, but we could just as well buy it here as there. On the other hand, the FBI by itself was a different story. The FBI men in their black suits were generally only interested in giving us a bad time, in standing in the background, dutifully observing and snickering, when we got into trouble, and in sometimes actively harassing us unless we could go over J. Edgar Hoover's head to the Attorney General. And perhaps we could this time.

*   *   *

"I'm sorry," I said to Miriam. "I shouldn't have let you come with us. Bernard is angry at me, and I'm worried about your mom's job."

Miriam looked at me. "You didn't do anything," she laughed. "I wanted to come. We'll be alright, you'll see, and Bernard and Thelma, they just worries theyselves too much. Thelma will be angry at me, I know, but she'll get over it. Beside, white boy, do you think I came because of you?"

"Well, if I hadn't offered . . . ."

"Maybe not now, but I would have come some day anyhow. I've been wanting to. I've been wanting to for a long time. And besides, them white crackers don't scare me.

But the crowd seemed to be getting larger, with more cars and pickups arriving and more white men and even some white women stepping out of them. After what seemed forever another black car drove up; then something seemed to be happening outside the station. I could see that one of the county policeman had been called over by one of the FBI men near the black cars. They were talking to each other, heads down, while the others – the FBI men, the cops – just watched them from their respective places. Then the county policeman returned to his group and talked to the others. After a while, they all stood up from leaning on their cars, they stopped laughing with each other, one threw away a cigarette he had been smoking, and then they came toward the crowd of people. It seemed ominous at first. But then a fat cop, with an enormous belly, stopped, looked over at everyone and yelled, "Ok, Ok, you all." The crowd stopped talking, stopped shouting curses at us, waiting for the cop to speak. "Look, I know how you feel, I sure do, but you're going to have to let these people go on their way."

There were cries of protest and curses. Some of them apparently knew him, and yelled " Come on, Joe, let us be."

Joe just stood there, one hand on his belt, and said, "You're going to have to let these people go. Fun's over." Eventually the crowd parted from the entrance door to the bus station and let Joe approach it with some of the other officers behind him. "Orville," Joe yelled, pushing on the locked door. "Orville." The thin white man behind the ticket booth came out, holding a large bunch of keys and approached the door. "Unlock this damn thing, Orville. Nothing's going to happen and nobody's going to get hurt."

And so we walked out with cops on both sides of us – the citizenry parted like a proverbial sea. But they kept on calling us names and one woman, in a white flowery dress, spat on us. The hatred in their faces was frightening. They followed us a ways, with the cops still with us, quite a procession, dwindling in numbers as we moved along and as I guess the fun of scaring us was gone, until we made it to the railroad tracks into the black part of town near Hubert's. The kid on the bicycle had followed us too, and now, although the adults had dwindled off, he took to riding around all of us in a big circle, yelling, "Nigger lovers, nigger lovers, nigger lovers," over and over. Eventually he tired and rode away. But there was something about this innocent-looking kid repeating these words, like in a child's game, that has lived with me all these years even more than the angry look of those white adult faces.

The next few weeks were uneventful. There were no more encounters with the whites. Things had apparently calmed down. We went around our business registering black voters, accompanying them into the white part of town, sometimes in their Sunday best, to stand on a line which moved so slowly inside the courthouse and sometimes extended right outside. There was nothing more wonderful than the look on their faces once they registered. "Lordy," a matronly one would say fanning herself in the hot sun and turning to her friends, "I did it and am I proud." And a smile with broken teeth would spread across her face.

And her husband, thin as a rail, and wearing a dark suit and white shirt, the cords of his neck as prominent as the bark of a tree, and leaning on his battered wooden cane would say, "Mama, we are proud too. In fact, Mama, we both done it." And they laughed; and one could but wonder what long times of hardship, what experiences of demeaning by whites and the whole Jim Crow system, served as a mutually understood backdrop to this simple defiant statement. Moments like this were repeated and repeated. Each time, they moved me.

But things were different at Thelma's. I apologized to her for letting Miriam come to the bus station, and she said to my surprise, "Never mind, child. I suspect it will be o.k." But inside, I could not stop feeling that I had announced my difference, my trespass into her life, and that there was a level of trust that I could no longer earn from her. And yet, she took care of me like a mother, not only feeding me but being concerned with my appearance in a way that my own mother was not. But I was an impulsive boy still, and – although I knew better, I suppose – I enjoyed so much the kidding attention of Miriam that I could not resist. One day, when she was sitting in the living room on a rocking chair reading a magazine, I came up behind her and kissed her on the back of her neck. She giggled, and turned around. "What you up to, white boy?" she said. And then to my surprise, she gave me the softest kiss full on my lips. We both laughed.

From then on, we had our tender embraces. Exciting, sweetly erotic, but it did not really go further than that, and we were careful to hide it from Thelma and Bernard. I felt this welling up of closeness with her. But I thought Bernard knew what was happening because one time he almost walked in on us. He did not say anything, however, which puzzled me.

*   *   *

I should have known better. I blamed myself. It was just like this white boy who had no idea what it was all about, even if he had come down here. This business with Miriam would go no place. I wanted to slap her upside the head, slap some sense into her; I all but said to her, "What you think you doing with that white boy?" But something held me back, she would have to learn, however hard it was.

And yet, at the same time, I felt this strange thing with Minnesota. I remembered what Josea had said to him at one point, and as it came closer to the time Minnesota was supposed to go back North, I thought, "What the hell, you never know," and spoke to him one evening after dinner. It was warm with that sweet smell in the air from a sweet melissa bush next to the house, and we had come outside the house to kind of stretch.

*   *   *

"Come here, white boy," said Bernard. He pointed next to him on the wooden steps to the front porch where he was sitting. I sat down. The steps were warped and much of the white paint had come off, leaving a striated pattern, scratchy to the palm of my hand. Bernard kicked at the red clay dust with his one shoe, not saying anything, looking downward.

After a while, I said, "So, Bernard, what is it? Are you still mad at me for letting Miriam come with us."

"No, not that," he said with a wave of his hand. "I'm over that."

I felt relief. "So what is it?" I said.

He was quiet for a while longer. Then he said, "You know, I've been thinking, what with your going back North soon. Remember that talk you had with Josea in Atlanta."

"Oh," I said, "That. Yeah, of course I remember."

"I don't suppose there is any chance you will change your mind?"

There was no chance. It had both intrigued and scared me. Josea had asked me to stay on, to work for SCLC full time, and even more than that, to settle in the South – to forget about going back North for school there.

"You see," Bernard continued, "it's different here. Yes it is awful right now, but in the South we know each other, black and whites

know each other, in a way you do not in the North. We live with each other here. You don't in New York City, in any of those big Northern cities. You know what I mean? Maybe it will even change here in the long run quicker than up North."

This was the argument that Josea had made to me, in his gravelly voice, when he and Randy sat me down in Atlanta. I thought that in some ways they were right. And for a moment, I thought that I could do that; I could change the course of my life and stay on, working for SCLC. And in that moment, I got scared. How far could I really go in this wish I had to help? My life would change forever if I were to make such a decision. I truly loved it here in many ways, although I was not as sure as Josea was that things might change here in the South more than up North, but then, regardless, I knew that I had to flee back home: there was my safety and my comfort.

And so, a few days later, I said my goodbyes and made it back to Atlanta and flew back home. I had school to return to, I had my life to get on with. At first, I kept in touch with Miriam, a letter or two, but then I did not respond. Can I excuse it? I was young, busy, ambitious, my life returned to the usual track of getting on with education and career. I slid so easily into what my life had been before I went down South. But it was more than that, because there came a time many years later when I realized what I had done.

One early morning, I was ironing a white shirt before going on a business trip that would take me to the Atlanta airport. And suddenly, I had a vision of Thelma doing the same task for me, unbidden, before we went off to church so many years ago, with that slow and unhurried way about her, and Miriam, standing there in her pretty black polka dot dress with a white collar ready for church and teasing me about my unpolished, dust-covered shoes and my rumpled pants that surely could also have used ironing. And I had a feeling which took me a while to recognize: it was not so much nostalgia as regret, like a still standing pool that had been in my chest for a long time. For I realized I had in those intervening years abandoned Thelma and Miriam. And there was something much more. Something more awful, a thought lurking by the side of the *standing pool, like a dark shape. For suddenly I thought how often through the years I had abandoned the women I loved by leaving them. And I thought back to Margaret, Margaret whom I invoked when I went down South, Margaret the maid who had left me as a child. Did it all come back to that, to something so seemingly far away, to a child whose heart broke? Had I exacted a terrible revenge for the loss I had never fully acknowledged, the loss of comfort and connection and love from a black woman? I had abandoned Thelma and Miriam, yes, as I had felt abandoned. I had my revenge and at my expense too. I was shaken.*

As fate would have it, that very day when I was in the Atlanta airport, I thought I saw Bernard once again. No, I said to myself, it could not be, it is just because of my vision in the morning. But indeed, it seemed to be him: his kinky hair was grey near his ears, his black skin was duskier and he looked distinguished, in a black pin-striped suit, dragging the usual black suitcase on wheels behind him, and what was probably a computer bag resting on top of it. I approached him. "Bernard?" I said, with a little hesitation. He stopped, looked at me questioningly. I noticed how the skin beneath his eyes was dark now and crinkled. "Harry," I said, "remember, Harry from Minnesota."

"Oh," he said. "Sure." He propped his bag up and we shook hands. He had ended up working for the city of Savannah, he said, the Parks Department. "After all that, I became a company man," he joked. We laughed. "But I like it," he said, "even if I am a piece of the establishment now. Hard to believe, given all my arrests when work-ing for SCLC and my history, that they even hired me. But I still help the black community there. Now it's from the inside." There was an awkward moment. Finally, I asked after Thelma. Bernard said, "She passed five years ago."

"I'm sorry," I said. "She was a good woman."

"Yes," he said. I wanted then to ask after Miriam too. I had it on the tip of my tongue. And I wanted to apologize for disappearing, to try to explain, to dip into that pool in my chest but I didn't. "You're back North," he said.

"Yes."

He smiled knowingly, as if that said it all. We compared notes briefly: family, children, but there was a distant look on his face, careful, not at all like it used to be. We were separate now and had been for a long time, after all those years. He had to catch his plane, and when we exchanged phone numbers, we looked at each other full in the face and knew that neither one of us would call.

The Power of Berry Soup

Some of this story is true. It happened that way. A famous writer once entitled his story: "You could look it up," and you could look parts of this story up. You might even find that some of the dialogue is true, taken directly from the transcript of the trial of the Littleton 9. But for the parts of the story that are not true, that is not factually accurate, I would contend that in a way they are: the spirit is the same. But you be the judge or – perhaps more accurately – be the jury.

I. 1967: Jenny Leading Cloud, Lakota Sioux, South Dakota

The recorder of stories had actually fled Germany many years ago, one step ahead of Hitler, who did not like the cartoons the recorder drew attacking the Nazi regime. The recorder had then had to flee Austria too, and eventually made his way to the United States, where he became amazed at and enamored of the Native Americans. He settled in New York City, but his heart was in the country of the Indians. And so it was today on the Rosebud Reservation in South Dakota that he turned on his tape recorder and asked Jenny Leading Cloud to tell the myths of her people, the Lakota Sioux. In a voice both cracked and strong, that spoke out from the snows of bitterly cold winters, Jenny told the story of berry soup, called "*wojabi*," and porcupine quills. She said,

> **"Somewhere at a place where the prairie and the Maka Sicha (the Badlands) meet there is a hidden cave. Not for a long, long time has anyone been able to find it. Even now, with so many highways, cars, and tourists, no one has discovered this cave.**

In it lives a woman so old that her face looks like a shriveled-up walnut. She is dressed in rawhide, the way people used to be before the white man came. She has been sitting there for a thousand years or more, working on a blanket strip for her buffalo robe. She is making the strip out of dyed porcupine quills, the way our ancestors did before white traders brought glass beads to this turtle continent. Resting beside her, licking his paws, watching her all the time is Shunk Sapa, a huge black dog. His eyes never wander from the old woman whose teeth are worn flat, worn down to little stumps; she has used them to flatten so many porcupine quills.

A few steps from where the old woman sits working on her blanket strips, a huge fire is kept going. She lit this fire a thousand or more years ago and has kept it alive ever since. Over the fire hangs a big earthen pot, the kind some Indian peoples used to make before the white man came with his kettles of iron. Inside the big pot, wojapi has been boiling and bubbling in the pot for a long time, ever since the fire was lit.

Every now and then the old woman gets up to stir the wojapi in the huge earthen pot. She is so old and feeble that it takes her a while to get up and hobble to the fire. The moment her back is turned, the huge black dog starts pulling the porcupine quills out of her blanket strip. This way she never makes any progress, and her quillwork remains forever unfinished. The Sioux people used to say that if the old woman ever finishes her blanket strip, then at the very moment that she threads the last porcupine quill to complete the design, the world will come to an end."(1)

The recorder of stories will disappear from this tale. But his record – the Lakota myth spoken by Jenny Leading Cloud – endures. It expands. As you will hear, it will mark this tale too.

2. September, 1864: Camp Weld, Colorado

This, then, is a story about history, how it circles around, spirals, comes back to the same place transformed but recognizable and, all too often, ugly and inescapable and heart-wrenching. At the same time in this spiral of history, there are threads, quills, glimmers of hope that bind together those who struggle.

Wynkoop struggled. Tall, patrician, well-spoken, and standing ramrod straight – some said that he looked like President Lincoln himself – he knew that here at Camp Weld, just south of the new town of Denver – it was a gamble on whether he could get a peace settlement. Black Kettle was an honorable man who seemed to desire peace not war, and Wynkoop had grown to admire him. After all, it was Black Kettle, one of the principal chiefs of the Cheyenne, who had sent an emissary to Wynkoop, at Fort Lyon, Colorado, where Wynkoop was in command, asking him to travel 140 miles west to Smoky Hill, Kansas, where Black Kettle would release to him four white hostages who had been captured by the Dog Soldiers. This was Black Kettle's overture, an offer that he hoped would show good faith and result in a peace negotiation with the whites.

Perhaps any other commanding officer would have rejected the overture. Indeed, when One-Eye, the messenger from Black Kettle, appeared before the Fort, he had not been sure whether he would be well received or simply shot. But the tall Major Wynkoop did receive him, read Black Kettle's intriguing proposal in a letter drafted by the mixed blood George Brent, who traveled between the two worlds, and then – when One-Eye urged him to come immediately to the Cheyenne camp before the Indians, including the Arapaho who had also camped there, dispersed – Wynkoop made the decision to go. Then and there; no time to get permission from Colonel Chivington, his superior, in Denver. He took it upon himself to advance; impulsive, he knew, but the overture for peace he believed overrode discretion. One hundred twenty-seven of his men and two cannon would be enough to protect them should Black Kettle and the Indians prove hostile.

He had been terribly wrong in this regard. On the fourth day, having ridden his men hard, early in the morning, they approached the village. They came up to a hillside, and when they looked over it they found themselves face-to-face with a battle line of seven hundred fifty painted and screaming warriors with bows strung. Wynkoop was stunned as he gazed at them. Had he jeopardized his men? Had he been a fool after all? For if the Indians attacked, Wynkoop saw immediately that, even with their cannons, they would not stand a chance. All he could do was brazen it out and hope that his first instinct when he read Black Kettle's letter had been the right one.

It was not easy. The warriors were shouting, creating a din so it was difficult to hear. Then one Cheyenne advanced toward him and asked what the soldiers wanted. Wynkopp said he came to talk. And then, "Why do you bring cannon and warriors if all you want to do is talk?"

Wynkoop, surprised for a moment, paused. Then, carefully he answered, "We come in peace, but we had to be prepared to defend ourselves in case of any treachery." For the moment, this seemed to satisfy the Cheyenne, so Wynkoop and his officers were escorted to a grove where they sat in a circle with twenty Cheyenne and Arapaho chiefs. A peace pipe was passed around. Then Black Kettle, whose Cheyenne name was Make-tava-tah, now fifty-two years old and who had been through many battles, losing his first wife nineteen years ago when the Utes captured her in a fight at Cimarron River and subsequently becoming a leader of her Wuh'tapiu clan, announced himself. And he looked directly at Wynkoop, his face impassive but his eyes bright, and with what Wynkoop felt was not hostility, but, rather, encouragement.

After the pipe was passed, again the same question was asked over and over by various chiefs about the cannon and Wynkoop's motive for being there. Wynkoop – worried – carefully answered again and again, and then finally he pleaded for the immediate release of the prisoners of whom Black Kettle had spoken and for a peace treaty. But at the same time – he was out on a limb just because he had not had time to get the permission of his superior when he set out so impulsively on this venture – he also explained to the assembled chiefs that he could not provide a treaty himself because he did not have the authority. The chiefs would have to come to faraway Camp Weld, and a treaty there could be signed by Colonel Chivington.

Now Wynkoop's response only seemed to evoke further questions and suspicion. For hours on end, as the day passed and then evening came – a soft wind now rustling the silvery leaves of the cottonwood trees in the grove – Wynkoop talked and listened while the warriors outside their circle grew increasingly restless. And then inside the circle, the Cheyenne Dog Soldier war chief Bull Bear suddenly jumped up, making a full throated yell, "This white man talking to us here," he screamed, "this white man, thinks we are children, but we are warriors and chiefs. He says, 'Give me the white prisoners right now,' but he promises us nothing in return. He thinks we are fools. He comes here only to laugh at us. He is not to be trusted. Whites cannot be trusted!" A number of the chiefs assented. Some of the Cheyenne warriors outside the circle were exclaiming loudly. Wynkoop thought that the game was over and they would be lucky to escape with their lives.

But now, Black Kettle, who after announcing himself had said nothing further, rose to his feet. He waved his hand for silence. Everyone stilled and again only the sound of the wind in the cottonwood trees could be heard. Black Kettle crossed the circle to Wynkoop, took his hand, pulled him up, embraced him, and led him to the center of the circle. He said to the chiefs, "I have been listening to this white man for this long, long time. This white man is not here to laugh at us. Unlike most of the white race, he has trusted our word and comes with confidence in the pledge we gave him. His tongue is not forked nor does he have two hearts; instead his words are straight, his heart single. If he had told us that he, alone, could give us peace when we delivered the white prisoners to him, he would have lied. Instead, he told us the truth: he cannot guarantee us peace because there is a greater chief at

Camp Weld. But we can do what we said we would do, give up our prisoners, and then go to Camp Weld and sign a peace treaty there."

Dusk had come. Black Kettle finished speaking, and the circle was completely silent. And then, without anything further, the chiefs simply arose without speaking and slipped away to their village beyond the hill, and the Indians outside the circle disappeared too. Wynkoop and his men were left alone. They did not know what had happened. Night came on. The moon and the stars shone bright in the wide black sky. Exhausted, everyone turned in, but most of them slept fitfully that night. Frightened. The next day, Wynkoop and his troops remained camped, waiting, wondering whether Black Kettle would return. Wondering, too, if they would be attacked by the Indians so much greater in number than they were. And then another night, and still, still no word.

Finally, early the next day, Black Kettle returned with the other chiefs. They brought with them four white hostages: fifteen-year old Laura Roper (who witnessed nine members of the Ewbanks family attacked, murdered, and scalped when she was taken prisoner), Daniel Marble (whose wagon train was attacked in Nebraska and eleven people killed and mutilated by Bull Bear's Dog Soldiers), Ambrose Asher (who had been rendered mute since his capture), and three-year-old Isabelle Ewbanks, survivor of the Ewbanks massacre. When handed up to Wynkoop on his horse, little Isabelle raised her thin arms and then clung tightly to him, saying, "I want momma." Wynkoop held her gently against his chest and turned his head away from the Indians to hide his tears.

The next day, Black Kettle (gambler that he was, too) and the Cheyenne and Arapaho chiefs, as well as twenty warriors, began the long journey with Wynkoop and his troops to Camp Weld. Wynkoop was joyous; he felt as he rode his horse leading the way under a cloudless blue sky that his impulsiveness had paid off after all: he had fashioned a peace with the Indians and all that remained was to cement it at Camp Weld. He and his troops would enter Denver in triumph and would be greeted with celebration. And in addition, he felt he had made a friend of Black Kettle, who had dared as Wynkoop had and who had trusted him and who – he did not know how – had convinced his own people, even the fierce Dog Soldiers, to give up their hostages in exchange for an enduring peace, a new way that would express their mutual humanity despite the brutality that Wynkoop knew both sides at various times had embraced. It would be so fine.

But it was not so fine. Not fine at all, for now, now at Camp Weld, things were not as he thought they would be. From the moment of his return, Wynkoop encountered trouble. The two powerful men whom he had thought would be pleased with what he had done, bringing about peace and the possible end of hostilities, were not. With the first of these men, Wynkoop thought he shared a lasting friendship. It was Samuel Chivington, a formidable figure, charismatic and – as it turned out – dangerously ambitious, standing six-foot four and 250 pounds, who even made Wynkoop look small when they stood side by side. Chivington had been a Methodist minister in Missouri, passionately and vocally anti-slavery, which prompted his largely pro-slavery parishioners to threaten such hostile actions against him that he had to preach his sermons while toting six guns – for which he acquired the nickname "The Fighting Parson." The Methodist church, thinking discretion in this case the better part of valor, transferred Chivington to a parish in the more anti-slavery environs of Ohio. But Chivington really *did* care more for fighting than for ministering from the bible, and eventually he had become a colonel in the Colorado regiments. In fact, he and Wynkoop together had successfully fought the Confederates in a phase of the Civil War at Glorietta Pass in New Mexico in March 1862, two-and-a-half years previously, registering a decisive Union victory and, Wynkoop thought, cementing their friendship in the process.

And of course Chivington was the superior officer whom Wynkoop had not informed of his gamble before he set out so hastily to meet with Black Kettle and the other Indian chiefs. Wynkoop did not realize how displeased Chivington had been on hearing the news of a "peace settlement," how envious he was of the attention accruing to Wynkoop, nor was he aware that, when informed of the impending arrival of Black Kettle and the other chiefs in Denver, Chivington had immediately written to his superior General Curtis in Kansas that these Indians – who had committed such bad actions in the past – "should be chastised" rather than rewarded. They were only suing for peace, he claimed, because they must know that the Third Colorado Volunteer Regiment, newly organized, was now prepared for battle against them. To put it differently, Chivington was attempting to sabotage Wynkoop's efforts even before his friend had returned to Colorado. And on this very day of the Camp Weld meeting, Chivington, to his pleasure, received the reply he wanted from General Curtis, a reply he did not share with his friend Wynkoop. Wrote General Curtis, "I want no peace till the Indians suffer more."

The second powerful man was Governor Evans. Not as powerful as he wanted to be, however. In Wynkoop's absence, the populace had voted down a proposition that Colorado become a full state, which Evans backed and which if it had passed would have made him a Governor of a state rather than of a territory. He was smarting just now from this defeat. In addition, the Third Colorado Volunteer Regiment had been organized by Evans and Chivington to battle the Indians but had seen little action. When Wynkoop proposed to bring Black Kettle and the other Indians into Denver in what Wynkoop thought would be a triumphant arrival to be culminated by their meeting with the Governor and the signing of a peace treaty, Evans at first refused to even meet with them. Over and over, Wynkoop urged him to meet and not to exact punishment upon the Indians, which Evans proposed as a condition of peace. In exasperation with Wynkoop, Evans explained: "I have created the Third Regiment. They have been raised to kill Indians, and they must kill Indians. What shall I do with them if I make peace?"

It took even more persuading, but Evans and his staff finally did meet with Black Kettle and the other chiefs at a council. When Black Kettle rose to speak, everyone – Indians and whites – fell quiet. He began by explaining why the chiefs had traveled four hundred miles to Denver. "We have come with our eyes shut," he said, "like coming through the fire. All we ask is that we may have peace with the whites. We have been traveling through a dark cloud, a cloud that has darkened the sky ever since the war began. These braves who are with me are willing to do what I say. We want to take good tidings home to our people that they may sleep in peace. And we want the chiefs of the soldiers here to understand that we are here for peace."

But his words had little meaning to Evans, who felt he had been pressured to have council with the Indians. Evans then spoke. He accused Black Kettle of suing for peace because of the change in the seasons. "The time you can make war is best in summer time; when I can make war best is the winter. So you have had the advantage," he said, "and now my time is coming." And he added menacingly, thinking of his Volunteer Regiment, "My soldiers are preparing for the fight."

And then things became suddenly and decidedly unclear, fatally so. Rather than simply leaving it at that, Evans handed over the final decision – despite his belligerent words – to Chivington, whom he called "the great war chief." He stated that arrangements could be made with Chivington to forge the peace that Wynkoop had suggested. In conclusion, Black Kettle was to go to Fort Lyons with the chiefs and with the Cheyenne and Arapahoe people, where Wynkoop would be in charge, and Chivington then would work on making final peace arrangements. At least that is what Black Kettle and Wynkooop understood. And so, they departed relieved, expecting the best and that a peace had begun and that only the final touches were necessary to make it a lasting one.

In fact, a formal photograph had been taken to memorialize the peace process at Camp Weld. Wynkoop had his father-in-law, a photographer, arrange it as a way to pressure Evans to meet with

Black Kettle and the chiefs. You can still see it, more often than not labeled as "participants at the Camp Weld council on September 28, 1865," although neither Evans nor Chivington, crucial to any negotiations, appear in it. The Indian chiefs are seated and standing – the Dog Soldier Bull Bear, White Antelope, Black Kettle – all Southern Cheyenne, and the Arapahos Neva, No-ta-nee, Heap of Buffalo, and Bosse. A trader/interpreter and even the Secretary of the Colorado Territory are there as well. In front, in the center, seated almost on the ground, is Wynkoop in regimental clothes: a broad-brimmed hat on his head, looking jaunty. The photograph seems to presage a peaceful future.

But what lay ahead could not be foreseen from the photograph. Wynkoop returned to Fort Lyon. Black Kettle and the Southern Cheyenne and Arapaho made camp near there at Sand Creek, where they were told they would be under military protection and should await the final establishment of peace. And then Wynkoop was accused of "having left his post without orders" to meet with Black Kettle from the very beginning, and, in addition, he was falsely accused of distributing "goods, stores and supplies to hostile Indians in violation of orders." He was promptly relieved of his command and told to report to the district headquarters of General Curtis hundreds of miles away in Kansas, where he would be called upon to defend his actions. Two days after Wynkoop's departure, who should arrive unannounced at Fort Lyons but Chivington bringing with him troops from a variety of battalions including four hundred fifty troops from the Third Colorado Volunteer Regiment. Seven hundred men in all. The die was cast.

That night, Chivington and his troops quietly made their way to the Cheyenne-Arapahoe village on Sand Creek. Five hundred Indians slept there, two-thirds of them women because some warriors were on a hunting expedition and, on top of that, the Dog Soldiers had not trusted the protection of the whites and had left. There were one hundred tipis and tents. Unsuspecting were the people inside, some of whom dreamt, some who shifted in their sleep uneasily. Black Kettle's tipi was the most obvious. From a pole near it, an American flag with its 34 stars on a blue ground and 13 red and white stripes flew in a slight breeze. It made no difference.

At dawn, Chivington and his troops attacked.

Black Kettle left his tipi and yelled for his people not to run, for they were at peace and under the protection of the white man. And then White Antelope, a brave warrior and one of those who posed for the peace photograph at Camp Weld, walked toward the soldiers, his hands held high asking them not to fire. He stopped. He stood there, his hands folded across his chest, hoping his actions would signify his peaceful intentions. Instead, the soldiers immediately gunned him down. At this point, Black Kettle and the rest fled. Many succeeded in escaping.

But so many could not successfully escape. The carnage of the attack was immense and lasted six hours. Those soldiers who took part in it justified their savagery as pay back for Indian savagery in the past. Little children on their knees pleaded, mothers on their knees with their arms around soldiers begged for their lives – but they were shot, hatcheted through their brains. A pregnant mother's body was cut open and a child taken out of her. And all – women, children, warriors – were scalped often four or five times so that each soldier could get a piece. Fingers and ears were cut off the still warm bodies to get the rings off. White Antelope's body, lying in the creek bed where he had fallen, was a prime target: soldiers cut off his nose, ears and testicles – the last for a tobacco pouch. Other soldiers cut off the vulvas of the dead Indian women and stretched them over their saddle-bows and wore them on their hats when they returned to Denver.

Chivington's reports of the event claimed he had achieved a great victory. The reports were filled with inaccuracies and fictions. He wrote that he had attacked "one of the most powerful villages of the Cheyenne nation" and killed five to six hundred people, implying they were mostly warriors and that he had effected "an annihilation of an entire tribe." The death total actually was somewhere between 60 and 160. Chivington also bragged that of course he had taken no prisoners. He made no mention of the savagery of his men nor of the children and women massacred.

The *Rocky Mountain News*, the first Colorado newspaper – founded five years before above a saloon by William Byers, who had himself ridden with Wynkamp and Chivington at Glorieta Pass and who initially had approved of the peace agreement at Camp Weld – now changed its tune. Byers hailed Chivington's accomplishment in his editorials, claiming that Wynkoop had been actually been "hoodwinked" from the beginning by the Indians to take part in peace negotiations. Byers contended that the rumors of the savagery of some of Chivington's troops were exaggerated. "Besides," he further wrote, "if committed, the Indians deserved them for the predations that the Indians had previously taken on whites." And so, when they returned to Denver, the Fighting Parson (who had once so nobly upheld the rights of slaves and preached a godly message) and his troops were greeted with celebration by the townspeople for his amazing and brutal "victory."

This, then, was the culmination of the Camp Weld peace agreement.

1865: Three Hearings To Find The Truth

In fact, eventually the truth did out, although there were those who never ceased to contend that Chivington had been justified. No less than three hearings about the Sand Creek Massacre, two military and one by the U.S. government, were held. Not all of the troops had taken part in the massacre. Some, including Major Soule, Wynkoop's companion, had refused Chivington's attack order; they told their stories of horror and labeled Chivington's contentions of how he had won a battle against hostile warriors as false.

The Joint Committee of the War issued its findings without mincing words. It said:

"As to Colonel Chivington, your committee can hardly find fitting terms to describe his conduct. Wearing the uniform of the United States. . . he deliberately planned and executed a foul and dastardly massacre which would have disgraced the veriest savage among those who were the victims of his cruelty. Having full knowledge of their friendly character, having himself been instrumental to some extent in placing them in their position of fancied security, he took advantage of their inapprehension and defenceless condition to gratify the worst passions that ever cursed the heart of man. . . .

"He surprised and murdered, in cold blood, the unsuspecting men, women, and children on Sand creek, who had every reason to believe they were under the protection of the United States authorities, and then returned to Denver and boasted of the brave deed he and the men under his command had performed."

If only words such as these could have stopped the unending cycle.

November 29, 1868: En Route to Fort Cobb, Oklahoma

It is four years later, four years to the day since the Sand Creek Massacre. Wynkoop has been vindicated by the government. Not only has he been found not to have violated orders by attempting to initiate peace with Black Kettle, he has been found worthy of appointment as "Agent for the Indians of the Upper Arkansas Agency" by the new president, President Andrew Johnson. He is now in the official position of acting to protect the Southern Cheyennes and Arapahoes, whom he has spent years helping. Chivington, relieved of his command, for the rest of his life does not live down the disgrace of the Sand Creek Massacre.

But since the Sand Creek Massacre, Black Kettle has lost much of his power as a peace chief. The young and angry Dog Soldiers no longer trust his judgment and they have gained more independence, although at times they return to Black Kettle's camp. They have gone on rampages of their own, killing whites. Wynkoop himself has felt betrayed by some of them, who have committed these depredations. In addition, the Southern Cheyenne and Arapahoe tribes have been confined to less and less land by the United States Government: first, in the Little Arkansas Treaty of 1865 where they agreed to stay on a reservation between the Arkansas and Cimmaron rivers in Kansas and Indian Territory (present day Oklahoma), and then in the Medicine Lodge Treaty of 1867 where their assigned territory was simply cut to less than half of what it had been. This slow diminishing, this undoing of peace treaties, this confining of Indians to smaller and smaller reservations often in places not native to a tribe, would characterize the United States's actions from here on out.

And Wynkoop, finally, is tired.

He understands that it is often difficult to separate peaceable Indians, those that General Sherman calls "well-disposed," such as Black Kettle, from the younger ones who favor war. He wants Black Kettle to receive protection by moving his people to Fort Cobb. However, he now learns that five columns of troops are converging on Washita River, where Black Kettle is camped. He fears the worse. En route to Fort Cobb, he reluctantly writes his resignation. He writes:

> *The troops have expressed their determination to kill under all circumstances the Indians of my agency. . . . The Cheyennes and Arapahos will readily respond to my call to come to Fort Cobb, but I most certainly refuse to again be the instrument of the murder of innocent women and children. All left me under the circumstances, with the present state of feelings I have in this matter, is now to respectfully tender my resignation.*

November 27, 1868: Washita River, Oklahoma

But it is too late. Far too late. Unbeknownst to Wynkoop, 180 miles away at the Washita River, what Wynkoop feared had already come to pass two days before.

George Armstrong Custer, known as "Ringlets" for his strawberry blonde hair which he fashioned into curls by wrapping it around candles when he slept at night and who always smelled of cinnamon, because each morning he liberally sprinkled that same curled hair with cinnamon oil – George Armstrong Custer, last in his class at West Point, yet a hero of the Civil War, where he had fought and led his troops bravely if at times recklessly, so courageously, in fact, that he was honored at the end of the self-same war at Appomattox by being awarded the desk on which the terms of surrender were signed by Generals Lee and Grant (terms drafted by non-other than the adjutant to General Grant, a Seneca Indian named Ely Parker) – George Armstrong Custer who wore around his throat a red cravat that inspired his troops of the 7th U.S. Cavalry to wear the same red cravats – traveled with his troops to the camp of Black Kettle and the Southern Cheyenne, next to the Washita River. On the morning of November 17, 1868, following the orders of General Sheridan, who specifically requested him, – "Custer I rely on you in everything" he wrote – Custer and his troops brutally attacked Black Kettle's encampment.

The regiment galloped through the tipis, firing indiscriminately and killing men and women alike. One cavalry unit pursued a group of women and children and shot and killed them without mercy. Any of the Indian men who lay wounded, no matter the extent of their injuries, were promptly shot to death. Some of the warriors retreated to trees that surrounded the encampment. Custer gathered together the captured women and children and used them as human shields so that his troops were not attacked. Meanwhile, seven hundred Indian ponies were shot and killed by the troops. And Black Kettle himself?

Black Kettle and his wife mounted one of the ponies. They attempted to flee. They were shot, shot in the back, and they both died that day.

This, then, was the ending to Black Kettle and Wynkoop's effort four years ago, at Camp Weld, Colorado to create a peace: the distant and tragic goodbye between two brave men. The Battle of Washita River became known as a massacre by many, but by others it was celebrated as the first U.S. victory in the Southern Plains War, initiated by Generals Sherman and Sheridan, destroying the fabric of the Southern Cheyenne society and forcing the Cheyenne onto an Indian Reservation.

Again and Again

The old woman sits beside the big earthen pot and stirs the berry soup. Outside the cave, it is nighttime; there are sudden cracklings of thunder that seem to split the world, and then flashes of lightning which expose the interior of the cave, casting the old woman's long shadow against the back wall. Then it is dark again, except for the light from the low fire under the pot. Shunk Sapa, the huge black dog, is now huddled on the ground against the old woman, shivering uncontrollably with each thunderous clap. She speaks softly to soothe him. The tumult outside makes it too hard for her to work on her blanket strip. She puts down the stick that she has been using to stir, and with both hands cradling her face, she stares out into the dark and listens to the rain.

4. March 14, 1970, BIA Littleton Office

The only reminder of Camp Weld on this day – over a hundred years after the failed peace treaty – is a small stone marker with a bronze plaque at 8th Avenue and Vallejo Street in Denver, erected in 1934. It simply says that Camp Weld was headquarters against the Indians, 1864-65. There is no mention of Wynkoop, although a street in Denver bears his name, no mention of the meeting with the Cheyenne and Arapaho over one hundred years ago that seemed to promise peace between Indians and whites, and of course no mention of the noble peace warrior Black Kettle. The streets of Denver are no longer dirt, dry and dust-blown when the wind turns up, and there are neither horses nor horse-drawn buggies. Cars whiz by instead. Everything is concrete. The wind blows silently across the road and the buildings. Today, in a kind of irony, a page from the Rocky Mountain News, still in print, has been forced by the wind against the monument, obscuring the words of the plaque.

Nine miles away, at 1100 West Littleton Boulevard, a nondescript three-story building which houses the Bureau of Indian Affairs liaison office, the sidewalks are crowded with Indians from all over. Native American protest now is different from one hundred years ago. Dressed in heavy jackets against the cold, they carry signs such as "Stop BIA Paternalism" or "BIA what are you?" Young and old, men and women, grandparents and infants are all here. Eventually, the Indians occupy the B.I.A. building itself.

What Were They Protesting?

Sometimes today the issues appear from the outside so much smaller than the simple and yet tragic loss of Native American land one hundred years ago. Land carries with it heft and concreteness. But time has passed – the land is gone – and now intangible and more complex issues have become, for Native Americans – beholden to this behemoth entity, the Bureau of Indian Affairs that measures their lives with bureaucratic paper, bureaucratic rules and regulations –- as important as the issue of land.

And here is an example. In 1934, John Collier preparatory to becoming Commissioner of Indian Affairs – the august title given to the director of the Bureau of Indian Affairs – helped fashion a legislative bill that dealt dramatically with Native American land by preventing the Dawes Act, that is by preventing the continued sale of portions of Indian land by individual Indians through allotments, a process which had by then decimated some reservations and created a crazy quilt of reservation land and white enclaves when individual Indians sold off newly allotted land to whites. The new Act that Collier fashioned was called "The Indian Reorganization Act," or the "Howard-Wheeler Act," or even "The Indian New Deal" (as part of President Franklin Delano Roosevelt's New Deal). It overturned the idea of "assimilation" of tribes that lay behind the allotments created by the Dawes Act. Instead, it made Native American land now solely within tribal control. In effect, it sought to preserve and save reservations rather than divide them up. And it permitted and urged tribes on their reservations to fashion their own governments. Also, necessarily, it strengthened the role of the Bureau of Indian Affairs in the lives of Indians, a mixed blessing, but the consequence of a defeated people living within a structure, fashioned by the majority society, which had echoes and shades of colonialism.

And within its provisions of this new Act were two curious sentences. They were:

> *"The Secretary of the Interior is directed to establish standards of health, age, character, experience, knowledge, and ability for Indians who may be appointed,* **without regard to civil-service law,** *to the various positions maintained, now and hereafter, by the Indian Office, in the administration of functions or services affecting any Indian tribe. Such qualified Indians shall hereafter have the* **preference** *to appointment to vacancies in any such positions."*

In other words, the Indian Office, as it was called then (later to be called the Bureau of Indian Affairs), was no longer to be controlled and run by white men and women – that is, by often prejudiced Southern white bureaucrats who had for years populated the Bureau in its many offices and made their way to the isolated and now largely hard scrabble reservations throughout the West and South of this country. This new Act was to encourage hiring of Native Americans themselves, creating a less bureaucratic application process and insuring through "preference" in hiring and promotion that Native Americans could govern their own lives.

For the Native Americans, whose every aspect of life was now controlled by the Bureau of Indian Affairs – from schooling to social services to welfare to employment – it was crucial that Indians control their own destinies as much as the system permitted, and this had not happened at the Littleton office.

Most particularly, it had not happened to Enola Freeman, a Native American who had been passed over for years in favor of white workers despite the fact that she had been evaluated as "best qualified" and "well-qualified," as had fellow Indian employees. The irony was that Freeman and the other Indians who worked with her at the B.I.A. office in Littleton had been urged to leave their reservations and settle in Denver as a consequence of the Indian Reorganization Act of 1956. They had done so. And then they had been left high and dry by the white management of the B.I.A. office in Littleton. This, then, is what the protest is about. It might not have the excitement of a land dispute, but to the Native Americans who depended on the B.I.A., not just in Littleton, Colorado but throughout these now United States, it meant a great deal.

The Arrests

Eventually, as I say, the Native Americans go from marching in the street before the Littleton offices to occupying the building itself. They all come in. They take over. The leaders sit at the desks meant for the bureaucrats. Everyone comes into the conference room: adults, elderly, young, and old. This goes on for a number of days.

In the evenings, most of the Indians go back to their homes, or to friends' homes, in Denver, but the younger Indians actually sleep at the Bureau. And so, one evening, as might be expected, the police come and arrest the young Indians who have remained as a result of a complaint brought by the bureaucrat in charge of this liaison office. Nine Indians. They are from different tribes, in different parts of the country. They are Patty Baker (Mandan-Blackfoot), Lynda Bernal (Taos Pueblo), James Jones (Cherokee), John Gill (Sioux), Rick Buckanaga (Sioux), Virginia Reeves (Navajo), Linda Benson (Sac and Fox), Madelyn Boyer (Shoshone-Bannock), and Duane Bird Bear (Mandan-Hidatsa), a collection representative of Native Americans in general. And of course – and predictably – what are they arrested for? Trespass.

On Trespass

Trespass: how ironic. Think of it. Native Americans being tried for trespass. Like the fallen dry leaves of autumn, the whites had covered the lands of their ancestors. Occupied them. Built towns. Established boundaries. Made treaties, then each time, after a while, simply broken the treaties they had made in order to get more land, to create homesteads, to build the railroad, to search for gold in the rich earth, to go forth in the manifest destiny of the European races. And slowly the Native Americans – those that survived and were not slaughtered or did not die from white man's diseases such as the running face sickness which the whites called smallpox (and in some instances in early examples of biological warfare was intentionally given to Native Americans with gifts of infected blankets and handkerchiefs from smallpox hospitals) or had not starved in the cold winters – were pushed away or herded to reservations, often far from their original homes. And so, today each of these putative young alleged trespassers at the United States Bureau of Indian Affairs – *their* bureau, that now regulated *their* lives on *their* reservations – each one had in his or her cultural core, in his or her blood, the not-so-ancient memory of these attempts to deprive them of their land.

One could trace the meaning of "trespass" for any of the nine young Native Americans from very different tribes who have been arrested at the Littleton building. Let us take two of them, but any two would do and have similar stories For example, here is Virginia Reeves, a sweet-faced Navajo woman, whose ancestors had been captured by the subsequently mythologized (even during his lifetime in children's books for white readers) Captain Christopher "Kit" Carson – Kit Carson who, in Canyon de Chelly in northern Arizona (with the help of some of the Navajos' enemy at the time, the Utes) in 1864, near the same time that Wynkoop was trying for peace in Denver, had employed a scorched earth policy, slaughtering the Navajos' sheep and goats and destroying their plots of corn, their bean and melon patches, burning their hogans, filling their water holes with rocks and dirt, starving them out, so eventually 9,000 of them – including Virginia Reeves' great grandparents – were forced to leave their land and begin the Long Walk to Bosque Rondo, 400 miles away in the cold winter, women and children dying along the way. Took them from their magical and strangely fertile home of sandstone shapes and great expanse, from the majestic Canyon de Chelly, the place of cultivated peach trees – which Carson also destroyed – and clear water and high sandstone cliffs – a land bounded by the Four Sacred Mountains – to a confined space where corn would not grow and where the brackish water from the Pecos river was so alkaline that it caused severe intestinal problems. And, of course, many more women and children died there, starved there, at what the Navajos would always call thereafter "the place of suffering."

Yes, to his credit, Carson years later regretted what he had done and, gravely ill, he nonetheless argued in Congress to return the Navajos back to their rightful ancestral land, which – unlike other Native Americans – they actually *did* get back, but they had not only been decimated in numbers, they had been traumatized – those able to survive – in the intervening years. The Navajo treaty returning them to their land was finally signed on June 1, 1868. Carson had died eight days before. The Navajo: who had been treated as trespassers in their own land by the true trespassers. Here was Virginia Reeves, Navajo great granddaughter years later, accused of trespass.

Or take another one of the nine, Duane Bird Bear, Mandan-Hidatsa, a slow-spoken and stolid man, one of the most articulate of the young alleged "trespassers" at the Bureau of Indian Affairs in Littleton and a leader of the group. Bird Bear had made his way from Mandaree, North Dakota, on the Fort Berthold reservation to Phillips Exeter academy and then to the ivy league northern college of Dartmouth. He knew first hand about trespass from an early age. In 1954, when he was six years old, he saw his home and the entire town of Independence, North Dakota – *Independence* that could not live up to its name – slowly disappear beneath the water created by the newly built Garrison Dam. One hundred fifty-six thousand acres of Hidatsa homeland drowned. Homes, rich farm land, burial grounds, sacred places, a hospital, schools, churches, community centers – all drowned. The towns of Van Hook and Old Sanish drowned. Some said when combined together they spelled "Vanish." And also the villages of Red Butte, Lucky Mound, Nishu, Beaver Creek, Shell Creek, and Charging Eagle – all flooded. The gooseberry woods that flourished in the Missouri River Valley, the gooseberry woods around the village of Elbowoods, Elbowoods itself – drowned forever.

Near the end, on a moonlit night, a group of former Indian basketball players, armed with flashlights, assembled a flotilla of rowboats, rowed across the new rising lake to the Elbowoods high school, and then literally rowed down the school's main corridor to the trophy case. There they removed the state championship trophies won by the Elbowoods Warriors before the trophies too would have sunk beneath the dark waters. And rowed back in the moonlit night, clutching the symbols of their youth and of a warrior tradition transformed and of their life. And many of the more elderly Indians, who had never known or played basketball, stood at the edge of the rising waters that night, having been persuaded against their wishes by others not to let themselves be embraced by the dark water; not to let themselves be drowned as their home drowned.

And from these dark waters, a reservoir was formed, called at first Garrison Lake and then renamed in 1965 – there is no end of irony in these stories, irony that one could cut with a knife if it were palpable, irony that brings salt tears to one's eyes – renamed in 1965 Lake Sakakawea. In their wisdom, North Dakota renamed the lake that destroyed the very homeland of the Hidatsa after a Native American, after Sakakawea, after "Bird Woman" – Sakakawea who was the Soshone Indian woman who helped Lewis and Clark explore the lands of the Louisiana Purchase. She was actually a child-woman, kidnapped by the Hidatsa when she was 11, with whom she lived until she was sold to a Frenchman at the age of 13 who took her as his wife, both of them then accompanying Lewis and Clark on their journey westward. As if an Indian name, her Indian name, could redeem the loss of the land below the waters, could, in some magical way, undo the injustice of the drowning of the sacred earth of the Hidatsa.

And injustice it was: the fact was that originally the Hidatsa in the Fort Laramie Treaty of 1851 were guaranteed 12.6 million acres – *12.6 million!* – covering most of their original territory. Then, in 1870, the Fort Berthold reservation was established and suddenly the boundaries were much smaller – 7.8 million acres. And then in 1889, the Northern Pacific Railroad was given all of the southern part of the reservation to sell to incoming white settlers. Without even an act of Congress, the Hidatsa now were confined to only 1.2 million acres. In 1891, the Dawes Allotment Act simply abolished parts of the reservation further, opening them up to white settlers and 160 acre allotments, and this was followed by the Curtis Act of 1898, which applied the Dawes Allotment Act to the Hidatsa, explicitly overriding the force of the original Fort Laramie Treaty. The shrinking of property by paper missive, by words penned on foolscap, by signatures that might as well have been written on the waters of Lake Sakakawea itself, for all the meaning and endurance they had.

Of course, the final blow – the Garrison Dam – could have been avoided. There was an alternate plan. But the alternate plan would have affected the white town of Williston, and the Army Corps of Engineers in charge of the construction surreptitiously and on its own, without referring the matter back to Congress, decided to spare white Williston and destroy almost all of the Hidatsa reservation and its villages instead. In a photograph of the 1948 signing of that Garrison Dam agreement, George Gillette, chairman of the tribe, stands in his pinstripe suit and tie surrounded by white men in their suits and ties as J.A. Krug, Secretary of the Interior, sits at a large wooden desk in front of them signing the contract for the dam's construction. Gillette stands and weeps, his head slumped, his face covered by one of his large hands. The white men look on impassively.

And yet, if trespass held a poignant meaning for Duane Bird Bear, for Virginian Reeves, in fact for all of these young "trespassers," it was another irony to begin with that they were now all together at this nondescript government building in Denver in mutual and defiant purpose – Sioux and Hidatsa, Navajo and Taos, Shoshone and Blackfoot. For, if one looked into their ancestral past, one could find a history full of permutations and rearrangements as various tribes in this vast land that eventually was called the United States periodically fought each other, made peace, fought again: killed, scalped, took child hostages from each other whom they raised to be their own (as the Hidatsa captured and raised the Shoshone Sakakawae), sought revenge, attacked and were attacked, and, at the same time, had their peace chiefs and peaceful villages where the knowledge of the natural world permeated their very beings from the time they first opened their eyes on the sky and the plains, the mountains, the semi-desert and the animals of the wilderness. Perhaps it would have gone on forever like that, if it were not for the whites, who pushed and ultimately punished them all, whether they befriended the whites or opposed them. So that now, the Native Americans were drawn together, separate nations but all under the control of one gigantic entity: the Bureau of Indian Affairs, a behemoth of a bureaucracy, a sinecure largely of Southern whites, who by way of a quasi-colonialism, ruled a great deal of the Native American lives, although each tribe that survived and had a reservation had some control of the usually diminished land now allotted it; and administered services for its people and legally retained its unique and idiosyncratic status as an independent "nation."

So that now, too, there were Indian pow-wows in Denver or in Albuquerque or Bismark – "All-Indian," "Inter-Tribal" – which featured tribal dancing, the various tribes now amicably attending, each tribe bringing its traditional dance. Dancing – which had initially been banned by the Bureau of Indian Affairs in a misguided attempt to suppress traditional culture and then the ban lifted by the Commissioner of Indian Affairs, John Collier, in the 1930's, so now one could hear the hard drumming of feet on the ground, the sound of the drums themselves, the clicking of the gourd rattles and see elaborate costumes of feathers and animal skin, at the Indian Pow-Wows. And so it was that today at this unremarkable Bureau of Indian Affairs office in Littleton, Colorado, participants in the "sit-in" from so many different tribal societies, joined together in protest and celebrated, yes, celebrated as if they were at a pow-wow dance.

More About Trespass

Funny about trespass. What possible defense could these nine Native Americans have to the charge of trespass at the Bureau of Indian Affair office? They could hardly cite the long history of white trespass. Poignant, compelling as it was, it was not legally relevant at all. This trespass at the Bureau of Indian Affairs office would seem to be an open-and-shut case. Convict the Native Americans. Lock them up. A "sit-in," as it was characterized by the Rocky Mountain News, the very paper that wrapped itself around the plague commemorating Camp Weld, is, after all, a "sit-in." These Indians were occupying a building where they were not permitted to be. They had clearly been out of control and had violated the law. Trespass, pure and simple.

But, legally, trespass requires "intent." Say that you go to a friend's house, you enter, and when the friend returns he says, "Good to see you. Stay. You have my permission." And he sits down with you and eats. "Stay as long as you want," he says. "You are my guest." He leaves, and then, to your surprise, the police arrive and arrest you. For trespass. But you say, "Officer, my friend told me I have his permission to be here. Why are you arresting me?"

And *that* is your defense. And so it was for the nine young Native Americans. But the thing was, could they prove it? And how?

How Curious Are the Ways of Men

On its face, it would seem that these Indian protesters must be guilty – how could they not be? After all, they simply took over the B.I.A. building.

And yet, the reality was strange. For whites or for that matter blacks, the occupation of buildings in these times – as in the demonstrations of the Free Speech Movement at the University of California at Berkeley in December 1964 where over 800 students were arrested for occupying Sproul Hall, an administration building, in protest against the banning of the Congress of Racial Equality (CORE) from soliciting on campus or at Columbia University four years later in April 1968, where 700 students protesting Columbia's involvement in weapons research for the Vietnam War were arrested – these occupations or sit-ins invariably involved college-age students. Thus, one might expect that the Native American sit-in at the B.I.A. was similar. But it was not. It was a Native American gathering which, by its nature, was vastly different.

True, those arrested were all young adults, as in those other student sit-ins, but this was because these young adults had remained in the Littleton building in the evening when the vast number of Native Americans who had participated in the sit-in had returned home. And the vast number of Native Americans who occupied the building during the day was in character so very different than a white student sit-in. And this was very important to demonstrate to an all-white jury.

For, if the white members of this midwestern jury equated the sit-in with the student sit-ins at Berkeley or Columbia – which had received intense media attention not so long ago, and which were likely viewed with alarm and distaste in mid-America – it would be very difficult to get the Indians on trial in Littleton acquitted. They would be thought of as "wild Indians," the kind who take over government buildings. In fact, this was the government prosecution tactic: "Yes," they said, "we will depict these nine Native Americans arrested as dangerous and out of control and, thereby, scare the jury into finding them guilty."

And so it was essential for the defense of these Native Americans to show this white jury how different this sit-in was: to show that all generations of Indians participated – young adults, parents, grandparents and elders – and children and babies, too, as is common to Native American gatherings, to show that a spiritual elder had inaugurated the sit-in by holding a religious ceremony for everyone; and that members of the Indian community – members of all the different tribes – had brought vast amounts of Indian food to the Littleton office for the participants to eat.

But that in and of itself would not be enough.

For the most important thing to show was an interesting event that had happened. The protesters who occupied the building invited the Commissioner of Indian Affairs himself, Louis Bruce, to meet with them at the very building they occupied. In fact, the food they brought to the building was a celebration of the Commissioner of Indian Affairs meeting with them.

Louis Bruce was the third Commissioner of Indian Affairs to actually be a Native American; the first was that very same Ely Parker, the Seneca Indian who helped draft for Generals Grant and Sherman the terms of surrender of the South to end the Civil War. Parker had subsequently been appointed as Commissioner of Indian Affairs when Grant became President. Louis Bruce, this third Indian Commissioner, was a full-blooded Indian, too, the son of a Mohawk chief (who had actually played for the Philadelphia Eagles baseball team in 1904) and an Oglala mother. And now invited to meet with the Native American demonstrators, this Commissioner Louis Bruce actually accepted!

And so Commissioner Bruce came to the B.I.A. office in Littleton. When he entered the conference room there, he found the room completely filled with Indians from all different tribes. They were prepared, and after greeting him and asking him to speak, they presented him with a document to sign. It asked for the removal of three white management supervisors at the Littleton B.I.A. And Bruce, after changing the wording to "temporary suspension" and ignoring a box where he could have checked indicating that he did not have authority to make this decision, signed the document. All those present were delighted.

In court now, what did the prosecuting attorneys, what did the government say to this? "Yes," they said, "all this is true." The Commissioner of Indian Affairs himself *had* entered the building in Littleton occupied by the Indians and signed that document. But make no mistake, he signed that document under extreme duress. He was frightened of the Indians gathered there. He was afraid. And as a result, any document he signed had no validity. And for that matter, anything he said, any indication he conceivably might have made to the protesting Indians there such that they might *remain* in the B.I.A. building – that he invited them to stay – had no significance either. For Commissioner Bruce was simply afraid of the mass of Indians, that wild protesting horde. Surely an all-white jury would understand that.

5. Arapahoe County Court, June 23, 1970

And now for a moment, put yourself in the jury box at the Arapahoe County Court on June 23, 1970. Already you have heard from Phyllis Culbertson, an Assinboin Indian from Montana, a defense witness, matronly in appearance who speaks directly and without flourish. She says she was at the meeting in the Littleton B.I.A. building when Commissioner Bruce entered, and that he had addressed the gathering saying that he knew there was discrimination in the Bureau, that "he was glad to be there and to meet with us." After he finished his greeting to them, Culbertson herself presented to Bruce a typed statement asking for the removal of three white supervisors at the B.I.A. office and requested him to sign it.

After she has completed this part of her testimony, the defense attorney, Mr. Barbarica, asks Culbertson to explain to the jury what the Commissioner of Indian Affairs means to the Indian people. "What is that position?" he asks.

Says Culbertson, "The Commissioner of Indian Affairs to the Indian people is like the President of the United States to people who aren't Indian. All of these years, people from the tribes and the reservations go to Washington, and this is the man they look for to talk to. The Indians hold him in high esteem, and his word is final with them."

And when Barbarica asks further, "What does it means to Indians that Mr. Bruce is himself an Indian," Culbertson responds,

"Indian people would like to be involved in policy-making decisions that affect their lives, and they feel that it is important that the Commissioner of Indian Affairs be an Indian."

And so, now, you in the jury have heard the most legal part of the defense's argument, providing, in addition, information about what respect Native Americans had for the Commissioner of Indian Affairs, particularly Bruce.

But the defense continues to attempt to allay any fears you might have about this Indian horde by adding more and more information about the character of the sit-in at the Littleton office, as if the defense is trying to put you there, in the midst of the sit-in. For the next witness is an older Indian man with weathered features, thin, softly spoken, and tending to such one-word answers that he does not make a good witness. His name is, appropriately, John Holy Elk Face: he is the religious elder of the Indian community, from Standing Rock, North Dakota. Twenty-five years ago, you would have seen him as a younger man in his private first class uniform, studious in appearance and entering battle in World War II (where his brother Thomas was killed in the Pacific theater, toward the very end of the war). Today he wears an ill-fitting grey suit.

But he provides a certain gravity to the proceedings, explaining briefly that he held a religious ceremony for all the Native Americans who attended the sit-in in which he himself also took part. And when Barbarica, eliciting from him that he is a full-blooded American Indian who speaks his native language, asks him how many children he has, he responds "I've got ten. Eleven, but one is in the service."

To which Barbarica, to laughter from the audience, says, "I believe that means that you still have him." But this is important for you and the jury: a Native American giving his son to the United States army. It means something, even if the irony of it – giving himself to the forces that hounded his own people – may escape us. Gingerly, at the end of the examination, Holy Elk Face steps down from his chair, looking around with a certain sense of awe at the entire proceedings.

The key witness has now to appear, although no one, including the defense, is yet aware how effective she will be. Her name is Nelly Baker, the mother of one of the young people arrested, Patricia Baker.

Nelly Baker is a sharp-faced woman seeming in her forties and dressed in an unassuming way. She settles into the witness chair, and after being sworn in, she begins to answer Mr. Barbarica's questions. Picture her there.

From the beginning, Mr. Allcott, the prosecuting attorney, appears impatient with her and determined to oppose her testimony. When Mr. Barbarica asks how many children she has, and she answers four, and then is asked whether any of them are in court, Mr. Allcott foolishly steps in and says, "I can't see whether her children are in court matters," to which Barbarica says, "I think you will find it relevant, your honor." Barbarica then has Nelly Baker indicate that she is the mother of Patricia Baker, one of the defendants, who is indeed in court and who stands up so that you the jury can see her.

And then Nelly Baker's testimony proceeds, but in ways that might be unexpected in a courtroom. Barbarica asks, "Can you please tell us what you were doing on March 21st in the morning?"

A. That morning I was preparing food for the feast that we were going to have for Commissioner Bruce. I was one of the ladies that was asked to bring food.

Q. Can you tell us what kind of food you were preparing?

A. Well we had cornbean soup, cornbeans and dried meat with a little kidney fat. That is a favorite soup of ours, and berry soup, fried bread I brought.

Q. Just so the jury may know, what is fried bread?

A. Fried bread is Indian bread that we usually have at our feasts. It is fried. You can make it with bacon powder or you can make it with grease.

Q. And what is berry soup?

A. Berry soup is wild berries that we pick, and we dry and we usually put a little batter with it to make a soup, sort of a sauce.

Q. Now I forgot to ask you this but I think it is obvious. Are you an American Indian.

A. Yes I am.

Q. Can you tell me what tribe you are from?

A. I am five-eighths Blackfeet Indian from the Blackfeet Indian reservation in Browning, Montana.

Q. And do you speak your native language.

A. Yes I do.

Q. Can you please tell us what you did with this food after you finished preparing it? Excuse me, let me change that. How long does it take to prepare one of these?

Mr. Allott: (who now has had it, intervenes again) If it please the Court, may we approach the bench?

The prosecuting and defense attorneys together approached the bench. The courtroom is quiet except for the whispering of spectators. In a low voice, which you the jury cannot quite make out, the prosecuting attorney says to the judge that continuing this line of questioning by the defense is absurd. "Your honor," he concludes, "I simply cannot see that the time it takes to make berry soup has any relevance whatever to this case; it has no meaning. How long will the defendants be permitted to go on like this?"

The judge looked down quizzically at the defense attorneys, over his thick glasses. "So?" he says, "How do you respond?"

"Your honor," says Harris Sherman, the lead defense attorney, "trespass requires criminal intent, and we are trying to show that the defendants had none. The defendants believed they had permission; they prepared food for the Commissioner of Indian Affairs and he agreed to break bread with them and he willingly ate with them. The intent of these defendants was not criminal; it was welcoming and celebratory. One of the ways of showing intent – which, after all, is a state of mind – is to introduce the actions of those who are accused of trespass, to introduce the defendants' actions to the jury, and one of those actions was food preparation with the intent to serve to the Commissioner, to serve him traditional Indian food that required time and effort to make. Mr. Barbarica believes, *we* believe, the preparation of berry soup goes to intent."

The judge waited for a moment. "I'll allow it," he finally said, "but Mr. Barbarica, *please* do not draw this out any longer."

Barbarica does not let on that he may have made a classic blunder. He does not know the answer to his question! Any good attorney knows one should know the answer to your question when your own witness is testifying. On a wing and a prayer, he continues:

Q. Would you please tell us how long it took to prepare these dishes?

A. It takes about four hours, maybe longer. Five hours, we'll say.

The courtroom buzzes at this response.

Q. Can you please tell us what you did with the food after you finished preparing it?

A. Well, we brought it down to the Littleton offices at 1100 West Littleton Boulevard.

Q. Was Mr. Bruce there?

A. Yes. He was there.

Q. What did you do with the food?

A. We brought it in. We put it on a table that was arranged for the food.

Q. Was there other food there as well?

A. Yes.

Q. Was that food specially prepared for this occasion?

A. That is true.

Q. Now, after Mr. Bruce signed the documents, what happened?

A. Well everybody rejoiced. They were very happy he signed.

Q. And did Mr. Bruce begin to leave, or what did he do next?

A. Well, he spoke to different ones as he was going down the aisle.

Q. Did you speak to him?

A. Yes, I did as he passed me. I said, "Commissioner Bruce." He heard me, and then he came back. I shook hands with him and I introduced myself, and I told him, I said, "Mr. Bruce, are you going to have these kids put in jail?" And he said "No. Why should I? They haven't done anything wrong, have they?" And I said, "No, only what they thought was right."

Nelly Baker's voice cracks somewhat as she says this.

Q. . If you would like to wait and take your time, that is all right.

She shakes her head. Mr. Barbarica continues.

Q .Now, after Mr. Bruce said these words that no one would be arrested and they hadn't done anything, what did you do?

A. Then I asked him if he would like to have something to eat with us. He said, "Yes," and he went on over to the table and the ladies served him.

He sat behind me. I looked to see if he had coffee. He didn't have any coffee, so I asked him if he would like to have a coffee, and he said, "Yes," and I said, "What would you like to have in it," and he said, "A little sugar."

Q. Now I would like to show you Defendant's Exhibit Number 5 (a photograph). Will you describe what you see there?

A. Yes. He was eating Indian food, and enjoying it.

Q. Will you please tell the jury what it means to eat Indian food. Why you took so long in preparing it, and what it means to offer food in the Indian culture?

A. That is the best friendship that we could offer anyone – our food.

Q. Is that why you took such a long time in preparing it.

A. Yes, sir.

Q. Now would you describe the people in the meeting? Were they old, were they young?

A. They were all ages, all ages.

Q. Were there babies there?

A. Yes.

Q. Were there elderly people there?

A. Yes.

Q. Now I would like to specifically direct your attention toward the elderly people. In Indian culture, at least in our language, elderly people are called elders. I don't know how you express it in you language, but could you tell the jury what the meaning of elders is and why it was so important that they be present at this meeting?

A. If you are Indian, from the time you grow up you will always respect your elders. That is one thing that you will learn from the cradle up.

Q. Was John Holy Elk face, who testified yesterday, in Indian terms, an "elder?"

A. Yes, sir.

Q. Would he be called something of a spiritual leader?

A. That is true.

Q. Could you also describe why children were at this meeting, too?

A. Well, wherever we go, we Indians, we take all our families with us.

Q. In other words, this was a typical Indian meeting?

A. That is true.

Q. In reference to this meeting, was any Indian ceremony held?

A. Yes, earlier that morning there was, earlier that morning, but I was not there.

Q. Will you please explain.

Mr. Allott: May it please the Court, your Honor, unless she has personal knowledge of this. . . .

The Court: Sustained, sustained.

Q. After Mr. Bruce had eaten, what did you do?

A. Well, I and the other ladies cleaned up the hall.

Q. And did you tell them what Mr. Bruce had said concerning the fact that there would be no arrests? Did you tell that to anybody?

A. My daughter came in later and I told her. I said, "Don't be afraid because he told me that he wouldn't have you kids arrested. I am going home now, I'm tired."

Q. And did you go home at that time?

A. Yes, my husband and I went home.

Q. What happened at approximately 4:15 later that day?

A. Well, after I got home, I went and laid down. The phone rang. My husband said I have to get down there, they are giving them five to fifteen minutes to get out of that building, and then they are taking them. I said I didn't think I could make it. I laid there on the bed and my heart was so heavy because he *lied* to us.

Knowing he has hit a crucial point, Barbarica waits for a while, so her last words stand alone, and then he says, "No more questions, your Honor."

Nobody could say what moved the all-white jury. What would have moved you? Was it the description of the gathering there, with women and children and babies and the elders, all together? Was it the documentation that Bruce signed in front of all the Indians? Was it the compelling testimony that Nelly Baker gave when she talked of getting coffee for the Commissioner and then so heartbreakingly said, "He lied to us"? Or was it the long drawn out moment, the challenge by the prosecuting attorney following the question about berry soup, and Nelly Baker's final answer about the soup and how that opened up for the defense the continuing questions about the nature of the sit-in. Or, perhaps, it was even the power of berry soup itself?

Regardless, the jury found all nine defendants not guilty. For Native Americans, this was a signal victory, not only because they had won, but because of the way they had won: by showing who they were, by showing their customs and their culture. Against the terrible force of passionless bureaucracy, with its faceless power; against the dehumanizing construct inherent in Western law that reduces each man to the "reasonable man," which tends to read "reasonable *white* man," by which a man's actions are to be judged – "reasonable man" a construct devoid of anything but words, that is devoid of the scents and the intricacies of food and soup and the common tribal decency of breaking bread, devoid of history, "reasonable man" that all too often, if you let it, extracts the very soul out of human interaction while aspiring to justice. Against these forces, they had won.

And perhaps in winning they had followed the same path taken so many years ago by two men who tried so hard to know each other and each other's culture: Black Kettle and Wynkoop.

6. Cannon Ball, North Dakota, October 27, 2016

Forty-six years later. Two hundred fifty miles down the Missouri River from Lake Sakakawae – the lake that drowned the home of Duane Bird Bear and inundated the rich land of the Hidatsa – there lies another lake. It is named "Lake Oahe," after the old Arikara Indian village Ti Tane Ohe that lies beneath its still waters. Another irony in the making of a name, for this lake drowned 55,993 acres of land of the Standing Rock Sioux Reservation. Perhaps it would have been more accurate to name the lake "Eminent Domain." The dam that created the lake, authorized in 1946, and called, of course, Oahe Dam took many years to build. And then, fourteen years later in 1960, the dam was finally completed, and, with little warning, the government told the Sioux they had to abandon their homes. It was the bitterest of North Dakota winters: Indian families with children and with no place to go were forced to leave their homes forever, as the chill waters slowly rose. Two years later, and sixteen years after its initial authorization, the newly-formed lake was dedicated by an ebullient President of the United States, John F. Kennedy.

To make the lake, the 55,993 acres of reservation had been seized by the Federal Bureau of Reclamation, despite the Treaty of 1858, with the compensation awarded a fraction of what the tribe requested. The Standing Rock reservation's richest soil for cattle grazing, the dense timber stands on rich bottomlands which the Indians harvested, the wild fruit and berries that they gathered and dried, the wild birds and animals that they trapped: all were gone. The Sioux were left with their remaining land, whose soil had a higher clay content and had no timber stands and fewer wild animals. Like the Hidatsa of Fort Berthold, the Standing Rock Sioux's way of life: destroyed.

Today, the 2016 South Dakota tourism website advertises the wonderful fishing that takes place on Lake Oahe, where walleye are plentiful, as well as smallmouth bass, white bass, northern pike and perch, and expounds with apparent pride that Oahe is the Sioux Indian word meaning "a foundation," or "a place to stand on." A place to stand on, indeed. The darkness of those words apparently escaped the advertising person who wrote them. Of course, there is no mention at all of the land of the Sioux that lies beneath the lake. Perhaps one *could* stand solidly on this drowned land, on this foundation, feet deep in the mud, surrounded by silt, and minnows tickling one's toes and fish swimming around one's legs, if one carried a large weight to make oneself sink deep beneath the watery surface. Although the Standing Rock Sioux now fish this lake for subsistence, they would have preferred to have their bottomland back.

And today near the lake, in Cannon Ball, North Dakota – named after the Cannon Ball river that flows into the lake, where natural and perfectly spherical grey sandstone concretions of different sizes are scattered in the riverbed, like cannonballs from a long ago battle (perhaps you could use one of these to weigh yourself down so you could stand on the silt-covered land underneath the water without floating) – one can see hundreds of white tents and makeshift wooden structures and pickup trucks and campers and cars spread in the meadow. There are Native Americans camped here from over 100 tribes (it is like a pow-wow to end all pow-wows) and Vietnam veterans, and people from all over the country, perhaps 2,000 people in all. It is cold, the field is muddy, everyone is milling about bundled and gloved. At various points, smoke and steam rises on the vast field, from fires and pots of cooking food. There is a low hum of people talking or shouting, and at times the sound of singing or a guitar playing. The scene is surreal.

They are all camped there in protest against the route of the Dakota Access oil pipeline. The pipeline is being built to carry 470,000 barrels of crude oil *daily* from the Bakken oilfields in North Dakota down to a terminal in Illinois. The pipeline was diverted from a path that would have taken it near Bismark, North Dakota to go instead within 500 meters of the Standing Rock Sioux reservation and near Lake Oahu. The Standing Rock Sioux questioned why the Army Corps of Engineers refused to make a compete review of the direction of the pipeline, for if there was a leak, it would threaten the water source of the Standing Rock reservation leading out of Lake Oahu, and, in addition, cultural sites on the reservation were being threatened, including burial grounds, by the construction. In one sacred area, those large stones were in a formation representing the big dipper, and the stones (referred to as Inyanwakagapi) served as oracles for the Lakota. Of course, the Army Corps of Engineers in their survey of sacred sites completely missed this important one.

What began as a small protest has expanded dramatically because the issue was so characteristic of what Native Americans have encountered in these United States. From all over the country, Native

Americans – in fact people in general – have come to protest the construction. Among them is Johanna Holy Elk Face, originally from Standing Rock Reservation, as was her father. She is the sixty-three-year-old daughter of John Holy Elk Face, the elder who testified at the Littleton trial in 1970, forty-six years ago, the spiritual leader at the Bureau of Indian Affairs sit-in at Littleton. John Holy Elk Face died in 1987. Johanna is one of the eleven children, now grown, that John Holy Elk face testified about in Littleton.

And now, in fact, Johanna herself is considered by the Native Americans to be one of the spiritual elders, like her father years ago, one of the "water protectors." Today, she is sitting on a log near a ditch with two other Native American women, also spiritual elders. The three of them have tried to calm some of the younger Native Americans who, by their words – their words only – were provoking the Morton County police. In fact, some of the younger Indians have little use for spiritual elders in general, thinking of them as misguided, not unlike the way the Dog Soldiers thought of Black Kettle so many years ago.

Johanna and her two friends are simply sitting there, on their log, tired. And all of a sudden, *they* are the ones who are confronted by the Morton County police who surround them, as if they are dangerous, with four black SUVs. The police proceed to handcuff these three elderly women with plastic ties and then take them to the County jail in Mandan, North Dakota. The three women are charged of course with trespass. They are kept overnight with other protesters in what look like large dog cages.

And the inside of their arms are marked by the police with blue indelible ink, with numbers, a supposedly efficient way to make sure that they can ultimately be reunited with their confiscated belongings. When they are released the next day their arms look chillingly like those of concentration camp survivors.

And how does berry soup figure here? Where is it?

When they are released, the three women make their way back to the giant campsite that spreads over a meadow. They are hungry.

They find "Winona's Kitchen" run by Winona Kasto, from the Cheyenne River Sioux Reservation, which was also affected by the Oahe Dam. Winona is a large woman slowly but perpetually in motion.

Winona has been here for so many days that she cannot keep track. She is used to the cold that sometimes seeps through the multiple bundled jackets and sweaters she wears. Since she arrived here, she has been cooking constantly, much of the time outdoors over a wood fire. She makes soup or stew every day in a 50 gallon pot over the fire, serving more than 400 people a day. She left her job to do this cooking. Someone donated an RV to help her. From her vehicle there are thin strips of venison that she has carefully sliced that are hanging from horizontal strings to make venison jerky or what the Sioux call "papa." In addition, along the side of the vehicle hang great bunches of yellow corn cobs drying in the sun. And, of course, Winona has made a giant pot of *wojabi*, gathered today from strawberries from the supermarket in Mandan but originally made from the chokecherries and wild berries that she had picked from her reservation.

And so Johanna Holy Elk and her two women friends greet Winona with much emotion, and joke about the food in the jail. They sit on aluminum chairs and they feast, glad to be back and hoping that their protest will succeed. And they end their meal, appropriately, with white plastic spoons made red by the berry soup: they eat the *wojabi* in a kind of celebration.

Almost two months later, there is a seeming answer to their prayers, as the outgoing President orders that construction cease on the pipeline until a fuller and more complete review by the Army Corps of Engineers takes place. The giant camp grounds erupt in cheers and whoops, even though this victory may be tenuous as the new President may rescind it. Nonetheless everyone in the giant meadow treats it as a victory.

7. January 20, 2017, Inauguration Day, Washington, DC.

But it was not to be for Johanna and Winona and for all those others – from far and wide – who protested in the cold winter at Cannon Ball. For today, another white man with a great swatch of blonde hair (which he, too, preens as Custer did before him), sporting a red tie that rests on his wide frame like a singular exclamation point, is sworn in as President of the United States in Washington D.C. He stands there, solidly, in the cold air, waiting, his yellow hair ruffled by the wind.

Before this new President is sworn in, a preacher addresses the assembled crowd, intoning the sentiments of the Gospel of Saint Matthew. In a mellifluous voice, he says:

> "*God blesses those who are poor and realize their need for him. God blesses those who are humble for they will inherit the earth. God blesses those who hunger and search for Justice for they will be satisfied. God blesses those who are persecuted for doing right . . .*

His voice is carried by the loudspeakers over the assembled crowd and by television to the people of the United States.

It is a stirring message, but it is a message ignored. Four days later, this new President with the yellow hair, sitting at his desk, signs an order that rescinds the order of the previous President and permits the completion of the Dakota Access pipeline under Lake Oahe, guaranteeing that the oil will flow and that sacred sites be ignored, and, not incidentally, announcing to his followers his intentions toward others different than him. The new President then displays the order to the white men standing around him, who are smiling and nodding with approval as television cameras record the scene. There are no Native Americans around him, no proud chief who silently breaks down in tears. Other than that, the scene is the same.

A month later, the last of the protestors, including Johanna Elk Face, abandon the All Nations camp after threats of arrest for. . .

trespass. The meadow is left with scraps of paper, abandoned tarps, a muddied backpack, a child's doll whose motionless eyes stare at the sky, and a torn flyer saying "we will not be moved."

Over and Over

This, then, has been a story about history: how it circles, how it spirals, how it brings with it the anguish of Black Kettle, the destroyed hope of Wynkoop, the fragile wishes of those who sought – and still seek – justice and fairness in the land that we now call America.

The old woman gets up painfully from the ground. She moves to the fire that has gone down, adds wood to it, and then – again – slowly stirs the wojabi in the big earthen pot. It bubbles and a berry sweet smell fills the air. The old woman does not notice that the Shunk Sapa once again has pulled the porcupine quills from the blanket strip she has been preparing for the buffalo robe. When she sits back down, she pushes her white hair away from her eyes with one gnarled hand and looks at the blanket strip for a long, long time. Her eyes are grey. There are tears in them, perhaps from the smoke of the fire, perhaps not. Then, sighing, she sets to work once again.

Notes

1. The wonderful White River Sioux myth imparted by Jenny Leaning Cloud was recorded by Richard Erdoes and appears in Erdoes, R. & Ortiz, A, (1984) *American Indian myths and legends*, New York: Pantheon Books, pp. 485-486. Only the initial myth appears there; the other renderings of it in this story are mine.

2. The legal aspects of this case, the issue of Indian "preference," that lay behind the sit-in dragged on and on for many years, although the Indians in the end won. The amount of legal fire-power that the Department of Interior, the Bureau of Indian Affairs and non-Indian employees of the B.I.A. brought against the Indians was a sight to behold. First, Enola Freeman and three other employees, despite the Littleton sit-in, had to sue the Department of the Interior to enforce Indian preference for them. The Department of Interior tried to contend in court that the "preference" only applied to "initial appointments" (contorting the import of the statute which stated "appointment to vacancies" of any kind). Then, seeing they would lose this argument, the government tried to refine it to say that preference did not apply to "transfers and reassignments." The Department promptly lost this argument in Federal District Court, and then – despite the loss – appealed to the United States Court of Appeals, which almost four years *after* the sit-in ruled in a class action suit for Enola Freeman and her colleagues. (Freeman v. Morton, 499F.2nd 494 (1974))

But the legal attack on Indian preference was not over. This time the non-Indian employees of the Bureau of Indian Affairs, in Albuquerque, challenged the constitutionality of the "preference" in hiring required by the Indian Reorganization Act itself. They contended that such preference violated the newly passed Equal Employment Opportunity Act of 1974 as well as the due process clause of the Fifth Amendment. The Supreme Court four months after the ruling in Freeman v. Morton found unanimously in a decision by Justice Blackmun that the Indian "preference" statute was constitutional. Blackmun wrote: "*The preference, as applied, is granted to Indians not as a discrete racial group, but, rather, as ·members of quasi-sovereign tribal entities whose lives and activities are governed by the B.I.A in a unique fashion* " Morton v. Mancari, 417 U.S. 535,(1974).

Indeed, it was that uniqueness of the B.I.A. in the lives of Native Americans which the attorneys of the Littleton 9 tried to explain to the all white jury and apparently succeeded in doing. And, fittingly, the attorney who argued the Morton v. Mancari case before the United States Supreme Court was Harris Sherman, who in conjunction with attorney Barbarica, represented the Littleton 9 in their trial. For a full explication of this case and surrounding circumstances, including the guidance and involvement of the dynamic Native American leader Tillie Walker, see the excellent chapter by Carole Goldberg (2008) "What's race got to do with it? The story of Morton v. Mancari." In, R.F. Moran & Devon W. Carbado (Eds). *Race law stories* (Thomas Reuters/Foundation Press, New York (Pp. 237-273).

References

This tale derives from personal experience and from a variety of references in which the reader might be interested. The history of Native Americans is heart-wrenching and any one of these references is a story in itself. I have taken some artistic liberties here, although the basic outline of history, past and more recent, is accurate. For those interested, essential reading is Kraft's book on Ned Wynkoop, not only a well researched and well written document but an extraordinarily moving depiction of a time and place in American history too often neglected. In addition, the transcript from the trial of the Littleton 9 has been introduced into the story with neither change of the participants names nor much change of the words they spoke. However, the name of the attorney Barbarica who conducted the examination is an alteration; in fact, it was me.

The references used included:

Bird Bear, Duane, T. Knife Clan, Mandan-Hidatsa, Retrieved from Virtual Museum: http://www.nahmus.org.duanebirdbear.html

Daily, J. (1998) *Sacred beauty, Quillwork of Plains women*. Bismark: State Historical Society of North Dakota

Gilman, C. and Schneider, M. L. (1987) *The way to Independence: memories of a Hidatsa Indian family, 1840-1920*. St. Paul: Minnesota Historical Society.

Goldberg, C. (2008) What's race got to do with it? The story of Morton v. Mancari. In R.F. Moran & Devon W. Carbado (Eds.), *Race Law stories,*(pp. 237-273). New York: Thomas Reuters/Foundation Press.

Hidatsa, Mandan, Arikara earth lodges. Retrieved from www.kstrom.net /isk/maps/houses/hidatsa.html

Kraft, L. (2011) *Ned Wynkoop and the lonely road from Sand Creek.* Norman: University of Oklahoma Press.

Morton v. Mancari, 417 U.S. 535, 94 S.Ct. 2474, 41 L.Ed.2d 290 (1974) (Unanimous decision written by Justice Blackmun)

Running Wolf, M. (2016) At Standing Rock no one goes hungry. Retrieved from www.yesmagazine.org/people-power/at-standing-rock-no-one-goes-hungry-the kitchen-that-serves-traditional-lakota-food-and-values-20161216

Sand Creek massacre. Retrieved from en.wikipedia.org/wiki/Sand _Creek_massacre

Wynkoop, Edward W. Retrieved from www.kclonewolf.com/History /SandCreek/Bio/edward-wynkoop-biography.html

Vandevelder, P. (2005) *In the name of the fathers*. Retrieved from https://stanfordmag.org/contents/in-the-name-of-the-fathers

Schnapps

When Jerome ripped the shiny silver paper off the birthday present that Jennifer had gotten for him, with a presentiment of what it was, he was delighted. It was a wire metal cage. Inside, looking up at him with very dark eyes, sat a black and white Norwegian rat, nose and whiskers twitching. Its tail extended more than half again the length of its body. Jerome hugged and kissed Jennifer to thank her. The rat replaced the one Jerome had to relinquish at the end of his psychology laboratory course at the university in Greeley, a short distance from Denver where they lived – a rat which had run flawlessly through the maze Jerome had built and to whom Jerome had gotten very much attached. He had not named that one,. But this new rat, they decided together to name "Schnapps." Somehow, it fit him.

Whenever they were home, they opened Schnapps' cage and gave him the run of their one bedroom apartment. Schnapps responded to their voices when they called him. He played hide and seek in the book case with their dog. Schnapps would pop up at certain places between books, his nose twitching, and then disappear when the dog, Jiggers, barked and jumped excitedly, only to reappear between other books. The dog, whose nose was better than her aging eyes, sniffed away to find him again. In actuality, even if her eyesight were better and her years less, the dog was harmless to the rat. In her younger days when the dog had gone on hikes and camping overnights in the mountains near the city with Jennifer and Jerome, she disappeared for minutes, crashing through the underbrush, chasing squirrels and chipmunks, having a joyous time of it, but, more than once, when they saw her actually catch up to a small animal and the animal was frantically moving under her feet, she stood completely still, looking down at it and sniffing, curious and all but confused, as if to ask, "Now what do I do?" Of course, the frightened small animal beneath the her feet,, who must have thought that all was over, discovered that by a seeming miracle it was unharmed and simply skittered quickly away again. And so now yet again the dog was no actual danger to the rat Schnapps .

After they let out Schnapps for a while and he had played with Jiggers, they would always make sure to put him back in his cage. In fact, when called, Schnapps swiftly waddled forward into the cage and appeared happy to have returned to it. Everything about him seemed to belie the preconception that Jerome and Jennifer had about rats: certainly he was smarter than they expected. Perhaps the intelligence of rats was something that made people uncomfortable in general and people preferred to deny it. Perhaps too people preferred to think that rodents were impervious to affection, attachment, playfulness, or routine. Or perhaps Schnapps was just an exceptionally bright rat. Jerome and Jennifer did not know, but they grew increasingly fond of him. He was a welcome addition to their small family.

They were a young couple. During the day, Jennifer worked in an art gallery, which was at times simply boring, with few customers, and at other times, as when they had to hang a show, an exercise in frustration as the owner was anxious and bossy and, in Jennifer's opinion, had little sense of how things actually looked when they were placed on the walls. When they disagreed, Jennifer reluctantly always had to accede. And so, when she came home, she took delight in settling in and relaxing with her new spouse, and of course, Schnapps now became a much needed source of relaxation. And at this time, Jerome was completing his psychology studies and often tried to work a late shift at the local cab company. What time they had together felt precious to them.

In the morning, they let Schnapps out of his cage while they had breakfast, enjoying his antics, and then made sure to put him back before they left. And in the evening, Jennifer greeted him, opened his cage, held him, and then let him play with the dog in the bookcase. One morning, however, what with Jerome rushing to school, and Jennifer to work, they forgot to place him back in his cage before they left. This was a mistake, not because of what he might do in the apartment but because he had an uncanny ability to squeeze under doors, when there only seemed to be a little space. And so, finding the way clear and no one around, but Jiggers, Schnapps waddled to the front door, sniffed under it, and, without further ado, slid under it so that he was outside on the landing. Jiggers, finding her friend gone, barked a handful of times at the closed door, and when her barking brought no result, circled the living room carpet, lay down, curled up, her woeful eyes focused expectantly on the door, hoping that Schnapps would reappear.

Meanwhile, Schnapps had no intention of reappearing. Sniffing around on the landing, he wiggled under the next door he encountered. This brought him into a small waiting room in which he found nothing of interest, and so , continuing his adventure, he slid under the next door in the waiting room Now he discovered he was in the presence of two people, who at first seemed not to notice him There was a woman seated in a chair, quiet and listening. She had taken off her glasses and was rubbing the bridge of her nose. Then there was a man lying on a couch, face up, his eyes closed. His voice was raised and he was saying with evident annoyance that the woman let him talk on and on about his emotional pain upon losing his lover and seemed to him cold and uncaring when it was clear to him that he needed something more from her, some sense of who she was. The woman, in actuality an analyst in training, was intent on trying not to respond – she had heard this all before, for two years now in an analysis that seemed to her to be going nowhere. Saying nothing, she put her glasses back on and rolled her eyes, glad that her patient could not see her from the couch. All of a sudden, she let loose with what sounded to the patient like a muffled scream, and the patient then heard a strange movement from her. Startled, he opened his eyes and discovered that she was standing with one foot on her chair as if she were going to climb onto it (which he could not help noticing provided him with a surprisingly pleasant view of her thighs). He sat bolt upright. He saw she was flushed and speechless (but that her silence was no longer determined by analytic protocol). She pointed silently to the floor near him. He looked down and saw Schnapps, who had stopped in the middle of the room to observe them. For a moment, no one said anything, certainly not Schnapps, whose whiskers were moving rapidly as if he wanted to sense with them what was going on.

To the analyst's equal distress, her patient now burst out in great hoots of laughter, so much so that it took him a moment to catch his breath. Still without speech, she stamped the foot that had been on the chair angrily on the floor. Having finally caught his own breath from laughing, her patient — who happened to be a medical research scientist – explained, "It must be someone's pet rat. It's nothing to be afraid of." She now said something garbled and choked which he took to mean, how did he know? "It's a Norwegian rat, black and white, not one of those gray things," he explained. "It's harmless and probably not diseased." At this point, Schnapps swished his long tail on the carpet two or there times. "Arggh" said the analyst, or something like that, almost shivering.

The patient, who could not resist, said "Quite a phallic symbol," which made the analyst so angry that tears of frustration came to her eyes.

"Out," she managed, "Out," not knowing whom she disliked most at that moment, and not much caring which one left, although as she thought of it, both would have been fine.

"Alright," said the patient, "I'll see what I can do," apparently unaware of the extent of his analyst's distress with him and her initial thought that he would actually leave. Carefully, he got up, tried to step around Schnapps, which only startled Schnapps. Schnapps ran toward what looked very familiar to him, a bookcase in the room near the analyst's chair. Immediately, the analyst started to scream again. At the same time, the patient opened the door to the waiting room, and then the outer door, leaving the analyst frighteningly alone with Schnapps, now hidden somewhere in the bookcase. For a moment, the analyst thought her patient was going to leave her entirely. "Come back," she now found herself saying absurdly. "Please don't leave me here." Schnapps had poked his head out, to see what was happening, between a book on dreams and another on love in the analytic space, his whiskers twitching even more rapidly. He waited there quite a while as the patient made yelling noises designed to frighten him, then he disappeared once again. The analyst and the patient waited, anxiously looking at each other. Schnapps reappeared between a book on gender and another on psychoanalytic technique. Now the patient banged one side of the bookcase, which startled Schnapps. Finally, seeing that there was no dog here with whom to play, eyeing the open door, Schnapps tilted his head to one side, looked at both of them rather sadly, and, without warning, scampered straight away, his long tail following him. The patient also followed him through the two open doors, and by the time he made it to the hallway, he saw Schnapps waddling down the staircase, on his way to the second floor. For a moment, the patient wondered what the right or ethical thing was to do at this point: to follow the rat and try to entice him out of the building or to warn people on the second floor. But by then the rat had disappeared around a corner of the second floor hallway, and the patient decided to return to his session.

When he re-entered the treatment room, after closing both doors carefully behind him, he found his analyst seated on her chair once again, smoothing out her dress, a handkerchief in her hand. "Thank you," she breathed, barely able to look at him and clearly embarrassed. He lay back down on the couch. "Well," he said, again not able to resist, "I am glad you decided to say more today." Against all her training advice, she said, "You, you ..." in an accusatory tone, whereupon, after a moment when neither spoke, they both burst into laughter for a long time. In supervision the next day, her supervisor, a reserved man who was always impeccably dressed in a jacket and bow tie and who spoke with a ponderous authority, was highly critical of her. "What, indeed, were you thinking when you called him back so plaintively?" he asked and implied that she might have jeopardized the treatment irremediably by revealing so much about herself. In fact, it was a turning point and the analysis, which had seemed so bogged down, became infinitely deeper with mutual respect, as if they both recognized that the other was human after all, and ended up being a stunning success.

But to return to Schnapps, he had made it to the second floor, the hall of which looked very much like the third floor, and here he found another door, which he squeezed under. It was the apartment of George and Augusta, both near retirement age, who acted as managers of the building in exchange for a vastly reduced rent. It happened that George was in the midst of preparing an early dinner for the two of them, a tradition they had adopted to celebrate their anniversary, this being the day of their fortieth. Augusta had dressed up somewhat, another part of their tradition, wearing her good pearl necklace and a black dress, and George was just about to bring wine and cheese to the living room when Schnapps made his entrance along the edge of one living room wall, running along quickly, stopping suddenly as if to check things out, and then running along quickly again. Augusta let out a cry. "George, look at that rat!" For a moment, George in the kitchen wondered why Augusta was so loud, she often got this way when they watch t.v., often needing to add her own colorful commentary, so that at first he thought she was denouncing some devious cad on a t.v. show. Then he realized that she did not have the t.v. on, and it dawned on him that she meant what she said. He put down the tray with wine and cheese and rushed into the living room.

George saw the problem:Schnapps standing still for a moment in the center of the rug.

"Well," said George to Augusta, "look at that."

"I am," said Augusta, "looking at that, which is exactly the point."

"I cannot believe that we have a rat problem in our building," said George.

"It's never happened before," said Augusta.

They stared at Schnapps accusingly.

"What are we going to do?" Augusta asked.

"We could try to kill it," said George

"George, no. There must be another way."

"Hmm," said George, "you know I have this cardboard box from the liquor store."

"You mean, capture it?"

"Why not?"

"You might get bitten," said Augusta.

George was feeling particularly confident, and it made him feel very close to his wife, that she relied upon him, as she frequently did when push came to shove in their marriage. "I think I can do it," he said.

"And then what do we do with it?"

"I could just bring it to the park and let it loose," said George. "That would take care of the problem."

"George, let's see you do it," said Augusta.

George took this as a challenge.

And so this was how it came about that Schnapps found a nice chunk of fresh cheese suddenly dropped in front of him, as if heaven itself had opened up. He thought his fortune so very good, and he set to eating. He was not prepared, then, for the sudden descent of the cardboard box, or the deep blackness, or the paper that was then slid beneath his feet, nor the sensation of being raised up and moved.

*   *   *

Jennifer came home. She busied herself putting away some groceries. When she walked past the living room to the bedroom with the intent of freshening up, she noticed that Schnapps' cage door was open. She did not see him, and Jiggers, who had greeted her with her usual jumping when she came into the apartment, was now curled up near the bookcase and certainly not involved with Schnapps. Jennifer had a sinking feeling. "Schnapps," Jennifer called. Jiggers looked up in what seemed a rather soulful way, and her tailed thumped loudly on the floor as if she thought that Jennifer's call would magically raise her rat. But nothing happened. Jennifer called again, but Schnapps, who always came when called, usually peeking his head out from someplace in the bookcase, did not appear. Jennifer looked behind the bookcase, she then looked under the cabinets in the kitchen, opened the cabinet under the sink, went into the bedroom and looked under the bed, into the bathroom and looked behind the toilet. She then went carefully throughout the house, but there was no Schnapps to be found. A number of times before, when Schnapps was let out, they had both seen him squeeze under the front door, and they had opened the door and called him. She now opened the front door, but there was no Schnapps on the landing. She called "Schnapps" a number of times. Nothing.

When Jerome came home a short while later and Jennifer told him the news, he proceeded to search for Schnapps in all the places Jennifer had looked, despite the fact that she assured him that she had checked them, but there was no result. Jiggers actually got herself up and began following him around, but then she lost interest and returned to the bookcase, lay down again, her eyes more soulful than ever, as if she realized that Schnapps was gone.

"What should we do?" Jennifer finally said.

"I think we should check with the landlord, " said Jerome, "Maybe someone saw him or maybe he went into someone's apartment."

And so it was that Jerome found himself in front of George and Augusta's door. He felt some trepidation, for although there was, as far as he knew, nothing in his rental agreement that forbid him and Jennifer from having a pet, it was (at best) going to be awkward to ask whether anyone in the building had reported seeing a black and white rat that squeezed under doors. He took a breath and knocked.

Augusta answered his knock, opening the door and now dressed in a silken light blue bathrobe, with purple silhouettes of naked girls and Chinese symbols that made her look like an aging Las Vegas dancer. "Oh, Jerome," she said, "It is getting late. Whatever can be the matter at this time?" Jerome hesitatingly started to explain his plight, apologizing profusely about the late hour, and then leading up to how Jennifer had bought him a pet rat to replace his lab rat.

He was about to go on, apologizing again, about how they had mistakenly left the rat out and did not realize that the rat had a truly remarkable ability to squeeze into small spaces, when Augusta let out with, "So." Her arms were now crossed in front of her formidable chest, and there was clearly a disapproving look in her face.

George then appeared. He too gave him an angry look. Gruffly, he said, "I put him in a cardboard box and brought him to Hanford Park and let him loose. The box is still there." Augusta looked at him with approval, as if he were a hero.

"My George, he always knows what to do," she said.

But Jerome was oblivious to this. He thanked them and hurried back to Jennifer, told her the news and said, "Let me see if I can find him."

He drove quickly to the park. It was not a large park, he thought to himself hopefully as he got out of his car and walked across the grass. He now entered a meadow.. There was a mass of trees that extended a long distance and extended around the meadow in both directions. He walked near the trees and, to his delight, he found the cardboard box lying on its side on the ground, open. No Schnapps, however. What now?

All he could think of doing was to stand there and call. Wouldn't Schnapps come if he heard him, as he came when they called for him at home?

There was no help but to try.

"Schnapps," he called, his voice tentative at first, and then louder, calling into the dark, beneath the star-filled sky. There was no answer but the rustling of the trees The lights of Denver shone in sparkles on the edges of the park. "Schnapps, come home," he yelled stronger and stronger, and now over and over, walking in circles on the grass, envisioning his rat lost and trembling beneath some leafy tree. "Schnapps," again, a cry into the darkness.

He had roused a drunken man who had fallen asleep on the edge of the meadow, and now approached him, carrying a bottle of wine in a twisted paper bag. He was originally from Riga, Latvia; that was a long time ago, and when he heard the call of Schnapps in the dark night, he thought he was back home or that he was hallucinating, but then as he got nearer, he saw it was a man either drunker or more desperate than he. When he reached Jerome, he saw how distraught he was. He offered him his bottle. "I only have wine," he said, like an apologetic host, in the hope it would satisfy the man's apparently strange alcoholic craving and ease his pain. Jerome thanked him and tried to explain it was his pet rat, but he was so upset that it came out somewhat garbled. The man retreated backward, holding one hand palm outward while the other held the bottle, as if to ward off Jerome, and then turned and walked silently away, shaking his head at the man's story.

And on the sidewalk, at the rim of the park, the analyst, who felt she had a particularly difficult and long day, had decided to walk home, enjoying the soft night breeze. She thought it would be nice to relax once she got home, kick off her shoes, and, after a chicken salad that she had prepared the day before, listen to some Bach and have a drink. She deserved it. Then, in the distance she thought she heard someone yelling what sounded to her like "Schnapps" repeatedly, and she became frightened, hurrying her steps. She could not help wondering whether she had in some way lost it entirely. Years later, when she could recount what had happened to her colleagues and laugh about the rat in her room and the interaction with her patient, she often kept back this last vestige of that strange day because it seemed so inexplicable and haunting.

Meanwhile, in the park, Jerome repeated his plaintive cry, made all the more plaintive because he felt that he had betrayed his pet by leaving him out of his cage. After almost an hour, the dark having got darker and the cold getting to him, he turned reluctantly toward home, thinking of Schnapps, seeing in his mind an image of the rat: head cocked at an angle, looking at him with that curious intelligent look he had. Schnapps now was in a world he had never seen before, no doubt unprepared from his protected environment, unfamiliar with leaves and grass and bushes, vulnerable to predators he had never known. Lost. No longer yelling, Jerome walked slowly away, his head down, knowing he would have to report his futile quest to Jennifer. He found his way from the grass meadow to the pavement, and his footsteps now echoed in the night. As he walked, he lamented very softly and sadly to himself, realizing both how foolish he was being and, yet, how great the loss felt. "Oh, Schnapps," and then again, "Schnapps."

Termination

The sun shone through the white lace curtains, slanting onto the white plastered wall next to the open window and down to the polished wooden floor, throwing patterns that shifted as a slight breeze swayed the curtains again and again. It was autumn. He could see the huge oak tree outside, stalwart, as if it would never change even though many of its leaves were now brilliant yellow and orange. When the sunlight touched them, they shone so brightly that they appeared on fire. Beneath the tree, he could see by craning his head a bit on his pillow, that the still-green grass was strewn with colored leaves. Soon, he would have to call the landscapers and contract for leaf removal, a thought that made him chuckle.

He was dying. It was something that he both accepted and did not. It made him feel, peculiarly, that he belonged, that he shared something in common with people, as if it relieved him of that sense he had most of his life that he lived apart. And at the same time, he felt intensely alone. He did not want to leave this life, not yet, not ever. There were times that the beauty of it these days brought tears to his eyes, like now:, the autumn sunlit patterns on the wall, the bright leaves outside, all seemed so wonderfully alive that they made his eyes sting. Such intense beauty. So much of the daily routine of his life, the days dealing with the details of just surviving, the bills, shopping, watching television when exhausted in the evenings, worrying about this and that, seemed now to have been such a waste. He had the urge, suddenly, to walk outside, if he only could, and wrap his arms around the trunk of the great tree, and feel the rough bark against his cheek.

Textures now seemed to mean more to him than they had before, and smells. He could lie in bed and feel the white sheets, and they felt voluptuous and fascinating, with their folds and curves. Slowly, he would move his dry bony fingers (so bony that he could not reconcile them as being his) along them; they were unpredictable in their undulations, like a great snow-filled meadow, and then the perfumed smell that came from them reminded him of the smell from the lilac bush that had grown against the side of his grandparents house, just beneath the window of the room with the dark blue wallpaper on it, where he used to sleep when he visited them. His memories and day dreams would float like this at times, this way and that, as if they were on a giant ocean that carried them without direction.

But when he slept, his night dreams for quite a while had been awful – images of decay, his body seeming to decompose before his eyes; of pitch black night where he could not see; of great unbearable winds that threatened to blow him into an abyss – so that waking, sometimes sweating all over the bed and sheets, felt like arriving at a sudden safe haven. But now as he lay here, he found that when he slept he often came upon a continuing dream, a dream that he welcomed as a relief from the nightmares. It was not just a repetitive dream, although it often started out the same way each time, but each night the dream seemed to continue the previous one or advance it. It was all very curious. Now he found himself looking forward to dreaming when he was in and out of wakefulness.

Sometime the dream was just a fragment, stopping suddenly, and often there were other dreams interspersed. Each time, in the dream or the fragment of it, he seemed to return to his analysis of thirty years ago: his analyst would greet him, just as she always had, with a gentle nod, and he would lie down on her couch again, and he would talk on and on and sometimes he would hear her sensible, warm voice interrupting him – the voice that had seemed to guide him, challenge him, endure him, through all those twists and turns of his tumultuous time with her.

It seemed so strange, and yet, for some reason, he did not mention these dreams to his wife Sheila who with her heavy, sad eyes tended to him. Perhaps he kept it secret, he thought, just as he had the details of the analysis itself when it had happened. Then he did so for the sake of the analysis, so if he dreamt during that time, he made sure *not* to tell Sheila. His dreams then belonged to his analyst; together, the two of them adventured through the landscape of his internal life, his history, his wishes, his fears and – dredged up from his unconscious (he could not help but have the image of seaweed and mud attaching to obscure objects pulled from a river and dripping with water) – his dreams. But now, even though his present dreams were not during an analysis, and even though his analyst had actually passed away over ten years ago, somehow he still felt that he could not tell these dreams to Sheila. Strange.

Except for these dreams, he felt that he was managing to make a good exit. He had reconciled himself, he thought, to his death, and he felt fortunate that he was not in pain, that his faculties were more or less intact, even if his hearing had all but gone out of one ear. His son, who lived in Japan with his Japanese wife, had visited two or was it three weeks ago. He had been so glad to see him. He held his son's hand so tightly when his son leaned over to kiss his forehead as he lay on the bed; it was like their roles were reversed: he now was the little boy being kissed "goodnight" just before going to sleep. And his son looked strong and muscular, although he saw in his dark eyes how frightened he was. After all, he knew he made a terrifying sight – unreal, all skin and bones, a halloween cadaver with wide open eyes and an incongruous grin. When he looked in the mirror, even he gave a start, so why shouldn't his son be afraid too? It must have been such a change for his son, for the last time his son had seen him was six months before, when the disease had not yet ravaged his appearance.

It was so much more difficult with his daughter Marissa and her husband, who lived three hours away with their two young children, his grandchildren, Gregory who was only one year old, and Sonya who was five. Marissa had a look so much like her mother, but more open in many ways. When she saw him now, she would try to smile and then her eyes would well up with tears. He could see in her the young girl growing up through the years: how she would love to sit on his lap, and talk to him; how he taught her to ride her bike; how she would come to him with her arms wide open as a toddler. And now, too, there was Sonya, his granddaughter, who always approached him with questions : "Why granddaddy are your hands so bony?" or "What are all those medicines next to your bed?" She was so wonderfully direct; he actually loved her for it, while her mother would try to shush her. But oh how difficult it all was. How painful. And he worried that Sonya would remember him like this, and wondered what it would be like for her when he died.

At least (as he returned with some relief to the same obsessive internal subject) in his recurrent dream he remained healthy in appearance. And the consulting room in his analyst's house always looked the same as it had years ago; and the couch, with its intricate flowered pattern that made him fantasize at times that he was lying down on a river bank (that river image again) and looking at the sky – the ceiling he remembered was painted a light blue – looked the same too. And yet, he knew that the house itself after his analyst's death had been sold to another and non-professional family entirely, and the consulting room, no doubt, had reverted to its original use as a living space. He had actually, reminiscing once three years ago (before he had become sick) had an impulse to drive by the house just to see it; whoever lived there had changed the color of the house from yellow to white, and the trees that dotted one side of the house had all been removed, and a tricycle lay abandoned on the front grass. It was understandable, but it made him feel forlorn.

There were times he wanted so much to reassure Sheila by confiding in her what was happening to him inside so perhaps she would be less frightened (a fright he could see in those heavy sad eyes), but still, for some reason, he could not talk of this repetitive continuing dream, as if it were a real analysis about which one tended to keep silent. Maybe talking about it would sabotage the dreams in some way, he thought, just as talking about one's analysis could sabotage the analysis.

Instead, the two of them seemed to talk about their past or the children in tones very much like the tones they had always used, as if everything would continue the way it had been. He loved her simple laugh, with its lilt that rang clear like the sound of a bell, interspersed in their conversation whether she talked of a friend, or what she had bought at the grocery store, or the sweater she was knitting for Sonya. He wondered whether the sweater would be finished before he died, and whether he would ever see Sonya wearing it; but neither of them spoke those thoughts. And in this way, they seemed to him to converse right past Death, as if He were an undesirable guest who had gained entrance under false pretenses into their house and then taken residence in their bedroom. He smiled at the conceit, continuing it in his mind. They chose to ignore Him, despite his considerable and very dark presence, enjoying the feeling of being rude to Him, which (and now he found himself despite everything chuckling) He surely deserved.

The days ran into each other now. He dozed a lot. He held Sheila's hand at one point and they joked about how tentative they had been on their first date so many years ago at the Chinese restaurant that had been replaced numerous times by other restaurants (it was now Greek) and how he had tentatively reached over to touch her hand and managed to knock over his water glass. And yet, it had felt so right when their hands finally touched, as they did now. He raised her hand to his dry lips and kissed it.

It seemed a week had passed. It was Monday, he believed. And by this time, in his continuous dream, which had occurred almost every night, he and his analyst had arrived at what was to be his last session. They had agreed on it. And so, he entered the consulting room with a little hesitancy and glanced almost shyly at his analyst. But she was seated as always in her chair. She smiled in apparent acknowledgment but said nothing. He lay down as he always did.

This time when he lay on the couch in his dream, he talked of an early memory of his. He had been a young child himself (like Sonya). He had a brush full of viscous blue poster paint, and he remembered pushing it onto a news sheet on an easel, and the paper suddenly turned bright blue, and then the paint seemed to move as he moved the brush. His little easel was set up on the porch of his grandparents' house, the breeze made the leaves on the trees of the lawn whisper, and his mother sat in one of the white porch chairs. He was amazed at how clear the memory was. "My mother was reading," he said to his analyst, "always reading. I was so happy to be there with her, even if she seemed to pay no attention to me."

He had painted what he called a "little bool egg house," a little blue and white house with a blue smudge for a roof that seemed to teeter unsteadily on the page, as if at any moment it would fall over. He knew this because his father had framed the picture and liked to tell the story of his painting it. His parents said he had talked incessantly about his little bool egg house, but no one knew what it was. "To this day, I don't know what it means. .. little bool egg house. I guess the 'bool' means 'blue.' I'm not sure." He paused. " I wonder why the ceiling here is blue," he said to his analyst. She did not respond. "You know," he said, "it was just like my father to frame my picture. He did things, practical things. My mother was always reading a book and in her own world."

"You must be remembering this," she said, "because you want to remember your mother, even if she was in her own world."

Sometimes his analyst's words seemed just right.

"It was so long ago, you know, so long ago, and yet it is like only a moment too."

"I know, " she said.

They were silent.

"I love you," he said, suddenly, surprising himself.

All she said was, "Yes."

He waited quietly. He thought to himself – looking at the blue ceiling, tracing with his eyes a slight crack in it that made him

think of a crack in an egg, like a robin's egg that one found sometimes fallen in the grass – that he did not want to leave.

Finally, she said, "We've come a long way together." He started
to cry. She said nothing.

Then he had difficulty speaking, but, finally, catching his
breath, he said. "Thank you, thank you so much. I was so impossible."

"Yes," she said, and she laughed. "And you're welcome."

He waited again. Finally, she said in the same unchanging and
kind voice that she always used at the end of a session (even
though this was the last one), "And now our time is up."

When he rose from the couch, he found that she was already
standing. She smiled at him, and then she stepped toward him.
They embraced softly in what seemed like a delicate dance, and,
for a moment she was his mother and then she seemed to become
Sheila. He felt so close to her, so amazed by the softness of her
flesh that he did not want to let go. Then a white warmth spread
into him and seemed to go on and on forever.

When Sheila entered the room later, she saw that he was lying
very still. Both his hands lay unmoving and fully open on the
white sheet. He was vacant-eyed, his lips slightly apart as if in
anticipation. She remained standing, holding her breath. There
had been other times when this had happened, and she had seen,
after a long while, the almost imperceptible rise and fall of his
chest. But now, as she waited longer and longer in what seemed
like hours, nothing. She went to him and touched his hands. He
was unresponsive.

"Oh, Charles," she said to the still form, and then she heard an
impossibly loud sigh rush out of her own body. She knelt clumsily
next to the bed, her own eyes having gone so profusely wet that
she could barely see, and then she laid her warm cheek very gently
against his cooling one. "There, there," she said, patting his silent
chest over and over, "there, there," as if to reassure him.

Poems

I CARRY MY DEATH

I carry my death with me now
as one carries a child. It will be a while,
yes, but it grows each day, stretches,
yawns, sleeps on and off.
I feel its weight in my bones, in the interstices
of my knees, in the sometimes pain of my hip.

Not the way it was before.
When I run now, I move at a slower pace,
as in a dream, passed by a mother and her child,
moving in my own way,
cataloging the places where the pain lodges.
Only in my true dreams do I feel electric and soar between steps,
as I once did.

I carry my death delicately, respectfully
(it will not be denied, anyhow).
Once I had thought to rail
against it, lonely and heroic, but now
I want grace —
grace to outsmart it as long as I can
and to greet it when it is grown
as one would greet the new owner of one's house.
I carry my death with me now.

LOVE WITH A HINT OF SHAKESPEARE

I will be your trellis and your rose bush. I will come to you
 disguised
As a young girl. I will open to you like the wind, sudden and
 strong,
And carry you above the trees, the housetops, the town, in my
 human arms.

And place you down so softly, conscious in our circumscribed
 room.
These things I will try, and if I succeed, they will be no less true
For being fantasy. In return, I ask for something simple and
 dear:

Let me wonder at you. At the informed cadence of your voice,
 the way
You move through the transparent air, your deep tentative
 smile.
And in some quiet moment, when you gaze in the mirror,
 tilting your head

The way you do, your fingers softly on the nape of your neck –
Contemplative, searching, I ask that you see yourself as I see
 you.
Soft, high-cheekboned woman, be my dark lady. Be my muse.

THE EGYPTIAN COURIER TUMBLES

A long tumble of bones in the night
awakens me, and I scream "oh no, no"
and jump from bed, dash down the long stairs

yelling "Sunny, Sunny," peering
into the dark – switch on the light –
and hear your greyhound cry from the dining room.

Long-boned, delicate contradiction of a dog
more alien, more praying mantis than dog
with big eyes in a serious forehead
who cannot negotiate the stairs,

who climbs onto the couch each time
tentatively as an invalid,
your leg bones shaking uncertainly, and yet
when unleashed in the dog park

you suddenly uncoil like a spring and take off
in great impossible thunderous strides –
people stopping, pointing, in awe,

while other sensible dogs trail behind you –
– a fleet courier of some Egyptian god – and
then as suddenly stop, your great chest heaving –

how you are shaking now, crying, in the corner of the room.
You raise one sprained ankle. But you are, thank god,
bruised yet unbroken.

Tonight, noble creature, you must sleep downstairs.

ON GOING TO THE AMERICAN MUSEUM
OF NATURAL HISTORY WITHOUT YOU

Here in this cavernous museum without you
I find myself in a small room near a fragile reed boat
Looking at a diorama of Alexandria in the first century.
There are perfect small figures behind the glass bustling along
In the ancient streets, among the stalls of a market place,
With the curve of a sand beach and a blue plaster sea, seen from above.

So it must have been centuries ago, I wonder;
And suddenly I feel an unexpected fear: Like a trapped bird
It rises and beats the air inside me, with great tumultuous flaps,
As if its feathers were scraping and shattering against my ribs.
And I want so much to hold you, here and now.

For I see in my mind's eye, that this city, before me like a toy,
Is Manhattan this Sunday spring morning, and Columbus Avenue;
The Hudson River is brilliant blue plaster; and the people sit at their
Sidewalk cafes, sipping coffee and cappuccino, yawning, gossiping,
Rifling through their Sunday paper for the current news.
And these people too will die, this city too, as Alexandria did.

Love, you make me think long thoughts, and feel so fragile
That I yearn for your touch to quiet the great wings. You release
My body raw to the elements once again, so that I know sorrow
  physically,
Beyond words or before them; so I am young again. And I remember
What it is I once knew and made myself forget:
There is not time enough, there never was.

THOUGHTS PROMPTED BY A SEED

Does the dormant seed dream?
Seemingly dry and definitely small,
Does it dream what will become of it
Or insensate, knows not at all

Of time and bloom, of thrust and burst?
Does it lie in the hand blank as a stone
Or does it feel some terrible thirst?
Even if it could imagine being grown

How could it imagine such difference?
For my singular love from years ago
Couldn't have made any more sense
Of the burgeoning fullness I now know

Than the seed of the flower. I love you so.

THE MEANING OF CATS

She loved cats and rescued them.
This was not easy as her wheelchair
Scared them.

Found them in the debris behind strip malls,
Where they ate from the leftovers
Of Taco Bell and Dunkin' Donuts.

Feral, afraid, they nonetheless came to her;
Found her, wastrel to wastrel
Carefully, ceaselessly she tamed them
Day after day, and brought them home.

When Max disappeared, old and thin, one day
She assured me that he would come back.
And I wanted to believe her. Waited, but
No return, for a very long time.

Until one day, he was there, dead, desiccated,
A rag-cat, on the path to the front door. Thrown there,
By someone who read his tag, dragged there
By some animal who found him. Who knew?

Except I could not tell her.
How could I tell her?
Encouraging her as always
As she herself was struggling with her illness.
Worse than she ever struggled.

She died the week afterward.

And the omen of Max, spread flat on
The front path, irrevocable,
Haunted me and will forever.

And then one day over a year later,
An emaciated young cat appeared at the
Back door, feral, afraid.
Would not come near, hissed.

Day after day, we fed him, and he
Still hissed and ran away, but then
Ate when we were not near. For
Over a month, carefully, we coaxed
Him. Until one day, he actually
Ventured into the house before
Scurrying away. Until another,
He rubbed against my hand; until
Still another, he let himself be petted,
And another, he purred when moving against
My leg.

And we realized it was not only food he wanted,
But touch, but holding; a need as strong as hunger.
And now, Archie cannot be denied, lying on our
Laps, nuzzling our faces, his body vibrating, alive,
Even approaching fat.

And in this way, I learned from my daughter
The meaning of her love.

There are those
Who may prefer chance to fashion this story
But I settle on something else, something
Elusive and unknowable that mentors our
Lives

Like a cat, like Max, like Archie.

THE POPULIST

The flim-flam man with flaxen hair
Appraises with his gimlet stare

And grimaces his widening smile,
A fat, dyspeptic crocodile.

And how the folks just ooh and aah,
And laugh and clap his sisboombah,

Believe his flaccid gimmickry,
Love his disdainful mimicry.

They do not know the fate of those
Who choose to hold a monster close.

SEA SONG
(with apologies to Edward Lear)

I will dance with you by the sea
And somersault in the sand
If only you will be with me
Through the night.

I will breakfast at half-past three
And sing love poems upon command
If only you will stay with me,
Through the night.

I have fashioned a boat for tea
And to sail to distant lands.
Will you look at the stars with me
Through the night?

MARAIS-POITEVIN

Riding between corn and sunflowers
silently standing witness
to our passage;

Riding past quiet canals
covered in green algae,
we make our way.

The shadows of our bikes traverse the road
riding with us,
leaving no mark.

GUATEMALA

The wind flung bromeliads on our path,
And the blue sky mingled with the spume
Of the volcano. Through stands of corn

We walked, immersed in clattering green
Wands; sinking into the rich red clay we walked,
By sudden great pine trees that shot

Into the blue sky. Our guide touched the plants
Around us into shapes as various as the stars,
Naming them: plants that moved;

Plants that poisoned; plants that cut;
Plants that cured the same cuts, and salved
Our heartaches and our ills.

Follow me through these magical hills, my love;
Hold my hand. We will travel up and down
The mountain paths, wherever they lead,

Just as they led us here, until the dark night
Covers the forest, the corn, the rich red clay.

CHRYSALIS

You told me you are changing. I am too.
I do not know how, I only sense the process.
This must be how the chrysalis feels.

Nor does it help to wonder at the ending,
No more than were the chrysalis to plan.
This must be how the heart heals.

We are bathed in the sunlight and the wind,
Held tight by force and throbbings beyond us.
This must be how love reveals

Itself, or how lovers grow their wings,
And fly away despite the world protesting.

AT THE DOG TRACK

No one actually goes near the track
where the sun beats down. No one goes

near the dogs themselves. People watch through
this giant plate glass window, protected from the heat.

Except of course the handlers, who sweat in the sun
as they show off, one by one, each dog –

one handler per dog; and each handler a black kid,
probably from Bridgeport, which rises dark and grimy,

beyond the track. But the dogs – oh the dogs,
so beautiful and thin.

And when they take off, finally,
they seem to fly around the track,

and stop so suddenly before us,
their great chests heaving,

and hang their heads,
bound once again to this impenitent earth.

SOJOURNER IN CHINATOWN

I will always be a sojourner in Chinatown
where the fast-talking street merchant
sells lichees in paper-thin brown shells,

and custard apples, green and clumpy,
congregate on the painted wood of his stall,
successfully disguising their delicate insides.

I will be a stranger in the Chinese bakery,
sitting, watching, tasting my sweet bun
filled with red bean paste and sipping ice-cold tea

with tapioca balls through a too-large blue straw.
I will have you beside me. I will have you beside me,
watching with me, wondering with me at the people

who are shopping – oblivious, rushing.
These adventures that we have are different,
having them together. We take home the lichees,

custard apples, sweet buns, dried mushrooms,
and Chinese ceramic pots for the orchids
that sit near the window in our New Jersey home.

RIVER

It is strange to realize in my 54th year
I did not know what love is
Until now. And now I find myself carried
On a river, slowly but inexorably, downstream,
Through shade and sunlight, the muddy and grassy bank
First close then far away, moving in and out of eddies
As if on an inner tube – the water gurgling softly; and sometimes
Near, sometimes distant, you – on your inner tube – float too.

And I see floating down the river, other figures,
As if in a strange dance, sometimes crossing my path,
Sometimes circling with me in a watery dos a dos, then pushing and
Floating gently away: Here, don't you see, is your Russian grandfather,
On his inner tube, holding his rifle above the water to keep it dry;
And then my own Russian grandfather, smiling across the water as he
Passes me, exclaiming "*Wunderbar*," and disappearing around a bend.
And now comes your Ghanaian prince, looking wistfully at you again,
His royal wedding clothes sparkling brightly in the dark shadow;
And my Navajo woman, and her child, adjusting her long black hair,
Her elbows raised akimbo as she carefully places a silver barrette.

And now comes, as if surprised to be there, my first analyst
Looking jaunty in his silk cravat, and starting to explain, "You
    see . . . "
Before he drifts out of hearing range. And there are your girls,
Youngsters once again, kicking and splashing, so that the water
    droplets
Flash like gems in the sunlight, and they shriek with glee. And
    further on
Under that overhanging tree, my girl and boy float, singing,
    "Merrily we

Roll along, roll along," over and over as if the river will flow forever.
And there is my wife, and here your husband, on their inner tubes,
Passing near us, crossing, bumping and separating again.

And as my fingers trail in the cool water, and our inner tubes pass,
My fingers touch yours and I try to clasp your slippery hand in mine,
But the current pulls you away, and then back to me again.
And we are swept, whether we will or not, sometimes together,
Sometimes apart, downstream relentlessly, pulled by a force
Deep in the heart of the river
Never knowing where our journey will end.

Here, in my 54th year, it is so very strange I never traveled
This river before,
Nor knew its name.

LOST AND FOUND

You would have me lost with you, in the pine-quiet and the dapple,
The crackle of oak leaves underfoot, and the trodden path almost
  gone,
So that when the darkness comes and the shapes of trees and rock
Blur, we hold our breath, hoping for instinct to guide us out.

And I would have you in the sea with me, in those moments
Before the slowly forming, distant wave, approaches like a mountain
Alive; and safety is now only in moving to meet it,
To fling ourselves into its sweet watery wall; and pop out
On the other side, wondrous and out of breath.

We each have our metaphors, you and I, to hold us or pull us apart.

WORDS

Naming and words, you told me, cannot be trusted;
And only through the body can we show
Naturally and without deceitfulness
Shadows and intricacies of our soul.

I answered that it's only words we have,
Erratic, rough, and blunt as they may be.
In naming, now I find to my dismay
Love by words fails hopelessly.

Over and over, my body yearns for yours,
Very much as the green sea yearns for shore.
Evening or dawn, during the warmth of day,
Your breasts, your thighs, your love ask me for more.

Oh, your body that I sought, now casts its spell,
Upon my words, whose secrets to you alone I tell.

FOR NIKKI, ON HER 19TH BIRTHDAY

How does a father know his daughter
Or his daughter know him? Imposed as we were
By mystery upon each other, and growing
Together, like old vines and new tendrils,

And now growing apart – How do we know
Each other? Do we keep together by images,
Like photographs in a scrapbook: Jasper,
Chaco Canyon, Lettermullin?

Do we gaze upon our past like some
Distant land we visited together,
And reminisce? Or are our memories
Informed by a changed intimacy now?

On this your nineteenth birthday, straddling
Your childhood and adulthood like
A suspension bridge, I embrace you
And wish upon you the beneficence

Of insight, security and kindness
In your life. I see you move away
And watch with bated breath your wondrous
Progress, upon your own and with such telling grace.

I give no gift to you as great as you
Give me: a chance again to live and grow.
Daughter, flesh out of my flesh, soul
Dappling my soul, I love you so.

LOVE IN THE SECOND MILLENNIUM:
MARCH 13, 2003

Between the cracking of the towers
and the lie, serene and blatant,
flowing from the politician's mouth,

there is no room for flowers
today. The land is whitely vacant;
rabbits are in hiding; birds flown South;

and no one knows the morning anymore.
White-eyed, an hysteric man polkas
the suburban street, plays for applause,

and bangs with glee his tinny drum of war.
Distantly, the Beast fusses,
wakes from sleep; and whatever laws

protect, provide, are stretched upon the wrack.
In this bleak time, hold onto me my love,
for it is all we have to staunch these wounds.

Batten each door against each new attack
with your embrace. We are made of
sinew and of time beyond such sounds.

Let the Beast, the politician turn askance,
when we lie down together and when we dance.

THE PATTERN WE MAKE

The light spreads each morning
Onto the bed where you clutch
The comforter to you, asleep,

Adrift in its many colors –
Pink, blue, yellow, red –
Apart from me in an inland sea

Of your own. The birds try
Their disparate notes, tuning
For a symphony they never play.
It is beginning again, this day,
Outside the lace curtains,
Beckoning, warming, smelling

Of honeysuckle and damp earth.
Each day, you lie there anew,
And I kiss you again on the forehead
Where the skin worries itself
And on the bluish cast near your eyebrow,

And I place another tile,
Stroke another line
So close to me that I will not know,
(until the day my eyes close
And I fall backward softly)

the pattern we have made.

PUCK'S GLEN, SCOTLAND

It fell from a god's green dream,
This glen, steeped in water,
Replete with moss and fern.

From all over, rivulets
Empty into the stream,
Their water peaty brown.

Sometimes sheets of dark water
Fall from far above us,
Crash and spatter into spray.
I watch you descend with care
In front of a frieze of wet rock,
Like a stately myth of a lady

Born out of these loamy loins,
Born from the dark wet forest.
I watch silently as the crashing

Water overcomes all sound,
As you magically make your way
Toward me.

LAZY

I am languid in the old time
I am languid in the new
There is no thing
That I want to do.

LOVE IS DIFFERENT

It is different, it is the same,
Love is love, love is a name

For something wild,
For something tame

Like a cat that is roaring
Then contentedly purring.

I envision you stretching
On an unmade bed

Your body all curving,
It goes to my head,

Both lust and contentment
It is more than any sentiment.

When we first met
could we know we were meant

For each other? My beautiful flame
Our love is love both wild and tame.

ASCENDING

The trees this morning are in flame,
In flame with the light from the sun
Striking their ice-glazed branches

But only on the top, so that they seem
To be ascending toward the blue sky,
About to burst into a total radiance

That will make the world go white.
The snow too has a crystalline brightness,
Soft pillows that shape the ground but shine

Everywhere with grains of light.
We lie open and like the trees reach.
Perhaps we too shall ascend

Out of our morning bed, out of our
Individual dreams – the complex
Strata of loam and nightmare –

Holding hands, and rise through the sheer
Lace curtains, through the window.
For there is no ascension

Without the body. In your skin,
In your fingers, in the weight of you,
I arise, and only yearn toward the light

When I am held by you.
Like these trees I shall burst into brightness
Enwrapped by you, in my heart wood.

HUNTRESS

Stride for stride and elegant,
greyhound and lady take a walk.

The morning sun has barely burned
the frozen stubble near the lake,
and mist still rises silently.

Stride for stride, the two define
the air around them grey and taut.

FREE ASSOCIATION

Toward therapeutic ends
the analyst contends

even the smallest thought
will never be for naught.

THE ANALYST SLEEPS

It is nighttime and he lies upon the bed
watching the patterns on the ceiling
thrown by a streetlight against the leaves

of summer trees – content in his own pattern
and the beauty of the night, his companion
gently asleep, gently breathing, beside him.

And wonders: wonders –– how do his patients lie?
One so alone and wounded that her heart bleeds
upon the bed this night, clutching the sheets
around her so they form embracing arms, as she
does every night – abandoned by men, bereft
and alone, so awfully singular.

One fearful of touching the sleeping form
of the man beside her, wakeful, alone, too, nursing a furiously
cold grudge, borne of days and nights of disappointment.

One who holds himself so tight that he will sink
into his bed as if it is the sea,
not caring for the hands that grab for him,
trailing seaweed instead and the deep, cold dark.

The analyst, the analyst:
How can he be their talisman? How translate their fears,
transform the silent falling of their tears?
He turns and finally sleeps, and dreams
of voices calling to him through the night.

SITTING IN A MEADOW

Sitting on this rock, the green moss in clumps and wet with dew,
I embrace you, and hold you for this moment. It is our breathing
Together in this morning air and the way time slows as we breathe
That beguiles me – and you, who have shown me that leaving

Things behind is a painful grace that attends each beginning.
How alive I am with you in this place: the horse in its corral
Stares at us, stolidly, as if trying to make sense of our love;
The sour purple grapes, now wild, on their sinewy vine, planted

By some hand long ago – promise a sweeter tomorrow, if only we
    return.
("Be patient," you tell me always, "be patient.")
And over and over, the spiders on this rock enter our backpack
As if they had together conferred and decided to come home
    with us.

Curious, you lift one soft moss disk, surprised at how easily
It detaches, and suddenly discover a scurrying of ants, now frantic,
Trying to save themselves and their children;
And so, very gently, you replace their roof, and we wonder

Whether they sigh collectively when their world rights itself.
And there *are* worlds here, worlds beside worlds, worlds within
    worlds,
Worlds we have yet to explore, and time as various as these
    worlds:
The time of the ant, and the time that the stolid horse knows;

The time we measure by minutes, and the time we measure by our
   dreams;
And most of all the time of our love, that together we create
With our bodies and our touch and our unfamiliar words we speak,
When we open the hidden places of our souls, gently, to one
   another.

REVENGE

The body is its metaphor
When words are stopped or never known.
The scream that's caught in a surprise
Waits in the fiber and the bone.

And the raised fist of the loved child,
By terror stilled too suddenly,
Shakes hidden in internal night,
Waits like a switch yet to be thrown,

Then crashes down to murder, maim,
– Adult, unrecognized and grim.
The scream that was too long delayed,
Autopsy will not find in him.

LET MY HANDS BE MAGICAL

Let me touch you into sleep
As your mother did.
Let me wish my hands her hands
When your head was small,
And touch your brow so slowly
And press my fingers through your hair.

Let me massage the future from your brain,
Fling wide the door of the deep cage,
Where blackened birds with iridescent wings
Flap against the bars;

Let me release them to the midnight air,
To fly softly away and disappear,
And leave you here with me,
Your body eased into a somnolence.

Let my hands be magical to you.

DRIVEN TO ABSTRACTION

I know you around. I know your shape.
But I cannot see your shape at once.
I know your body from the concept
Of "aroundness"

And only when I plunge into abstract,
A plunge that happens all unknowingly,
Do I create from image and from touch,
You, illusively, inside of me.

And I cannot see my love for you
Nor fashion it from twigs or thread or clay,
And yet whenever I encounter you
– My body knowing and my bones –

You press intangible upon my soul
A love abstract and make my body whole.

TIME TRAVELS

Time travels in the daytime on a road
Or so it seems, going from place to place,
Inexorably, if sometimes fast or slow,

But always crabwise clacking as it goes.
It does not turn around, retrace its steps,
But fashions forward in a lurching mode.

Should we accept this daytime prodigal?
Not wonder at its grim intrepid ways,
Its flat indifference to connectedness?

Or should we puzzle at the tenderness
Of night, when hues and borders softly blend,
And dreams make sequence dim and fallible,

And Time has shed its bearings and its form?
For where is Time when sleep slips Time away
And enters into us or we to it?

When I lie down beside you and commit
Myself toward absence, wander from the bend
Of both your legs, your haunch sensuous, warm;

Take leave of both your breasts, your breathing slow,
And fall unfettered into inner space,
Where is Time then? Can sequencing explain

Our intertwining love? Do we retain
An augur of the possible in lips
That tentatively met six years ago,

And do our bodies find in their abode
A secret – needing neither Time nor road?

ASSIGNATION

Meet me in the rain,
With the mist everywhere,
And I'll kiss you on a dare
On your soft lips.

Let it be our refrain,
In the night or during day,
That I'll caress you every way,
With my finger tips.

Your are as wild as wind-blown rain,
As sweet as sudden sun,
And I love you like the one
Orchid the hummingbird sips.

A TONE DEAF LOVER TO HIS LOVE

I heard today on public radio
a tree frog inside a misting forest
in Borneo adjust in pitch his song

of a single note through trial and error
to resonate to the tree hole in which
he sat. It took Darwinian eons to perfect
this technique to trumpet his amphibian
love. Even the cricket, less versatile,
unable to adjust its pitch, sculpts out

an earthen hole with cricketly aplomb
that resonates perfectly its one-note
love song. Next to the bird who ornaments

a melody of passion to enthrall
his mate, these two seem amateurs. But I,
less talented than all: than frog, cricket

and certainly than bird in making song
of passionate love to draw you to me
can offer only this, a winter's poem.

VOYAGE

I did not know what it meant to leave
And arrive, my body lived by a force
That pulls toward you without recourse,
Beyond reason. Now the shore recedes

Slowly, its intricate pattern dims
As substantial rock, fir trees, quartz sand
Fade to pastel. I feel upon my hand
My grandfather's touch on the skin

Between my thumb and forefinger,
Unseen, gentle, ghostly, he guides me
Toward you, across this darkened sea;
And I turn from past regret or anger.

I yearn for more than I did before,
And to mingle my vision newly with you.
Breathless, arrived, I fall into you,
Joyful and spent – dazed immigrant on your shore.

SONG OF A WHITE
CIVIL RIGHTS WORKER

I remember her seated in the kitchen
In her grey maid's uniform, her dark, large bulk
Slow moving, and my mother, white, hurried, thin,
Leaving me with a quick goodbye and the thud

Of the front door
And I, only four at the time, not knowing history.

Locked arms and swaying.
We shall not. . .
Struck.
We shall not be moved.
Struck John.
Just like a tree. . .
Struck. Robert.
Standing by the water.
Struck. Martin.
We shall not be moved.
Struck down. All my illusions.

Dear America, cruel and untrue dream.
Struck. Me.
Let me go. Yes. Let me go.
Free – ee – dom,
Free – ee – dom,
Free – ee – dom,
Freedom.
Freedom.

Nameless, she left one day and did not return
And I missed her.

But I was only four at the time, not knowing my history.

THE HERO WITH A THOUSAND FACES

The hero with a thousand faces
And fifteen thousand eyes
Advanced upon the mountains
Like a person mesmerized.

And if you saw the sudden burst
Of the receding sun,
Or if you walked the fabled road
Through the forest gloom,

You would have seen him standing there
And would have been afraid,
For who alone can bear the heat
From which our vision is made?

I DON'T DISCOURAGE

Don't send me off to other women's arms,
Extol their nubile charms;
It's you I want, and you only;

Or wonder if you still can fascinate
Or think that by a mood you can escape
It's you I want, and you only.

Anger, annoyance will not discourage me.
Being yourself is all you need to be.
It's you I want, and you only.

FABRIC

This fabric we are making is so fine,
That my heart aches when you are gone,
And yet, the absences are threaded there
And play their part. Would that the words
I speak were made of flesh and action.
Weaving takes time, I know, and passion
Must find its place and pattern.

But I love you so and yearn to see
If flesh and lust will make this mystery
Greater or less. I am afraid, as you
May be, for either one. But what to do
If this proves more silk than gossamer,
And the pattern that we weave each day
Turns so beautiful we cannot turn away?

THE LAWYER

He was impeccable in dress
and spoke in sentences so full
of nuance and care and clarity
that we were all impressed.

His tie coordinated
with his shirt, in pastel shades
of blue or green or mauve;
and silver cuff links understated.

He would assure of writs and laws,
precedents and rule,
establish a client's good intent
within a reasonableness clause.

So all seemed safe and sane with him,
this game of moneyed odds;
he would not blink nor sweat in court,
nor brook an angry whim.

But when he slept, he loved the cries
of enemies, both near and far.
he knifed, and gouged and blooded them;
cursed fiercely and anatomized.

And so the verity it seems
we sensed from all his days of court:
However suave his counsel was,
He was no gentleman in dreams.

POEM FOR NICOLE, MY DAUGHTER
Who died at 35 from complications of spina bifida

When she was young, she walked.
She walked
Toddling on her braced legs
Smiling
Her arms out
Coming to daddy

But it was not to be
Gradually time took over
First with double canes
Then with a walker
Then with a manual wheelchair
Then with a motorized chair

As others embraced possibilities
Hers dwindled.

And still – how did she do it? –
She smiled and always,
I can hear her now,
Always said, "Daddy,
Daddy,
Don't worry"
And held her arms out.

BODY SURFING

Love, I cannot, try as I might, easier as it might be,
Turn this force aside. It drives me beyond myself
Like a wave, in wind and roar and salt; I body surf
On your love, my love on yours. I dream of your nipples

Engorged. I dream of your ribs and chest. I dream of your voice
And your cry. And I am drawn by a force in you, in spite of what
You may want, pulled onward in gravity so fierce and constant
That my heart pounds with the rush, my body bending toward
   yours,

Searching for you. It is too late, and too early, to stop, even
If I could. For my mind bends to yours too, my history changes
With your love, my soul transforms with the scars of your body
And their history. And when finally this wave flings me

Onto the beach among the opalescent shells and the sand dollars
And the starfish, and I lie spent on the cool indifferent sand,
I will weep with joy and sadness that it ever came to me
To know such a wild ride: and I will lie there listening

To the roar of the ocean, until the stars and moon sprinkle
Their dust in the long night, and I close my eyes dreaming of you.

THE DAYS ARE COMING FAST NOW

The days are coming fast now
no matter what you say.
I feel the crouching presence
is never far away.

See how in the dark corner
with eyes as bright as cats'
it waits in patient posture,
knowing that "that is that".

Let's bargain with the daylight
let's quarrel with the moon
let's hold our hands and dance
let's make the backyard bloom.

I do not want to let go
of you, both soul and skin.
Our elongated conversation,
Our love, our bumbling

are the only poultice
and are the only cure
for whenever the presence
justifies its purr.

LOVE HAS ITS PHASES

It's different now. Love has its phases,
As the sea has weather.
I can breathe, my heart no longer hurts

The way it did when I gave you chase,
And when your absence severed
My abdomen, divvying my core

As if I were an apple. I've beached
Myself upon you and your love.
The storm that crackled, lashed and spun,

Is spent. I need not beseech
Its rage, but enter to our bed as to a cove.
I sleep; your thigh soft and translucent,

Calms my hand. Your gentle voice subdues,
Compels the wind, and in the morning now,
Sets the table for our timeless love.

IN ANSWER TO A YALE COLLEGE REUNION REQUEST FOR INFORMATION ON MY LIFE

Your questions float from very far away,
To institutionalize my memory.

Just print: "I learned some poetry, some Freud,
How to search a wound and heal it on the couch,
The wondrous meaning of a woman's sigh,
How a child's happiness can make me cry.

Protect me still from hale, hearty and well-met;
I have so much further to go, to unlearn yet."

KNOWING

I know now these are love letters. Let them be.
Shhh. I would stop your protest as it passes your lips.
Do not question, say they are not real, say I do not know you.

I know, afterward, I carefully place the memory of each time
  together
Like a delicate shell in a silver bowl;
I know that I felt your hand against my chest and your heart beating.
I know the slim hardness of your back and the cushion of your
  abdomen.

And I know that I yearn for you, that I have images:
Mango, peach, persimmon – honey flowing from an orchid,
Crazy, mixed up metaphors that stumble and fall over themselves
In their rush forward, Latin, wonderful.

Wonderful as a waterfall, under or going over.

THE WAITING

And so you clothe the fig trees,
in burlap and cardboard
against the winter cold –
and they stand like abandoned children
outside the house – waiting.

And the brown leaves are gone
from the driveway, the bigger trees
stiff and bare in the back yard,
while the cat cuffs with each paw,
one stray leaf
this way and that
in the dwindling light.

And we wait.

The snow will come , and the
drifts will fill the back door; and once
again, everything will change –
and transform into white beauty.

We too have transformed together;
ensconced with the seasons,
watching their regular course;
grown together, celebrated each other –
and yet the seasons in us shall not circle.

And when the last log is burnt in the fireplace,
and the snow has melted,
and the trees begin to bloom yellow and green again
and the figs swell slowly on their branches;
and the cat spreads himself, shamelessly, on the hot driveway
We will be filled with the beauty of it all.

And yes, we shall always wait,
As we do now: you and I.
And I shall love you again and again.

DREAMS FORETOLD

We are contained now, you and I
within our dreams,
We are constrained now, you and I
within the time we have but do not
know, fashioned by whatever drove
us magically together long ago.

The crazy quilt that we have stitched,
knowing and unknowingly
with patterns that beguile us every day:
I would not have you any other way.

Everything I see has you in it: the fig
trees in our yard, the music that you play,
the drawing of a child –
all are imbued with you.

Whatever I encounter, you are there.
I would not have it any other way.

BIRTHDAY PRESENT

I give my body as your birthday present,
For it is all I have to give. Take it,
It's yours, and its long history: smell the scent
Of mother's milk on my lips, drink a bit

My toddler's tears, and kiss my adult sweat.
Finger my chest scar, and feel the way
My heart, when I embrace you, quickly beats;
Take from me my eyes so that you too may

See the joyous beauty of your face; take
My hands, given to caress and turn you on.
Hold too my abdomen, and feel how it is raked
With emptiness (and anger) when you're gone.

I give you too my shoulder for your head,
When we are lying in the gentlest sleep.
And wish my body always in your bed,
To make the night so soft it is complete.

And last of all, my sex for you to know:
The surprising, rising organ of my love,
My tightened scrotum, sweet spasmodic flow
That merges with yours, when I feel you move.

Open this present, so we may explore,
In whatever years we have, beyond our skin.
Unwrap me, love, and til we breathe no more,
Enfold my soul, entire and within.

ON A GREEN RUG

As you lie there,
Your hands under your head
Your upper body bare,
Vulnerable,
With me seated beside you,

It is that meandering curve I follow,
From your elbow down,
Down past the proud muscle of your shoulder,
Past your soft upraised breast,
Past your abdomen.

And then I gaze at your face, your eyes
Looking at mine,
Looking at me looking at you,
Your accepting smile,
Your acceptance of my gaze.

My love, that curve goes inside me:
It is landscape, it is river,
It is conte crayon on the palest paper.
The curve and your acceptance of my gaze,
Grace me,
Invite me

Like music,
Like love.

IN THE GRASS, LOOKING AT YOU

Looking up at you with the sun shining
Through the leaves, I barely see you. Spokes and
Flares of sunlight, and your face disappears
Into whiteness. I shade my eyes with one hand

And your face reappears. Repeating the process:
You're there, you're gone. Sometimes our love seems
Like this, flitting from substance to chimera,
And back again. But for now, I lie content

Comforted by you. The breeze moves the leaves,
Then stops, then moves them again, sibilant
Like the sea playing with small stones, and the sky
Shines constantly, ceaselessly blue.

Nothing can preserve this moment, not words
Nor song, nor memory. Nothing so sweet
As now, nothing so painfully fragile.
Love me, hold me between your breasts and the grass.

CONTINUITY

It had seemed at first it was a force
That you released in me,
So strong that it would spend itself
In poetry.

And I would look back upon this time
As on a cataclysm,
With wonder at how my soul experienced
A spasm.

But last night as I lay awake
And wished you by my side,
I realized that my love for you
Could abide.

And suddenness could lead to time
And time to distant night;
Your love transform, still transport me
When my hair is white.

FINALE

Day of doom
Is coming soon.
Bring out the broom.
And we will go in the other room.

Afterword

I am a psychologist and psychoanalyst. For the past thirty years, I have had a private practice, treating children, adolescents, and adults, in Ridgewood, New Jersey, a suburban town not too far from New York City. My experiences play a part in all of these stories. Before becoming a psychoanalyst, I was a legal services attorney who lived and worked on the Navajo and Hopi reservations in Arizona and New Mexico, and – when practicing privately – also represented Native Americans in Denver, Colorado.

In addition, in the summer of 1965 I was a civil rights worker for the Southern Christian Leadership Council, Martin Luther King's organization, primarily working out of Atlanta and Fort Valley, Georgia, a small town south of Atlanta. For that matter, I have always enjoyed diverse cultures and have tried on vacations to explore other cultures than my own, cultures which figure in some of these stories and poems.

Last, I have an abiding interest in the study of psychic phenomena. I have written on the subject in my recent book *The Paranormal Surrounds Us: Psychic Phenomena in Literature, Culture, and Psychoanalysis (Jefferson, N.C., McFarland, 2018)*, taught the subject and advocated that psychoanalysts and mental health professionals be more aware of these phenomena. Psychic phenomena play a role in a number of the stories here.

The short stories and poems were written after a day of seeing patients or on weekends. In ways that are not at all obvious, my patients

237

over the years have inspired some of them. In psychoanalysis, in writing short stories, in struggling to put words into poetry, my hope has always been to approach the intimate heart of our lives, with its terror and beauty, and to question our assumptions of how our world is constructed.

CPSIA information can be obtained
at www.ICGtesting.com
Printed in the USA
FSHW020011021219